Stephanie Bond, Leslie Kelly, Michelle Rowen

ONCE UPON A VALENTINE

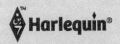

TORONTO NEW YORK LONDON
AMSTERDAM PARIS SYDNEY HAMBURG
STOCKHOLM ATHENS TOKYO MILAN MADRID
PRAGUE WARSAW BUDAPEST AUCKLAND

ISBN-13: 978-0-373-79667-0

ONCE UPON A VALENTINE
Copyright © 2012 by Harlequin Books S.A.

The publisher acknowledges the
copyright holders of the individual works
as follows:

ALL TANGLED UP
Copyright © 2012 by Stephanie Bond, Inc.

SLEEPING WITH A BEAUTY
Copyright © 2012 by Leslie Kelly

CATCH ME
Copyright © 2012 by Michelle Rowen

Recycling programs
for this product may
not exist in your area.

Printed in U.S.A.

*Look what people are saying
about these talented authors...*

Stephanie Bond

"Sex and humor blend perfectly...this fairy tale
of a story has the perfect magic ending."
—*RT Book Reviews*, 4 stars, on *No Peeking...*

"Red hot, deliciously wicked,
fantastically entertaining."
—*Joyfully Reviewed* on *Watch and Learn*

Leslie Kelly

"A hip contemporary romance
packed with great one-liners!"
—*RT Book Reviews*, 4.5 stars, on *Terms of Surrender*

"Another wonderful happy ever after."
—*Fresh Fiction* on *More Blazing Bedtime Stories*

Michelle Rowen

"A sexy, flirty romance with a supernatural flair...
Ms. Rowen certainly knows how to charm her
readers with a delicious story."
—*Fresh Fiction* on *Touch and Go*

"Michelle Rowen makes her Blaze debut
with this fun tale of ghosts, curses and
sizzling sex. Readers who like a hot paranormal tale
should look for this tasty treat!"
—*Affair de Coeur* on *Hot Spell*

Stephanie Bond has been reading Harlequin romance novels since she was a preteen, never dreaming she'd grow up to write them! Today, with more than sixty romance and mystery novels to her name, Stephanie still believes in happy endings. For more about her books, visit her website, www.stephaniebond.com.

Leslie Kelly has written dozens of novels for Harlequin Blaze, Temptation and HQN Books. Known for her sparkling dialogue and humor, Leslie has been honored with numerous awards, including the National Readers' Choice Award. In 2010, she received the Lifetime Achievement Award in Series Romance from *RT Book Reviews*. Leslie lives in Maryland with her husband and their three daughters. Visit her online at www.lesliekelly.com.

National bestselling author **Michelle Rowen** was the winner of the 2007 Holt Medallion for Best First Book and the 2009 *RT Book Reviews* Reviewers' Choice award for Best Vampire Romance. Michelle's hobbies include writing, writing and...well, that's about it (unless you count Twitter and Facebook as hobbies). She lives in Southern Ontario, but has never been a big fan of snow. Please visit her website, www.michellerowen.com.

CONTENTS

STEPHANIE BOND

All Tangled Up

This story is dedicated to
all the romantic insomniacs out there.

1

THE SIGN READ Welcome to Tiny, Tennessee, Population 1345.

Andrew MacMillan sighed and pulled his hand over his mouth—make that 1344. His father, retired veterinarian and widower, Barber MacMillan, had passed away sitting in a rocker on his front porch with a smile on his face. That was according to Red Tucker, his father's neighbor, accountant and best friend of seventy years who had found him the day before yesterday. Leave it to his father, Andrew thought wryly, to die as he'd lived—on his own terms.

Since Andrew's trip would be open-ended, to arrange the funeral and settle his father's affairs, he'd decided to drive from Manhattan to Tiny to have use of his car...and to think. He and his father hadn't been estranged, exactly, just cut from a different cloth. The fact that Andrew's mother had died when he was a teenager hadn't helped matters. She'd had a knack for mediating father-son squabbles with sugary words and buttered biscuits. Without her loving lubrication, the men had clashed.

But when Andrew had decided to attend college in Ohio, his father hadn't held him back. Then again, he hadn't made the trip to attend graduation. And although he'd congratulated Andrew on landing a plum job with a big advertising firm in Manhattan, he'd never once visited in thirteen years.

On the other hand, Andrew hadn't been the best at visiting, either. He'd tried to make it back to the MacMillan farm for a few days every year around the holidays, but last year things had been too busy at the firm and he simply couldn't get away.

Regret ballooned in his chest, but he couldn't pretend a trip home over Christmas would've made a difference in their relationship. In fact, it might've made things worse, since Andrew's suggestions that his father sell the fifty-acre farm and move to a place he could better maintain were always met with cross remarks. By the end of a stay, their tolerance for each other seemed to wear thin.

"Visitors are like fish," his father had been fond of saying. "After a couple of days, things start to smell."

Andrew tried not to take offense at the fact that his father considered him a "visitor" in the house he'd grown up in. It was just his father's way.

He slowed as he drove into the downtown area of Tiny, which consisted of three entire blocks of the most diverse and unusual shops one could imagine: Bitty's Bakery, Tiny Hardware, Harlowe's Musical Instruments, Tiny Town Grocery, West Drug Dispensary, City Hall, Dr. Berg, M.D., Flood Dentistry, Dolls & More, Shoes & More, Flowers & More, Watches & More, Biscuits & More, Books & More and…more. As customary, the shops' marquees featured personal messages to members of the community: "Congratulations, Wendy!" "Happy Anniversary, Maggie and John!" "Welcome, Baby Jenkins!" The windows touted Valentine's Day Sales.

Hadley's Funeral Parlor sat slightly off the beaten retail path, located in a freestanding former fast food building. No one seemed to notice or mind the drive-through window. Their marquee offered condolences to the Barber MacMillan family and the Sadie Case family.

Sadness tugged at him. Sweet-voiced Mrs. Case had been his third-grade teacher and had been around his father's age, he recalled. A generation of Tiny-ites was fading away as fast as the younger generation was moving away.

He wondered vaguely how long it would take to sell his father's farm, jokingly dubbed the Mane Squeeze Ranch by his dear mother, and preserved by his father for her sake. Years before, the adjacent state park had expressed interest in the Mac-

Millan land because of the limestone cave spring on the property, but things changed.

Andrew pulled his black BMW into the nearly vacant parking lot, his stomach tied in knots. He couldn't imagine anything more painful than for a child to arrange a parent's funeral, but conceded it was the circle of life, the last thing he could do for his father to perhaps make up for all the little things he hadn't known to do when Barber was alive.

He climbed out of the car and squinted into the warm winter sun. The weather in Southern Tennessee was always unpredictable, so it wasn't altogether surprising to find temperatures in the high seventies in February. He would enjoy it today. Tomorrow it could be snowing.

In the short walk to the double doors of the funeral home, he listened to the call of songbirds lulled out by the warmth. Hardwood trees were still bare, but the cedar, hemlock and white-pine trees offered plenty of cover—and color—in the otherwise gray landscape.

When he opened the door, a chime sounded somewhere in the distance to announce his arrival. The decor hadn't changed in the decade or so since he'd last been there—tributes to the local high-school sports teams and Tennessee trophy trout mounted on wood plaques. Hadley's Funeral Home was a social hotspot. This afternoon it was, um, *dead,* but if a viewing was scheduled this evening, it would be hopping with regulars who would sign the guest register, ooh and aah over the casket, and peek at the cards on the flowers to see who had sent roses and who had sent carnations.

Geary Hadley appeared, tall and gaunt in his black suit, but his droopy features lifted in recognition. "Andrew, how nice to see you. Well, not under these circumstances, of course, but you know what I mean. Your father was a good man."

Andrew shook the veined hand the man extended to him, wondering how many hands the man had shaken in his lifetime. "Thank you, Mr. Hadley. It's nice to see you, too."

"Let's go to my office," the man offered in a low, comforting voice.

Andrew's stomach churned as they wove past various rooms in the hushed building. By the time they reached the small, cramped office, he was ready to get the meeting over with. "Regarding my father's wishes—"

"Here you go," Mr. Hadley said, handing him a metal urn.

Andrew stared down at the urn, confused. "What's this?"

"Your father's ashes," Mr. Hadley said. "Those were his wishes—to be cremated."

Andrew almost dropped the urn, but juggled and caught it. "Since when?"

"Since always. Every time Barber set foot in this place, he apologized to me in advance for denying me a big crowd here at the funeral home." Hadley smiled. "That was his way." He opened a file drawer and rummaged through it, then removed a yellowed sheet of stationery. "Here you go. He made me keep a copy of it on file."

Andrew shifted the urn to the crook of his elbow and took the sheet of paper to scan.

I, Barber MacMillan, being sane and all of that, upon my death, wish to have my body cremated and my ashes scattered over the Mane Squeeze Ranch. No muss, no fuss, no funeral and no headstone.

Andrew blinked in surprise. "I didn't know."

"I'm not surprised," Mr. Hadley said. "Barber was an odd bird…but then, you probably know that better than anyone."

Andrew nodded. "Yes." He folded the paper and stared down at the urn. "So, how am I supposed to do this?"

Mr. Hadley shrugged. "Just unscrew the lid and start scattering. Make sure you're upwind."

Andrew pursed his mouth. "Aren't there laws against scattering remains?"

Mr. Hadley gave a dismissive wave. "If you don't tell anyone, neither will I."

Andrew nodded, remembering that in Tiny, Tennessee, laws were elastic. "What do I owe you for the, um, services?"

"Already taken care of," Mr. Hadley said. "Barber saw to that ages ago." He handed Andrew another piece of paper. "Here's an obituary for the paper. I think your dad would be okay with that, at least."

Andrew read the write-up about the man who had been a pillar of the community, a source of comfort and know-how for the farmers in the area who had depended on him to vaccinate their cattle against pink eye, treat swine pneumonia or birth stubborn foals. Barber MacMillan treated any animal that needed his help, but he was especially gifted with horses, a trait not passed on to Andrew, who had always worked in the stables, but didn't bond with the animals the way his father had.

> Barber MacMillan is survived by his son, Andrew Barber MacMillan of New York City, and a host of grateful friends and neighbors, human and otherwise.

"It's a fine obituary," Andrew said.

"Summer wrote it."

Andrew frowned. "Summer…Tomlinson?"

"One and the same."

The image of the coltish, towheaded teenager who lived next door came to mind. Summer was five—no, six—years younger than Andrew. He had a vague memory of her giving him a Valentine's Day card when she was a shy preteen. He hadn't seen her since he'd moved to Manhattan after college. Even though his dad spoke of her often, because she'd assisted him in the stables on occasion, she hadn't been around during his holiday visits. But apparently, Summer had been close to his father. He felt a rush of gratitude toward the young woman.

"Oh, and my daughter Tessa asked me to give you this." Geary handed Andrew a business card.

Andrew glanced at the real-estate logo and the picture of his former classmate—still pretty…and probably still as vapid. "How is Tessa?"

"She's done real well for herself," Mr. Hadley said, pride in his voice. "She thought you might be interested in selling your dad's place."

Andrew nodded. He'd seen his dad's will and knew he was the sole beneficiary. "That's the plan."

The man's eyes twinkled. "Tessa's still single, too."

Andrew coughed, then tucked the card in his pocket. "Thanks, Mr. Hadley. I'll give Tessa a call…about the property."

He shook the man's gnarled hand again and left, carrying the dubious burden of his father's ashes in his hands. Andrew settled the urn in the passenger seat of his car and shook his head. "You managed to throw me one last curveball, old man."

How could he in good conscience scatter his father's ashes over the farm and then sell it?

Andrew's mind clicked as he drove over familiar roads, past recognizable landmarks, and allowed nostalgia to flow over him. The high-school campus and the city pool looked incredibly small. He shook his head, thinking about how big and important they had seemed when he was young. Ditto for the movie theater and bowling alley, around which his social life had revolved.

The road leading to the Mane Squeeze Ranch was hemmed by overgrown foliage on either side of the paved road barely wide enough for two vehicles to pass. The closer he got to home, the more memories assailed him. The gigantic weeping-willow tree at the fork in the road where he used to ride his bike, tap the trunk then ride back, the wide spot in the road where he'd waited for the bus, now tangled with dormant blackberry bushes, the grouping of community mailboxes, all shapes and colors, lined up in a row.

As he drove by the Tomlinsons' house, he was distracted by the sight of a slender woman sitting on an upstairs balcony, combing her waist-length golden-blond hair.

Summer Tomlinson, he realized with a start. No longer in cutoffs and sporting a boyish pixie cut. She looked up and saw his car, then jumped to her feet, shouting and pointing.

Andrew looked back to the road and his heart leaped to his throat. Standing in the path of his car was a swaybacked gray horse that looked too old to move…and too big to miss.

2

SUMMER SCREAMED AND closed her eyes against the impact. After the crash, she opened her eyes and gasped at the sight of the black BMW sitting tilted in the ditch with its bumper butted up against a small tree. The gray horse—Max—lifted his weary head and whinnied at the vehicle that had spoiled his run for freedom.

Summer ran down the stairs leading from the balcony to the ground and rushed across the yard toward the car. Truman, Barber's setter-shepherd-mixed dog, was on her heels then bounded ahead, barking excitedly.

The car's airbag hadn't deployed, which was a good sign. The driver was climbing out from behind the wheel, another good sign, even though he wore a scowl on his face.

And his face was unmistakable—Andrew MacMillan. Dark hair, light brown eyes, strong nose, square chin. Rendered tall and sturdy on simple country food and hard work on his father's farm. She remembered the thrilling glimpses from her bedroom window of him, shirtless, riding a tractor across the MacMillan fields. Now dressed in tan-colored slacks and a long-sleeved collared shirt, he looked every inch the refined businessman. By comparison, she felt self-conscious in her cotton dress and bare feet and her drying hair loose around her shoulders.

Truman jumped up on Andrew to give him a lick and a sniff. The man took a moment to rough the dog's scruff before gently brushing him away. "Down, boy."

His voice was so similar to Barber's, she realized suddenly. Apparently, the dog thought so, too, because he immediately sat down, although his tail thumped the ground impatiently.

"Andrew, are you okay?" she asked.

He nodded, then jammed his hands on his hips. "I'm fine." His gaze swept over her. "Hello."

Her bare toes curled in the wiry winter grass. The ground was colder than the air temperature. "Hi. I'm Summer."

A smile curved his mouth. "I remember."

When their eyes met, her breath was squeezed out of her chest. Her ears popped and cracked as if she were being lifted to a higher altitude. Then a gust of wind picked up the ends of her long hair and whipped it into Andrew's face. He blinked, and she grabbed at the wayward locks. He lifted his arm, presumably to help, then she felt a yank on her scalp.

"Ouch," she murmured, tilting her head.

"Sorry. Your hair…it's caught in my watch."

"Ow, ow, ow," she said as the tension on her scalp increased. She lurched forward, following his hand, and suddenly, they were face to face.

She inhaled sharply. His eyes were so sexy, like drops of caramel, fringed with thick lashes and brows. His lips parted, then he gave a little laugh. "I think I'm making things worse."

Not from her perspective, she thought abruptly. But she couldn't seem to speak.

"Maybe I should just remove my watch." He moved his hand, but Summer shrieked in pain.

He winced. "Sorry."

"Let me try," she offered out of self-preservation. She gingerly turned her head toward the snarl and began to work methodically to remove a few strands at a time. But the proximity of his body to hers messed with her concentration.

He had nice hands—big and strong-looking, but well-groomed. She knew from Barber that Andrew wasn't married, but seeing up close that his ring finger was empty did something to her stomach. As she worked to free her hair from the stem of his watch, she realized it was probably a very pricey piece. She prayed she didn't damage it in the process. Just as she was getting ready to suggest the dreaded "cut it out" solution, the last of the strands came free.

"Sorry about that." She wound her hair into a rope and held it down. "It was such a nice day, I was drying my hair in the sun."

"No problem," he said, but he stepped back, as if he were afraid he might be entangled again.

Which irritated her because his protruding watch was at least half to blame. The air between them held the tingly remnants of their forced intimacy.

Behind them, the gray horse brayed to remind them he was supposed to be the center of attention.

"Hush, Max," Summer called.

Andrew's eyebrows went up. "Is that your horse?"

"No...that's Max. He belongs to your father." Then she caught herself. "He...*belonged* to your father. I'm sorry for your loss, Andrew."

He nodded, his face somber. "Thank you. And thank you for writing the obituary. Mr. Hadley gave me a copy."

"It's the least I could do. Barber meant so much to so many people around here."

He averted his gaze, but not before she saw pain and confusion there. She hadn't meant to imply Barber MacMillan had meant more to the town than to his own offspring. She'd gathered from Barber's remarks and Andrew's infrequent visits that father and son hadn't been close. Still, being orphaned...well, she knew a thing or two about that. She'd lost both of her parents in the past five years. On each occasion, Andrew had sent flowers, a thoughtful formality, she knew. But he couldn't have known how much his gesture had meant to her, how many times she'd written the thank-you cards to get the phrasing just right, just like the sentiment she'd written on the Valentine's Day card she'd given him when she was twelve. She was annoyed with herself that she'd cared so much what he thought.

She gestured to the lopsided vehicle. "I can call Red to bring the tractor down and pull you out."

He worked his mouth back and forth. "No need to bother

Red. I think I remember how to fire it up." He nodded toward the braying horse. "But him, I might need a hand with."

"I'll walk with you and put Max back in the stable," she said, then looked down at her toenails which were painted a vivid blue. "Uh…let me get my boots." She hurried back toward the steps leading to the balcony, feeling like a rube. She was relatively sure that women in New York City did not scamper around barefoot. As she climbed the steps, she felt Andrew's gaze on her. He was probably marveling over the fact that she was still there. In fact, the farthest she'd moved geographically was from her childhood bedroom down the hall to the master bedroom in the home she'd grown up in.

But she didn't care, she thought, tossing her head as she walked across the timeworn wooden planks of the balcony to the French doors that opened to her bedroom. She'd had her chances to live elsewhere. She'd gotten a marketing degree from the University of Tennessee in Knoxville, but had passed up job offers there to work at the Tiny Caves State Park just a few miles down the road. And she'd never regretted her decision— working at the Park and helping Barber in her spare time kept her busy and fulfilled. She preferred this place, where rush hour was Sunday morning before church and the closest thing to police sirens was the call of screech owls.

Summer entered her bedroom, wondering how much of a miracle she could perform on her hair in sixty seconds. She stopped at her dressing table and surveyed the tangled mess with a sigh. Some days the long locks were more trouble than they were worth, but lopping them off seemed even more daunting.

She ran a wide-tooth comb through her hair quickly, tackling the worst of the knots. Then she clasped it into a low ponytail, gave the length a twist into a loose, fat braid and secured it again at the bottom. From the closet she pulled her worn brown-leather boots and stepped into them, hooking her fingers through the pull tabs for a yank. A soft swish against her leg caused her to smile. Gabby, her butterscotch-colored Persian cat, sniffed her, sneezed then began to complain loudly.

"Yes, Gabby," Summer soothed, "Truman is a smelly beast,

but he's all alone, so you might have to get used to having him around—or at least the smell of him." She gave her beloved pet a tickle under the chin, then turned to the mirror and lamented her casual dress, limp and almost threadbare from countless washings. But she wasn't going to take the time to change now and make Andrew MacMillan think she cared.

As she secured the French doors from the inside, she glanced down and took him in against the landscape.

For a man who'd grown up here, he couldn't look more out of place. And it was more than his polished clothing and sporty car. It was the way he held his big body rigid and apart from everything else…as if he had no intention of being pulled back into a small-town lifestyle. His stance worried her because it didn't bode well for the future of the Mane Squeeze Ranch and stables.

She bit her lip. It also threatened to spoil her own personal fairy tale that Andrew MacMillan would return to Tiny and sweep her off her bare feet. To be sure, just looking at the man made her realize how quickly her teenage crush could balloon into full-fledged infatuation.

No, it was clear that Andrew MacMillan had outgrown Tiny… but maybe he would be in town long enough to satisfy her burning curiosity about what it would be like to spend one night under that big, strapping body of his.

He turned his head and glanced up to the balcony and she stepped back, lest he think she was watching him.

She jogged downstairs and headed toward the front door. Gabby sat at the top of the stairs, loudly venting last-minute complaints that made Summer smile. On the way out, she grabbed a soft cotton lead line from an assortment of tack hanging on a coatrack. As she strode across the front yard, she noticed man and horse were facing off, neither one of them moving. Truman sat, still planted, but whining to be released from obedience.

She approached Max with soothing noises. "Are you missing Barber?" she asked the aged horse. "Did you decide to look for him?" He whinnied softly as she slipped the lead rope over his thick neck. "C'mon, old man, let's go home."

She tugged him in the direction of the Mane Squeeze and he grudgingly turned and plodded after her. Andrew whistled for Truman, then retrieved something from the car and caught up to her with long strides. Under his arm, he carried a metal urn.

"I assume those are your father's ashes?" she said.

He nodded, his expression wry. "He wanted them spread over the farm."

"That doesn't surprise me. He loved it so."

Andrew didn't comment, just fell into step next to her. His shiny black dress shoes were in stark contrast to her scuffed brown boots. She was aware of every inch of him moving beside her, especially after they'd already had an up-close moment. Her heart rate accelerated, and her breathing felt constricted. Her mind raced for something to say, but she was also sensitive to the fact that, in light of his recent loss, he might prefer silence. The horse trudged behind them at a snail's pace.

"Do you live out here alone?" he asked, glancing around.

She shrugged. "I'm alone in the house, but the animals keep me company. Your father kept an eye on me after my parents passed."

"He spoke of you often. He appreciated your help in the stables."

"I helped Barber when I could. I work at the State Park five days a week," she offered, in case he thought she'd been mooching off his father.

"What do you do there?"

"My title is Community Relations Coordinator, but I basically do whatever the general manager needs for me to do. Your father told me you work in advertising?"

"That's right."

He didn't seem to want to elaborate, which made her feel as if he thought she wouldn't understand his job. Whatever.

Truman bounded ahead, then back, presenting Andrew with a found stick.

"Fetch is his favorite game," she offered.

He obligingly took the stick that dripped with drool and gave it a toss, then withdrew a handkerchief from his pocket to wipe his hand. A white business card whipped out and fell to the ground. Summer recognized it instantly as Tessa Hadley's agent card.

He bent to retrieve the card and slipped it back in his pocket.

"So you're going to sell the Mane Squeeze?" she asked, unable to keep the censure out of her voice.

"It's the only thing that makes sense."

"But what about the horses?" she blurted.

His mouth tightened. "How many horses are in the stables now?"

"Nine."

His eyes widened. "Nine? There were only two the last time I was here."

"Things have been tight around Tiny. Barber adopted horses people couldn't take care of anymore."

Andrew lifted his hands, obviously at a loss. "Maybe the new owner will want them." But he picked up his pace, as if he was in a hurry to get to his father's place. Summer clucked to Max so they could keep up with him.

They rounded the corner, and the entrance gate to the Mac-Millan farm came into view. Summer saw it through Andrew's eyes—wild and overgrown, the fence sagging, the mailbox rusted. In the distance, the stables looked dilapidated, the roof choked with tangles of woody grapevines. The building where Barber had once maintained his veterinary office was almost completely obscured by bushes. And the house itself was run-down, badly in need of a paint job, flanked by clutter and sitting in an unkempt yard that was more weeds than grass.

Andrew stopped and she saw his grip tighten on the urn. Emotions rolled off him. Sadness? Frustration?

"I had no idea things had gotten this bad," he murmured. "He didn't tell me and I…"

Didn't ask. The unspoken words hung in the air.

He reached into his pocket and pulled out the business card, juggling the urn while he pulled out a cell phone.

Panic sparked in Summer's stomach. "Andrew, everything looks ugly this time of the year. Please, don't put the farm on the market until you've at least seen the horses."

"I'm afraid that won't change my mind," he said, punching in a number from the card. "Hello, Tessa? Andrew MacMillan.... Yes, thank you....Yes, he was a good man....I was wondering if you had time to stop by my dad's place—"

Summer plucked the phone from his hand, then disconnected the call.

"What are you doing?" he snapped.

She held his phone out of reach. "Your father dreamed of turning the Mane Squeeze into a horse-rescue center. Don't you owe it to him to at least give it a shot?"

Andrew shook his head, clearly perturbed. "I'm sorry, Summer. It's a noble cause, but it would take a tremendous investment to turn this place into a rescue center. And all of my resources are invested in Manhattan."

The hard edge in his tone left no doubt he intended to sell the land to the highest bidder and hightail it back to New York. The horses would be left out in the cold...or worse.

She angled her head. "What if I told you your father and I had a plan?"

He frowned. "What kind of plan?"

"A plan to make enough money to fund a horse-rescue center."

He rolled his eyes. "Another one of my father's harebrained ideas, no doubt."

She pulled her long braid over one shoulder and held it up. "Not hare...*hair.*"

3

ANDREW STARED AT SUMMER. The woman had already knocked him for a loop with her golden good looks and lithe body. Now she was telling him she and his father had been scheming to turn the Mane Squeeze into a horse-rescue center…and it had something to do with her magnificent mane of hair?

"I'm not following," he said.

She held up the end of her thick braid. "Your father invented a hair formula we were going to market."

He squinted. "Come again?"

"He originally developed it for the horses' manes and tails, but years ago I noticed how long and silky they were and I started using it myself. When I told my friends about it, they all started using it, too. Barber couldn't make it fast enough. We were going to market it and use the money to fund the rescue center."

Andrew blinked. He vaguely remembered a generic spray bottle of some concoction his father always used to groom the horses, hanging on a hook in the stable. "A homegrown hair-growth formula?"

"More like a conditioner. In my case, it makes my hair stronger and it grows longer."

He couldn't deny she had gorgeous hair, but still…. "My father never mentioned anything about this to me."

"I know," she said, suddenly unable to make eye contact. "He didn't want to take advantage of your position."

Andrew frowned. "You mean he didn't want to ask for my help."

She sighed. "He was proud, and he was afraid you would laugh at him."

His chest tightened. "I wouldn't have laughed, but I would've explained how difficult it is to bring a hair product to the market."

"But that's your business," she said. "You know all the shortcuts."

He shook his head. "I'm in advertising, not marketing. By the time I get a product, it's ready to be sold."

"I have a degree in marketing," she said. "Together, we could—"

"Whoa, whoa," he said, raising his hands. "I don't have the time to devote to this. I have to get back to New York."

"But surely you'll be here for a few days," she argued.

"I have a couple of weeks of vacation I could take," he admitted, then gestured toward the sagging farm. "But it looks as if I'll need it all to try to clean up this place."

"I'll help," she offered. "You can leave the horses to me. In return, will you at least agree to take a look at what your father and I were working on?"

While the idea of spending more time with Summer Tomlinson was intriguing, Andrew wasn't interested in wasting time analyzing a homemade beauty concoction of his father's for its marketability. He opened his mouth to tell her so, but somehow the word "Okay" came out instead. And before he could correct himself, her face lit up like the sun.

"Great! I have everything at my house. Come over for dinner tonight around seven." She tugged Max toward the stables. "C'mon, boy."

Max complained, but followed obediently. Andrew frowned, knowing how the horse felt. He'd been home for ten minutes and Summer Tomlinson was leading him around as if he had a bit in his mouth.

Truman looked after her and whined, then looked up to Andrew.

"Go if you want," he encouraged, but the dog reluctantly stayed.

Andrew watched the sway of Summer's retreating backside and fought the same urge to follow her, turning his attention back to the matter at hand—retrieving his car from the ditch. But first things first, he thought, glancing down at the urn he held. He needed to find a place to store his father's ashes. He strode across the scraggly lawn toward the white clapboard house where he'd grown up, fighting the sadness that pulled at him at its state of disrepair.

The limestone walkway, once bright and studded with bouquets of mint, was now dull and choked with weeds. The porch that had been wide and inviting with white furniture and bright pillows was now cluttered with stacked furniture, rusting washtubs and miscellaneous tools.

The house itself looked tired and droopy, with peeling paint and falling gutters. He walked up onto the porch and made his way to the front door, fumbling for his key before realizing the door probably wasn't even locked. Sure enough, when he turned the knob, the door swung open. Truman rushed inside ahead of him, barking happily, calling out for his misplaced master.

Andrew walked inside and another wave of sadness swept over him. His father's life, interrupted—an overstuffed recliner, a newspaper folded to the crossword puzzle, a bowl of chocolate-covered peanuts on the table next to the TV remote control. A strange sense of déjà vu struck him and he realized with a start that if he substituted the plaid recliner with black leather, the *Tiny Gazette* with the *New York Times* and the old boxy television with a sleek flat-screen, he could be looking at his own living room. Pushing aside the disturbing revelation, he set the urn on the fireplace mantel.

Something on his wrist caught his eye. Wrapped around the stem of the gold watch his boss had awarded him for landing a particularly lucrative account was a strand of blond hair. He found the end of the hair and tried to pull it free, but it was as thick as fishing line. Afraid he would damage the stem, he opted to wait for a pair of scissors. But the sight of it reminded him of being wedged up close to Summer Tomlinson—close enough to kiss that bee-stung mouth. Beautiful women were common in New York, but he couldn't recall the last time one of them had scrambled his senses to the point that he was undressing her in his mind…wondering what it would feel like to lose himself in her body—

A noise sounded from the kitchen, cutting into his inappropriate musings about Summer Tomlinson. Andrew went to investigate and found Red Tucker bent over, peering into the refrigerator. His father's friend looked up and smiled wide. "Andrew! Hello!"

Andrew smiled and shook the older man's hand. "Hello, Red."

Red gestured to the back door. "I knocked, but no one answered."

"I just got here, myself. But you know you're always welcome."

"Didn't see your car in the driveway out back."

"I put it in a ditch in front of the Tomlinson house trying to dodge a fugitive horse."

"You okay?"

"Just irritated."

Red laughed. "I'll fetch the tractor and give you a tow directly." Then he nodded to a covered dish sitting on the butcher-block table. "Debbie sent you a chicken casserole—I was trying to find a place to put it, but it looks like the church brigade has already been by."

Andrew glanced inside to find the refrigerator packed with labeled food containers.

Red rearranged a couple of items and added his wife's casserole. "If you want my opinion, I'd skip Tessa Hadley's Mexican dip and Anna Kelly's potato salad. But Roberta Bride's apple pie is a keeper."

Andrew smiled. "Thanks for the tip."

The man closed the refrigerator door, then sobered. "Your father was a good man. He'll be missed."

Andrew nodded at the man's heartfelt words. "Thank you. You were a good friend to him, Red."

Red looked around the cluttered country kitchen. "Do you know what you're going to do with the place?"

In light of his recent conversation with Summer, he hesitated. "I suppose I'll sell it."

Red nodded. "Figured as much."

"I have to say, I'm a little surprised how rundown Dad let things get around here."

The man's expression turned pensive. "The last few months, your dad lost interest in everything but the stables."

"Listen, Red, did Dad talk to you about a grooming product for horses he was planning to market and sell?"

"No." Then Red pulled on his chin. "But that makes sense."

"What makes sense?"

"Odd business expenses I called him on that he was vague about—lab expenses and chemicals and such."

"How much money are we talking about?" Andrew asked, suddenly concerned.

"Several thousand dollars. Money he couldn't afford to spend, between you and me. Did you know he was behind on property taxes?"

Andrew straightened. "No."

"And that he'd taken out a mortgage?"

Alarm bolted through his chest. "But my parents paid off the property when I was young."

Red grunted. "You should be able to get more for the property than your father owed, but with the way real estate has dropped around here, it'll be close. And those taxes will need to be paid sooner rather than later."

Andrew nodded, shot through with frustration that his father hadn't let him know he needed money. Had he gone without things he needed to take care of those broken-down horses? Had Summer Tomlinson influenced him to spend money on the crazy hair conditioner?

When he went to see the distracting woman tonight, he intended to find out.

4

SUMMER WAS A NERVOUS wreck, second-guessing what to serve for dinner, what to wear, what to say to Andrew when he arrived. Gabby wasn't helping with her running critical commentary from her perch on the windowsill where she supervised and apparently found everything from the rosemary pot roast to the green wrap dress wanting.

"Shh!" Summer said to her vocal cat.

Gabby blinked, then lifted her chin as if to say it was a lucky coincidence she'd just decided she *wanted* to be quiet.

Summer glanced around the room to check last-minute details—the pot roast was sliced and sitting on the sideboard, along with mashed potatoes and gravy. The simple dinner wouldn't measure up the elegant meals Andrew was no doubt accustomed to, but it was the nicest cut of meat she'd had in the freezer and, she hoped, would remind him of the virtues of good home-cooking.

The women in New York had their tools of seduction, and the women in Tiny had theirs.

Next to the food she'd placed the binder containing the notes on the project she and Barber had worked on, and a container of the pinkish conditioner she and Barber had dubbed Mane Squeeze. Hopefully, she could convince Andrew their formula could compete in the marketplace.

The doorbell rang, and Gabby yowled in notification.

"Yes, I heard it, too," Summer said. On the way to the front door, she slipped off the scarf she'd worn over her hair while cooking. Her heart thudded against her breastbone. Tonight was supposed to be about business, but she'd be lying if she said she wasn't hoping it would lead to something else.

She opened the door and Truman rushed inside, licking her knees and her hands.

"Truman," Andrew chided, "we haven't been invited in."

Summer laughed to cover her nervousness. Andrew was so handsome in brown slacks and a cream-colored long-sleeved dress shirt that highlighted his dark coloring. Now that the sun had set, the early-evening air gusting around him was tinged with the bite of the waning winter. Goosebumps raised on her arms. "Please, come in."

He smiled, revealing white teeth. "I promise not to lick you."

Her cheeks warmed as illicit images leaped to her mind. She

stepped aside and tried to tamp down her pulse as he crossed the threshold.

He extended a covered pie plate. "I brought dessert."

"How thoughtful," she murmured.

"I can't take credit...Miss Bride made it."

Summer smiled, but before she could take the pie, the sound of barking and hissing followed by a horrific crashing noise from the kitchen ended the moment. She rushed in to find the meal, the notebook and the container of conditioner spilled all over the floor. The edge of the runner had been pulled down, Truman was barking furiously and Gabby was sitting on the sideboard, her teeth bared and her ears laid back.

"Oh, no!" Summer cried.

"Truman, be quiet!" Andrew commanded.

The dog stopped and whined, then retreated to stand next to Andrew. Gabby, however, refused to retreat. She continued to hiss in the dog's direction, leaning so far forward over the edge of the sideboard that it looked as if she might leap across the room onto him.

"Gabby!" Summer scolded. From a narrow closet, she pulled a broom and a few menacing motions sent Gabby bounding up the stairs. The Persian stopped at the landing to give everyone a piece of her feline mind, then lifted her tail in the air and walked away.

"I'm so sorry," Andrew said, gesturing to the mess. He glared at Truman who hid his head.

"I'm sure he was provoked," Summer said, frowning after her cat. Then she sighed and lifted her hands. "I don't have a plan B for dinner."

Andrew smiled and lifted his offering. "We have pie."

Summer laughed, relaxing a bit. "That does sound good. I'll put on some coffee."

"And I'll start cleaning up," Andrew offered, reaching for paper towels.

The ruined dinner actually helped to break the ice, although Summer was upset to find her notes soaked with gravy and the spilled conditioner. So much for a classy presentation. They moved to the living-room couch and coffee table, and over thick wedges of pie and creamy coffee, she reviewed sticky pages and described how she and Barber had refined the recipe for the formula.

"Your father told me the secret is how the aloe-vera gel reacts with the evening-primrose oil." She extended a rescued spoonful of the blush-colored lotion. "Barber made a new batch last week. He kept the inventory in the kitchen pantry, by the way."

Andrew sniffed the conditioner. "It has a pleasant scent," he admitted.

"We added rosemary oil for fragrance, and pomegranate for natural color. We found a cosmetology lab in Knoxville that doesn't test on animals and our formula qualifies to be marketed as organic."

He glanced over the reports that included a budget, his mouth pursed in thought. The pink-and-black lettering of the Mane Squeeze label and logo design she'd labored over now seemed painfully amateurish. She could tell he wasn't bowled over when he returned to eating his pie. Finally, he swallowed.

"What about tests to prove it actually makes hair grow longer? That's a big claim to back up."

"The lab has been conducting tests for three months," she said. "I regularly submit a few strands for analysis. The latest results are promising."

He set aside the reports and gestured to her hair. "And how long have you been using it?"

She offered up a lock of her loose hair for his inspection. "Over seven years. Hair typically grows about six inches a year, and my hair is about forty-five inches long. So the entire length is the result of Mane Squeeze."

He reluctantly took the proffered strand, then awkwardly rubbed it between his fingers. "It...has a nice texture," he said, then cleared his throat. "And I noticed earlier that your hair is, um, strong, but maybe that's your natural makeup."

She shook her head. "Before I started using Barber's conditioner, my hair would barely grow past my shoulders."

He was still holding the hank of blond hair, and the sight of it entwined in his large fingers sent a quickening to her breasts.

Erotic visions flashed in her head of his hands pushing into her hair and tousling it during carnal activity.

"So what do you think?" she asked. The words came out sounding more husky than she'd planned.

His dark eyes bore into hers. "I think you have beautiful hair." His husky tone matched hers.

She wet her lips. "Does that mean you'll try to market your father's formula? That you'll fulfill his dream to turn the Mane Squeeze into a horse-rescue center?"

His mouth opened. "I've decided to, um…do my best."

Excitement and happiness bubbled up in her chest. "Thank you!" Impulsively, she threw her arms around Andrew and kissed him on the mouth.

What started out as a sweet thank-you kiss quickly morphed into a deeper, harder exchange. Summer opened her mouth and welcomed him inside. His tongue delivered arrows of desire to awaken dormant erogenous zones. He wrapped his hand around the nape of her neck and slanted his mouth against hers. She moaned as her body came alive, shifting to loop her arms around his neck. He eased her back on the couch and moved his kisses to her neck. She sighed in his ear, relishing the warmth of his body pressed against hers.

This was unlike her, she thought distantly. She'd had her share of suitors, but no one had ever made her feel so wanton with a simple kiss, had made her feel as if she wanted to roll around on the couch like a teenager.

He kissed lower, nuzzling her cleavage, and she arched into him, urging him on. Her nipples budded in anticipation of his tongue's attention. He slid his hand down her back…and she inhaled sharply as her head went back in pain.

"Ow!"

He stilled his hand. "Sorry…I think your hair is caught again."

"Your watch?"

"No…my cuff link."

After some awkward levering, she sat up and he turned her around to try to loosen the wayward hair.

"Ow, ow, ow!" she moaned.

"I'm sorry." After several long minutes, he grunted. "Almost...there." At last he lifted his freed hand, then he laughed. "I keep getting tangled up with you."

Summer smiled, then, feeling bold, she tossed her hair in what she hoped was a coy gesture. "Maybe you should take off your shirt."

She saw desire in his whiskey-colored eyes, but then he glanced at his watch and pushed to his feet. "Actually, I should be going. It's been a long day."

Summer stood hurriedly and adjusted her clothing. "Of course. You must be tired. Thanks for listening...and for bringing the pie."

"No problem." He whistled for Truman, who came loping in from another room. He picked up the lab reports and headed toward the door. Summer walked with him, tingling with embarrassment. The man probably had a girlfriend—or many—back in New York.

"Let me know if you have any questions about the conditioner," she said brightly. She pulled her hair over one shoulder and played with it self-consciously. "I'll be over tomorrow after work to feed the horses."

He was staring at her hair, no doubt thinking what a complete nuisance it was. "O...kay," he murmured, then practically fell out her front door into the cool air...and was gone.

5

I'll do my best.

Andrew was taking a break, standing at the door of the kitchen pantry, drinking a tall glass of cold water after a morning of hot, tedious work cleaning up his father's property. He stared at the row of bottles containing the pink Mane Squeeze conditioner, along with a long list in Barber's handwriting of individual customers awaiting delivery. He'd been all set the previous night to tell Summer that although he respected her efforts, bringing a hair conditioner to the marketplace wasn't a project in which he was prepared to invest time or money.

Instead, he'd been mesmerized by that mane of exquisite hair, fixated on the thought of seeing her nude with her glorious golden veil all around her, and said he'd do his best.

He sighed, then wiped his sweaty neck and pulled out his phone. He scrolled through his contacts, stopping on an entry for an advertising associate in Nashville who specialized in direct-to-consumer sales and pressed the connect button. It was probably a waste of time, but...

"Andrew MacMillan for Charles Basker....Charles, hello.... Yes, long time, no see. How are you?...Good. Listen, I'm back in Tennessee for a few days, and I have a favor to ask. My veterinarian father recently passed away....Yes, thank you. The reason I'm calling is I just learned that he and a friend of the family developed an organic hair conditioner that's become a bit of a local sensation. I was wondering if you'd be interested in taking a look at it and giving me an opinion on its viability in a wider market?...You will?...Okay, I'll ship a few bottles your way. Thanks, man."

He ended the call, a little nonplussed, but not overly concerned, because the man probably said yes a hundred times a day and meant it a fraction of the time. Over the years he'd received his own fair share of similar calls from friends and associates and he couldn't remember a single personally referred product that had panned out. But he'd do this so he could in good conscience tell Summer he'd tried.

As long as he wasn't looking into those sexy blue eyes of hers, he might be able to pull off a half-truth. He hoped the woman had no idea how much he'd wanted not only to tear off his own shirt last night, but to relieve her of her clothing, as well. And lose himself in her eyes and her body and that amazing hair.

He touched the cool glass to his forehead.

But then what? He'd come back to Tiny to tie up all the loose ends, not to create more. He glanced into the living room where his father's ashes still sat on the mantel, mocking him. Yet another decision that needed to be made.

Andrew found a box and pulled out six bottles of the conditioner, then picked up the list of supplies he needed from the hardware store, grabbed the keys to his dad's pickup truck and left by the back door. Truman was waiting for him and happily jumped into the bench seat when Andrew opened the creaky door of the truck. Andrew felt a pang for the dog who had obviously fallen into a comfortable routine of accompanying Barber wherever he went.

When Andrew left, he'd have to find a good home for Truman. Summer would probably be willing to take him in, but that cat of hers would make his life miserable. Andrew looked at the sweet-faced dog. Yet another decision to make.

As he circled around to drive by the front of the house, Andrew surveyed the progress he'd made clearing the yard of overgrowth and clutter. He'd managed to uncover the building where his father had once maintained his veterinary office, resulting in a huge pile of bramble that needed to be burned or hauled away. He'd peeked in a dusty window to see furniture and equipment encased in covers and realized the building would be a perfect office for an animal-rescue center.

Then he quickly turned his mind elsewhere.

Retailers in Tiny were hyping Valentine's Day, reminding shoppers not to forget their lovers on their special day! Red balloons abounded. Andrew tucked his tongue into his cheek—over the years he'd enjoyed a few mildly serious relationships with women, but he'd always managed to avoid Valentine's Day by scheduling work travel. He rejected the idea that a made-up holiday could or should bring a couple closer.

He stopped by the post office and mailed the box of conditioner and copies of the ingredient-testing reports to Charles. The task took longer than he'd planned because people recognized him and stopped to give their condolences. It made him realize just how far from Manhattan he was. Here in Tiny, everyone knew everyone. And so it continued as he stopped by the hardware store to buy paint and countless other supplies, as well as when he stopped by the City Hall building to inquire about the property taxes due on his father's farm.

The clerk was Roberta Bride, who pinched his cheeks and said nice things about Barber. When she presented Andrew with the tax bill, he managed to hide his surprise at the substantial sum, but assured her he would settle the debt as soon as he got his father's financial affairs in order. And he thanked her for the apple pie. She dimpled and said it was nice to see he hadn't gotten "above his raising."

Andrew smiled, but on the way out of the building, his mind churned with all the decisions at hand. He was feeling overwhelmed and eager to get back to the relatively calm chaos of Manhattan.

He heard his name and turned his head. Tessa Hadley, dressed in a smart skirt suit, her dark hair bobbed, was walking toward him, wearing her "agent" smile.

"Andrew, I thought that was you." Then she gestured to his jeans, T-shirt and the old boots he'd pulled from the closet of his bedroom that had remained unchanged after he'd left home. "Even dressed like a local, you stand out." She stepped forward to clasp him in a hug and held on a little longer than necessary. "I'm sorry about your father."

"Thank you," he said, extricating himself.

"Did you like the Mexican dip I made?" she asked brightly.

"Er, yes," he said, deciding not to tell her about Red's warning and even Truman's subsequent refusal to eat it. "That was kind of you."

"You live in New York, I understand. How exciting! You're in marketing?"

"Advertising. I see you're doing well."

"Yes," she said, sweeping an arm down her figure as if she were a game show prize. Then she angled her head. "Our phone call yesterday was cut short."

He shifted from foot to foot. "Sorry about that. I was going to call you back."

She batted her lashes. "I would've called you back, but I've been busy getting poor Sadie Case's house ready for the market. My dad said you were interested in selling your father's farm?"

He hesitated, and the hesitation itself irritated him. He'd been humoring Summer Tomlinson with this idea of a horse-rescue center funded by a magic hair potion, but he didn't really have a choice.

"That's right," he said. "As a matter of fact, I'd like to get it on the market as soon as possible. Would you be interested in listing it?"

"Of course. If I remember correctly, the property shares a boundary with the State Park, doesn't it?"

He nodded. "At one time, my father said he'd been approached by someone with the state to buy the property for the limestone cave spring."

"I'll look into it," she said, her eyes gleaming with the promise of a sale. "Will you be home later? There is some paperwork you'll need to sign, and I'll have to take a few photos."

"You can bring the paperwork, but if you've seen the house, you know the property isn't very photogenic at the moment. I'm cleaning it up now."

"The photos can wait," she agreed. "But it's a date—see you later!" She gave him a toodle-loo finger wave, then twisted away.

He stared after her, guilt gnawing at his gut. But it couldn't be helped, and it's what he'd come here to do. The sooner the farm was listed, the sooner he could return to New York.

The errands had taken longer than he'd planned. By the time he got the supplies unloaded and organized, it was late afternoon. He decided to hook the bush hog to the tractor and make a few passes at the front pasture to improve the curb appeal of the farm. Truman kept him company, but maintained a safe distance from the mowing machine.

The weather had held, and the temperatures were still high. It was slow going—Andrew had to jump down from the tractor often, to remove rocks or branches that were too large to safely skim. Remorse plagued him. He'd forgotten how much work it was to maintain even a small farm. No wonder things had fallen into disrepair. He should've been more attentive, should've noticed his aging father needed help.

It didn't take long for him to work up a sweat and shed his T-shirt. He used it to wipe his neck and glanced around from this slightly higher vantage point. From here, he could see the Tomlinson house, and just like that, Summer was crowding his thoughts again. He wondered why a sweet, pretty country girl like her wasn't married, then reminded himself for all he knew, she might've been married a dozen times. And besides, what did her marital status have to do with him?

He continued mowing, but the mindlessness of the work combined with the unaccustomed activity of his body kept his mind fixed on Summer in that fetching green dress. And her *out* of that fetching green dress. And her *in* that fetching green dress… but mostly *out* of that fetching green dress. And her hair… Lust seized his body when he thought of running his fingers through that satiny blond curtain.

Truman's bark interrupted his thoughts. Andrew looked to see what had captured the dog's attention and saw Summer walking down the path toward the stables. She lifted a hand to wave, and he waved back. Truman abandoned him, making a beeline for her. Andrew couldn't blame him. Determined not to stare, he turned to proudly survey the work he'd done and bit back a curse—the strips of mowed grass were crooked and he'd missed wide swaths of weeds he'd have to redo. Summer was probably laughing at his haphazard job. Forcing his mind back to the job, he tackled the ground again. Later, when he drove the tractor back to the barn next to the stables, at least he was satisfied he'd put in a good day's work.

With a start, he realized he couldn't remember the last time he'd said that.

He turned off the tractor and jumped down to the dirt floor. The barn housed the tractor and a host of dusty implements, plus crates of old tools and miscellaneous clutter—more stuff to sort through and discard. As he exited the old wood structure, he was starting to feel the weight of his father's life pulling on his shoulders.

Truman appeared at the door of the stables and barked a welcome. Except for cleaning around the building, Andrew had managed to ignore the stables thus far, but decided he probably should check out the inhabitants. And saying hello to Summer was only polite.

He hung his T-shirt over his shoulder and walked through the open doorway of the faded red structure. On either side of a straw-covered hallway were rows of stalls, ten in all. The doorway at the other end of the stables also stood open. Summer stood there grooming a tired-looking brown horse whose hocks and knees were wrapped with gauze. She was crooning in the horse's ear...and she was spectacular.

The late-afternoon sun slanted in behind her, casting her slender figure in a golden halo. She wore slim jeans tucked into knee-high boots, and a gauzy white shirt that was transparent in the light. Her hair was pulled back into a low ponytail, leaving the ends to brush the top of her buttocks as she stretched to groom the horse, whose big eyes were nearly closed in abject appreciation. Eight more heads of all shapes and sizes were stuck out over the stalls, gazing at their savior. Max whinnied and tossed his big gray head as Andrew walked closer.

Summer turned toward him and smiled. "Hello."

"Hi." His jeans suddenly felt tighter. Could she be any more beautiful?

"You've been busy," she said. "The yard looks nice."

"It looks better," he corrected. "I've barely made a dent."

"Is there something I can do?"

"No, you're doing plenty by taking care of the horses." He gestured to the forlorn group. "Where did they all come from?"

She nodded to the corner stall. "Max's owner died, so Barber took him in. Same for Fila here, who came to us in pretty bad shape, as did Pippen, the little mare down on the end. Jax and Henna were found after a flash flood, caught in barbed wire. No one ever claimed them. Kuppa, the one wearing the bell collar, is blind. She used to belong to a customer of Barber's, and the lady just couldn't take care of her anymore. Same for Striker, Topper and Atlas. Their owners asked Barber to take them."

Andrew looked from animal to animal. Every story tugged on his heart. It had been kind of his father to take in the horses... but taking care of them had nearly cost him his home.

"I know you have a lot on your mind," Summer said, "but have you had time to think about your father's formula?"

"Some," he said, hedging. "I—"

"Yoo-hoo!" a woman's voice called. "Is anyone home?"

He turned to see Tessa Hadley come into view. She had changed into a red dress that was cut low and riding high.

"Andrew, there you are." Her eyes widened at the sight of his bare torso, and she fanned herself. "My, my...I didn't realize advertising was such a physical job."

"Hello, Tessa," he said, pulling his T-shirt over his head. "Do you know Summer Tomlinson?"

Tessa looked toward the end of the barn and straightened. "Of course. Hello, Summer."

"Hi," Summer said. "What brings you out this way, Tessa?"

Andrew's stomach cramped.

"Andrew asked me to list his father's farm," Tessa said, teetering on high heels.

Summer looked at him and drew back, her gaze accusing. Andrew wanted to defend himself, but what could he say?

"I brought the paperwork to sign," Tessa continued, then she patted the dish she cradled. "And since Andrew liked my Mexican dip so much, I brought my Mexicali casserole for dinner!" She bit her lip and eyed Summer warily. "There might be enough for three if you want to join us."

"No, thanks," Summer said with a little smile. "But I've heard about your casseroles—I'm sure Andrew will love it." Summer gave him a pointed look, then led Fila back to his stable.

Frustration welled in Andrew's chest. He didn't want to leave Summer, wanted to make her understand he had no choice but to put the farm up for sale. "Do you need any help with the horses?" he asked.

"No, I've got it covered." Her body language was stiff. "You and Tessa have fun."

"We will," Tessa sang. She took a step and wobbled in her shoes.

Andrew reached out to keep her from toppling, realizing too late he'd missed a chance to ditch the casserole.

Tessa clung to his arm and laughed throatily. "I can't believe I'm saying this, Andrew, but are you sure you want to sell this place? You would certainly improve the landscape around Tiny if you decided to stay."

Andrew's gaze flicked to Summer. She was in profile, stroking the throat of the blind horse, Kuppa, but he could tell she was listening.

Andrew looked back to Tessa and gave her a tight smile. "I'm sure."

6

FOR THE NEXT FEW DAYS, Andrew avoided Summer and assumed she was avoiding him, too, since she never ventured from the stables to the house. He kept his mind and body occupied with sprucing up the property. There was still plenty left to do, but he finally felt as if he was making headway. As difficult as Tessa had been to get rid of the night he'd filled out the paperwork to list the farm, she had been helpful in rounding up a crew of laborers to haul away the piles of debris and items for charity, and to prep the house. If the dry weather held, the crew would be back in a couple of days to finish the painting, then Tessa would be back to take photographs.

Today he'd made it out to the rear pasture on the property to bush hog the area around the limestone cave spring in case the state sent a representative to take a tour. It was, however, the one area his father had kept relatively clear. Barber was fond of putting his arthritic feet in the warm, deep aqua-colored pool that had formed underneath a shelf of limestone. In his lifetime, Andrew had never known the pool to be any larger or any smaller, come drought or flood.

He glanced around and acknowledged it was a beautiful place—the ornamental trees and plants his parents had planted around the spring were thick and mature from the warm water table. He hoped the state would agree the spot would make a popular tourist destination. Tessa had pressed upon him that his best hope of getting a selling price to clear his father's debt was if the Tiny Caves State Park annexed his father's farm into their property. If that happened, his hope was that the state would then agree to Summer's plan for the horse-rescue center.

Then everyone would be happy, including him, ensconced in his condo in Manhattan.

He was getting antsy about the work he was missing, experiencing withdrawal from his laptop because there was no internet connection on or near his father's property. Managing emails on his phone was becoming increasingly frustrating with the slow network speed and spotty reception.

Then again, just about everything about being in Tiny frustrated him.

When he drove the tractor back to the barn, he strained for a glimpse of Summer, but she wasn't in the stables. He did notice, however, that the horse trailer was missing.

He went inside to shower, picking his way through the boxes of clothes and other items he'd packed to be donated to charity. In his bedroom, the boxes were sitting in a row along the wall, filled with items from his childhood he hadn't taken with him when he'd moved away, but his father had never bothered to dispose of. He stripped off his work clothes and showered, then popped a couple of pain pills for his aching muscles. He winced when he flexed his arm, conceding that a gym workout couldn't compare to a day of hard work on the farm.

After he dressed, he noticed the blond hair still wrapped around the stem of his watch. He crossed his bedroom to the desk where he'd spent many hours doing homework, and opened drawers, looking for a pair of scissors. In the bottom drawer, he found a pair. When he removed them, though, he spotted something on the bottom of the drawer that stirred a memory chord. He pushed aside various relics from schooldays past—combination locks, headphones, a ball of rubberbands—to reveal a Valentine's Day card. When he picked it up, his pulse jumped. It was the card Summer had given him—he did the math in his head—eighteen years ago.

Even then, she'd been crazy about horses, as evidenced by the image on the front of the card, a cartoonish horse with a heart in its mouth braying, "Be Mine." On the inside she'd written, *Andrew, I think you are awesome. Summer.*

He smiled, then gave a little laugh. Had she been crushing on him back then? She didn't think he was so awesome now. He set the card on the top of the desk, then cut the strand of blond hair from his watch, marveling over the strength of it.

The woman's hair would probably support her weight—or even his. His mind skimmed over the implications if the Mane Squeeze conditioner really had made her hair that strong. It would be a bestseller, assuming they could cut through the retail noise to sell it. But who knew if the formula his father developed was the reason, or if Summer was using some other hair product with it, or maybe taking a supplement. She didn't seem like the kind of person who would be purposefully dishonest, but she wanted so badly to believe it worked, she might see a cause and effect where there was none.

He stopped in the kitchen to grab a beer, then wandered out onto the front porch to enjoy the view. Furniture sat stacked and pushed up against the house the way his father had left it. Near the rail sat an aged rocker. Andrew realized, with a jolt, that it was the chair Barber had been sitting in when he'd died. But instead of being repulsed, he was drawn to the chair. He sat down gingerly, then slid his hands over the smooth wood of the armrests and settled back. It was a well-made piece—sturdy and comfortable, with a gentle rock. As he drank his beer, he looked out over the valley tinged with the metallic glow of the sinking winter sun and realized, all in all, this was a pretty nice spot to take your last breath.

He understood why Barber wanted his ashes spread here on the Mane Squeeze, but he couldn't, in good faith, spread his father's ashes across the land then sign the deed to the land over to someone else. He'd find a nice place to store his father's urn.

The headlights of a truck came down the road and the vehicle slowed. When it pulled off and headed toward the Mane Squeeze, he realized the driver was Summer…and she was pulling the missing horse trailer. He pushed to his feet and watched as she drove around the curved drive, then veered onto the grassy road leading to the barn and the stables. She parked, then hopped down and walked back to the horse trailer. She was wearing a cowboy hat over her luxurious hair. His body reacted, just watching her move.

He set down his beer and started toward the trailer, wondering if one of the horses had taken ill and she'd had to transport it to the vet. But when the horse emerged on a lead line, he squinted.

A new horse?

Perhaps "new" wasn't the right word—the white swaybacked horse took lumbering steps, with its head hanging low.

"What's this?" he asked as he walked up.

Summer turned her head. "Hi…I didn't see you. This is Sallie."

"Summer," he chided, "we can't take in any more horses."

She bristled. "There's room for one more."

"That's one more we'll have to find a home for! One more that will eat its weight in feed every week until we do!"

Her eyes narrowed. "Sallie belonged to Sadie Case. Miss Case was my teacher and she loved this horse. I wasn't going to just let her be put down."

Andrew bit the inside of his cheek, contrite. "Miss Case was my teacher, too." He sighed. "Okay…Sallie can stay."

Summer smiled and led Sallie toward the stables, although he had the feeling the horse would've stayed with or without his permission.

His phone rang at his waist. He glanced down at the caller ID to see Charles Basker was calling. Curious, he connected the call.

"Hi, Charles."

"Andrew, hi. Listen, I'm pressed for time, but I have an opportunity you and your friend might be interested in for this hair conditioner of your father's."

"I'm listening," Andrew said.

"A vendor backed out of a fifteen-minute spot on a home shopping channel during beauty hour. If you can get a spokesperson to Nashville tomorrow before four o'clock, it's a sweet deal—three million impressions at eighty percent off the normal rate."

He told Andrew how much the spot would run and Andrew was impressed. The gasoline to drive there would cost more. "But we don't have inventory."

"That's the beautiful part," Charles said. "You have six weeks to fulfill orders. You can sample the market without committing to inventory."

Andrew pressed his lips together. Should he tell Summer about the opportunity, or simply pass? A successful advertising spot might open a can of worms and involve him in the project more than he wanted to be.

On the other hand, if the public didn't respond, maybe Summer would concede the Mane Squeeze conditioner wasn't a winning idea.

"Hold on, Charles. My friend is here, let me ask her." He put the phone on mute and strode inside the stable where Summer had coaxed the new horse into the remaining stall. She was scooping corn into a feeder.

Andrew explained that he'd sent the bottles to his associate and the opportunity being offered.

"You did that?" Summer asked, her face lifting in appreciation.

He nodded, uncomfortable with her gratitude. "It's your decision. Are you interested in the spot?"

"But we don't have a spokesperson."

"Sure we do...*you*."

Summer's eyes widened. "Me?"

"Who else are we going to get on such short notice? Besides, you're the one with the hair."

She shook her head. "I can't go on television."

He shrugged. "Then I'll tell Charles we'll pass." He held up the phone to push the button, but Summer stilled his hand with hers.

"Wait." She worried her lower lip. "Okay...I'll do it."

7

BETWEEN HER NERVOUSNESS over being the Mane Squeeze spokesperson in an impromptu stint on a home shopping channel and being in close quarters with Andrew in his sporty little car, Summer was sick to her stomach during the entire three-hour drive to Nashville the following day.

Valentine's Day, to be precise.

And Andrew's attitude didn't exactly soothe her anxieties. When she asked him to help her come up with talking points for the fifteen-minute commercial, he was cooperative, but his enthusiasm was a little flat. In fact, from his body language and grudging comments, she got the distinct feeling that he was regretting setting up the commercial shoot in the first place.

Or did he simply find her company objectionable on a day reserved for sweethearts? All the radio stations seemed to be playing every love song ever recorded—he'd finally put in a CD of jazz music. She reasoned he was probably pining for a lover he'd left in New York, and not in a humor to be babysitting her and her case of hair conditioner. Maybe he and his girlfriend had had an argument over the fact that he was spending the night at a hotel with another woman.

Not that they'd be sharing a room, but Summer couldn't help feeling an implied intimacy at their travel arrangements. She told herself it only made sense that they spend the night, since by the time the shoot ended and they tied up loose ends, it would likely be too late to drive back, especially if the predicted stormy weather materialized. It was her unrealized attraction to Andrew that made everything so…tangled.

She glanced at his profile, dismayed that the mere sight of him could send her pulse racing. Hadn't he practically run out of her house the other night after their kiss? How much more proof did she need that he wasn't into her?

She looked back to her note cards and silently reviewed the talking points, but kept stumbling over the order and forgetting the phrasing. The more she practiced, the more she panicked. Too soon, they were parking in the lot of the studio, a large non-descript warehouse on the outskirts of downtown Nashville. They were both quiet as Andrew pulled the case of product from the trunk and she removed her garment bag, but she could feel him bristling when her hips or hands came close to his. Knowing how much he didn't want to be there made her feet grow heavy as they approached the entrance.

Once they were inside, though, Andrew was congenial and professional as he introduced her to his associate, Charles Basker. Then Summer was whisked away to hair and makeup and to change. Separated from Andrew, she was unnerved and uncertain. Suddenly, she questioned everything, from the label on the conditioner she'd designed to the red dress she'd brought to change into. As far as the talking points, she couldn't remember a single one. By the time she was led to the set that was surrounded by cameras and illuminated with huge canister lights, she was almost paralyzed with fear. She stood off to the side watching the host interact with the current guest who was extolling the virtues of a mood lipstick that changed colors as a woman became more or less "interested" in her partner.

"Just in time for Valentine's Day," the woman said with a cunning smile. "The lipstick goes on pale red, but intensifies as she becomes…excited, shall we say?"

Summer watched the presentation intently, hoping to pick up a few pointers. But the guest seemed so poised and natural—a far cry from how she herself felt. She lifted her thumbnail for a nibble.

"Relax," Andrew said in her ear.

She turned her head to see that he'd joined her. She lowered her hand, desperately wanting to act cool in front of him, but conceding defeat.

"What if I blow this?" she asked, feeling dangerously close to tears.

Suddenly, his face softened and the tension that had held his big body rigid all day seemed to drain out of him.

"There's nothing to blow," he said, his voice gentle. "This is simply an opportunity to test the market—either the audience will respond to the product, or they won't. Either way, you'll have an idea of whether Mane Squeeze could compete in the retail arena. That's all we're looking for today."

His words calmed her. She smiled, then took a cleansing breath and exhaled. "Thank you, Andrew. And thank you for making this happen. Your father would be so happy."

His light brown eyes clouded for an instant, then cleared, indicating he was back to business. He gestured toward the set, where an attractive middle-aged man bantered with the elegant representative of the mood lipstick. "The host will ask questions and encourage viewers to call in." His gaze swept over her red dress and strappy high-heels. "Your primary job is to look good, and that's not a stretch."

Summer's cheeks warmed under his compliment. "Viewers won't be looking at me," she murmured. "They'll be looking at my hair."

"That, too," he agreed, nodding to the shiny length hanging

over one shoulder. "Even if you freeze up and can't say a word, your hair will speak for you."

She bit into her lip.

"Not that you're going to freeze up," he added quickly. "You'll be great. And it'll be over before you know it."

He stepped forward unexpectedly and gave her a bolstering squeeze. Summer turned her head in surprise, and suddenly his mouth was next to hers. She swallowed.

"How about a kiss for good luck?" she whispered.

His eyes became hooded, then he complied, capturing her lips with his in a smoldering kiss that conjured up sensations that ran deeper than platonic good wishes.

"All right, all right, break it up," came a sarcastic voice behind them.

They parted and Summer took in the man who wore headphones and a sardonic smile.

"I know it's Valentine's Day and all, but you two lovebirds will have to wait until later to celebrate."

Summer exchanged an awkward glance with Andrew and opened her mouth to protest, but was cut short when the man introduced himself as the producer and launched into what would happen during the fifteen-minute live taping. When the lights dimmed briefly, he frowned and spoke to someone through his headphones.

"Looks like we're getting a storm," he told them, gesturing to the ceiling of the insulated room. "But don't worry. If the electricity blows, the backup generator will kick on in ten seconds. The host will know what to do." He winked at Summer. "You're on in two minutes, little lady. Are you ready?"

She glanced at Andrew, who gave her an encouraging nod. She looked back to the producer. "Yes."

He ushered her forward to introduce her to the host, who was scanning the product sheet for Mane Squeeze as the lipstick was whisked away from the presentation pedestal and replaced with bottles of the conditioner. The host looked up and his eyes shone in appreciation as he shook her hand.

"The camera is going to love you," he said. "And what marvelous hair."

She didn't have time to blush because the producer was counting down from thirty. As the count dipped below ten, she sought out Andrew and found him, standing in the back of the studio next to a monitor. He gave her a thumbs-up, and she tried to smile.

"Three...two...one," the producer said, then pointed to the host.

The man was a seasoned professional. He introduced Summer, then oohed and aahed over her hair and picked up a bottle of Mane Squeeze to let viewers know the exclusive hair conditioner that Summer used was being made available for the first time to a nationwide audience right here on this stage. After a split second of stage fright, Summer recalled her talking points. She explained how a veterinarian had developed the formula to groom the manes and tails of the horses, then added that the net proceeds from the sale of the conditioner would fund a horse-rescue center. She smiled into the camera, but from the rear of the studio she felt Andrew's disapproving gaze on her.

Technically, he owned his father's formula and the distribution of the net proceeds would be his decision. But how could he refuse after she'd made a pledge on live television?

They were about five minutes into the commercial when Summer realized something was wrong. The host referred to a monitor that tracked phone orders so he could incite viewers to call by telling them how many fellow shoppers were jumping on the deal. When he glanced at the monitor, though, he looked concerned, then laughed. "I can see that some of you are skeptical about this organic formula. Can I ask you, Summer, how long have you used Mane Squeeze?"

She told him, avoiding claims that the conditioner stimulated hair growth, emphasizing instead that it made her hair stronger to withstand the wear and tear of the elements. And she assured him she wasn't wearing extensions, that what he saw was all her natural hair.

"Folks, look at this gorgeous mane," the host said. "We have a regular Rapunzel here in the studio." He picked up a lock of her hair and rubbed it between his fingers. "And you can't believe how soft and luxurious her hair feels. I'm sure those of you watching are eager to see what Mane Squeeze can do for your hair." He repeated the phone number and the item number over and over, and his sales pitch grew more exuberant—or desperate—as the time wound down. When the producer cued him with a "1 minute" card, the host was practically begging viewers to call in. "It's a small investment—less than the cost of a haircut. What do you have to lose?"

The producer was mouthing and fingering "three, two, one," as the host wrapped up. "And we're out." The producer clapped his hands. "Okay, clear the set."

The host winced at Summer. "Sorry that sales weren't better. It happens sometimes. Here, have a lipstick." He pressed a tube of the mood lipstick into her hand.

With a sinking heart, she thanked him and slipped the lipstick into her pocket, then took the box of conditioner a crew member handed to her and moved in Andrew's direction. He relieved her of the box, gave her a wink, then shepherded her out of the studio and into a small adjacent office where his friend Charles Basker studied a computer screen. The man hit a button on the keyboard, then turned to a nearby printer and pulled off a couple of sheets. He looked up and motioned them forward, but Summer knew from his expression that the news wasn't good.

"Well, we can't always have a homerun," Charles said with forced good humor.

"How many units were sold?" Andrew asked.

Charles extended the report. "About fifty."

Summer's stomach dropped. She'd hoped to sell ten times that much. She could sell fifty bottles around Tiny, without advertising.

"It's okay, Charles," Andrew said. "It tells us what we need to know." He glanced at Summer. "Doesn't it?"

Feeling like a chastised child, she nodded and thanked Charles for the opportunity. The men made more small talk, then shook hands and said goodbye. Summer's heart dragged as she and

Andrew backtracked to the entrance. She'd hoped to introduce Barber's formula to the world.

Outside, it was storming, with rain coming down in sheets. Andrew told her to stay in the lobby while he went to get the car, then he ran out to brave the weather. Summer surveyed the sky, lit up with neon lightning strikes, thinking it was good they were spending the night after all instead of trying to drive back in this soup.

Andrew pulled the car alongside the curb, then emerged with an umbrella that he held over her head when she walked out until she was settled into the passenger seat. When he climbed in the driver's seat and closed the door, he was soaked through. His sport coat drooped and his dark hair dripped down his back. He gave a harsh laugh. "Just another reason to dislike Valentine's Day."

Summer gave him a little smile, but inside she was shrinking. He was so handsome, he took her breath away. That kiss... she was sure he'd enjoyed it, had sensed his desire for her. But he seemed intent on avoiding all intimate contact with her. "Is the hotel far away?"

"Thankfully, no. I'll be happy to get out of these clothes."

His words conjured up images in her brain of him doing just that.

"Into something dry," he added, as if he'd read her dirty mind. "The hotel restaurant is supposed to be nice. We could have dinner there if you like."

"Yes, I'd like that," she murmured.

On the drive to the hotel, she remained quiet to allow him to concentrate on the road in the driving rain. The steamy interior of the car seemed more intimate than before. She felt as if the heat from her body was fueling the fogged windows. He kept adjusting the defroster to keep the windshield clear. She was relieved when they pulled underneath the valet canopy of their hotel.

At the registration desk, the clerk treated them like a couple, gave them sly glances when she handed over two room keys.

"Mr. MacMillan, Ms. Tomlinson, your rooms are...*close* to each other."

"Thank you," they muttered in unison.

On the elevator ride, Summer stared straight ahead, thinking the less she looked at Andrew, the less apt he was to guess what she was thinking—that she'd love to share his bed tonight. They alighted from the elevator and discovered their rooms were directly across the hall from each other. The bellman was behind them with their overnight bags.

Andrew tipped the man, then gave her a tight smile. "Give me twenty minutes to change?"

She returned a curt nod. "Knock on my door when you're ready."

It was the longest twenty minutes of her life. She refreshed her makeup, impulsively stroking on a layer of the mood lipstick. She pressed her lips together, noting the pale cherry hue that looked like a natural stain, doubting there was any truth to the assertion that the lipstick would "brighten" if a woman was attracted to her companion. More likely, it was a reaction to sunlight, or the bright lights of the studio.

She brushed her hair, opting to leave it loose around her shoulders. She adjusted her red dress again and again, wishing she had something else to change into, worried it was too formal for a platonic dinner in the hotel restaurant. After all, Andrew would probably change into casual slacks or jeans. She didn't want to look as if she was trying too hard to...what?

Seduce him?

The knock on the door made her jump. When she opened it, her mouth went dry and she was instantly glad she hadn't changed. Andrew wore a dark suit, with an open-collar cream-colored dress shirt. "Ready?" he asked.

She nodded, then fell into step with him to walk to the elevator, hoping he couldn't hear her heart pounding in her chest. She was being silly, she chastised herself on the ride down and the short walk to the restaurant. This was simply a business dinner between two associates…old friends…neighbors. Wholly platonic and completely unromantic.

But when they entered the restaurant, she did a double take—red hearts dominated the wall and table decor, sensual music played in the background and couples sat huddled in twos in low lighting.

She'd forgotten it was Valentine's Day and that the entire world would be paired up for dinner. And from the look on his face, Andrew had forgotten, too.

8

THE MAÎTRE D' EXTENDED a wide smile. "Welcome. You're in luck. We still have some choice tables left, and the chef has prepared a special menu to share for Valentine's Day."

Andrew took a half step back. "I don't think…I mean…" He glanced at Summer, hoping she'd step in.

"We're not dating," Summer supplied.

The maître d' angled his head. "This is your first time dining together?"

"Yes," they said in unison.

His smile beamed wider. "Even better. Right this way."

Summer looked at Andrew with raised eyebrows. Andrew hesitated, but realized his only choices were to leave, which would be rude, or to embarrass Summer by pressing the issue that they weren't a couple. He acquiesced with a lift of his arm to indicate she should precede him. She smiled and followed the maître d', and he followed her, marveling how the view of her from behind was equally as mesmerizing as the view from the front. She was a stunner in that red dress. Considering the way the studio crew had stared at her during the shoot, he was tempted to believe the reason more units of the hair conditioner hadn't sold was because TV viewers had been too riveted by her to listen to what was being said.

As if to prove his point, more than one head turned as they walked by. Andrew picked up his pace and held his hand at the small of Summer's back in case the louts with wandering eyes got any ideas. Her silky hair tickled his palm. He gritted his teeth against the urge to sink his hands into the thick curtain.

They were led to an intimate table that was more like a half booth and necessitated them sitting close. A waiter appeared and handed Summer a red rose. She smiled and held the bloom up to her nose for a deep inhale, then broke off the stem and tucked it behind her ear. The waiter nodded in adoring approval, and Andrew squashed a jealous pang. He listened as the man described the fixed menu of hearty bread, caprese salad, chateaubriand, side dishes and dessert. Andrew ordered a bottle of pinot noir. When they were alone, he cast about for a distraction from her luminous blue eyes. At a loss, he retrieved his phone and glanced at the screen.

"Expecting a call?" she asked.

"No," he said with a frown. "But I just noticed my network is down. Does your phone have service?"

She pulled a small phone from her purse. "No. Maybe it's because of the storm."

Heavy curtains were drawn over tall windows, but flashes of lightning lit up the edges, and rain pounded the roof.

"I wonder if it's storming in Tiny," she said, her voice thick with concern. "The horses will be stressed, especially Sallie, since she hasn't had time to acclimate."

Andrew was touched by how much she cared about the animals. "Red will take good care of them."

"I'm worried about what will happen to them now," she murmured. "I was so hopeful Mane Squeeze would be a runaway success. I guess I was a little naive."

He hated seeing her disappointment, but deep down, he was

relieved the sampling had failed. He could say they'd given it a shot and get back to his life in New York. "Success for a new product is like lightning in a bottle. As much as we professionals hate to admit it, sometimes it comes down to random luck."

"It's not the absolute end of Barber's formula," she said. "I'll still use it, and I'll groom the horses with it as long as they're around."

He toyed with the stem of his glass. "Tessa said the State Park is interested in buying the farm. Maybe they'll be willing to fund a horse-rescue center."

She gave him a tight smile. "I've worked for the Park for a long time. They simply don't have the funds to invest in a venture that doesn't generate revenue."

He inclined his head, conceding she was probably right.

She shifted in her chair, then gestured to their festive surroundings. "I'm sorry about the misunderstanding that we're here on a date."

"It's okay. I suppose to outsiders, we look like a couple."

A blush tinged her cheeks, and he realized that despite the letdown over the lack of interest in the special conditioner, she was enjoying the moment. She probably didn't get many chances to dress up and dine in upscale surroundings in Tiny.

When the music changed to a slow song and she glanced wistfully at the couples gathering on the small dance floor, Andrew told himself it wouldn't hurt anything to ask her to dance. But when she moved into his arms under the twinkling overhead lights, he realized he was sorely testing his resolve not to bed her. With her willowy body pressing against his and her golden hair swirling around her shoulders, it wasn't much of a stretch to imagine the two of them horizontal, indulging in a different kind of dance altogether.

The woman had him tied in knots, he acknowledged as the night wore on.

The food was delicious and the more wine Summer drank, the more animated she became. Over the shared meal, they conversed easily about growing up in Tiny, laughing over collective memories. She was well-read and plugged into current events.

Her values and beliefs mirrored his on many issues, but she was congenial and open-minded. He couldn't remember a more enjoyable meal.

"You're staring at my mouth," Summer said, lifting her napkin. "Do I have a smudge?"

"No, your mouth is just very...red. It's nice," he added quickly, then realized he sounded like an idiot. "It must be from the wine."

She touched her fingers to her mouth. "The host of the shopping channel gave me a tube of the mood lipstick they were selling."

He squinted. "I vaguely remember...it's supposed to change colors?"

She nodded.

"Depending on what?"

She arched an eyebrow and gave him a knowing look.

His body reacted, sending a rush of blood to his midsection.

"How red is it?" she asked, pursing into a pout and leaning closer. "Like a cherry?"

He swallowed painfully.

She leaned closer. "Like a strawberry?"

It was getting harder to breathe...and harder everywhere else, too.

"Like a siren?" she whispered.

Thank goodness, the waiter arrived with dessert, breaking into the red-hot exchange. Andrew lifted his napkin to dab at the perspiration beaded at his hairline. The woman was killing him.

Over a decadent chocolate dessert, their forks touched above the table while their knees touched underneath. And by the time they returned to their rooms, their hands and hips brushed at every step. When they stopped in front of her door, Andrew's reasons for not sleeping with Summer were in danger of being overridden by all the reasons he should.

He no longer had to worry about the complication of being tied to her over marketing his father's formula. In fact, since he'd be leaving soon, he didn't have to worry about any ties at all. After his father's land was sold, he didn't foresee a reason to ever return to Tiny.

Besides, he thought languidly, the way she toyed with her amazing hair and stared into his eyes told him she recognized the heat they generated. And her lips were so red and juicy, they looked as if they might pop. So why was he hesitant?

Because Summer Tomlinson was not one-night-stand material. She had that dreamy forever look in her eyes that scared him more than the thought of being mugged on a dark New York street.

"Good night," he said abruptly, then turned to go, only to be brought up short by a tug and a yelp.

Summer's hair was caught in a button on his jacket.

"Ow," she said, leaning toward him.

He fumbled to free the blond strands, but in the low lighting of the hallway, he only succeeded in making things worse.

"Ow, ow, ow."

"Sorry. Maybe you should try."

But she couldn't turn her head to see the button. "Can you take off your jacket?"

They twisted in every direction, but it was hopeless. Summer alternately groaned and laughed, holding her head. "Stop, please—I have scissors in my room."

She reached into her purse, then handed him her key card. He opened the door and awkwardly walked inside with her attached to him like a Siamese twin. She gestured blindly toward the bathroom.

"We need to move in that direction to find my toiletry kit."

They moved as if they were shackled together, giving in to bursts of laughter. After much clumsy rummaging, Summer finally retrieved the scissors from her bag and handed them to Andrew.

He balked. "I can't cut your hair."

"You'll have to. I can't see the knot."

Panic seized him at the thought of slicing off even a tiny section of her glorious hair. "But...will it grow back?"

She laughed. "Eventually. But if you don't hurry, I'm going to have a permanent crook in my neck."

He swallowed and positioned the scissors close to the tangle around his button. In two snips, she was free, leaving a strand of golden hair in his hand.

She surveyed the damage, dismissed it with a wave, then held up a trash can for him.

"You're just going to throw it away?" he asked.

She smiled. "If I were home, I'd put it in the garden for the birds to use to build nests."

He released the thatch of flaxen hair and watched it float into the can.

"I keep getting caught on you," she said with a laugh.

He nodded, thinking he should leave before something else of hers wound up wrapped around him.

"I should go," he said. But his feet wouldn't move.

Summer was twisting a lock of her shiny hair around her finger. Somewhere along the way, the rose bloom behind her ear had been lost. The golden mane was mussed from their earlier contortions with the jacket. Her blue eyes and red mouth were still soft from the wine. She was, without a doubt, the most sexy woman he'd ever seen.

He had to get out of there.

She lifted the twisted strand of hair and used the silky end to caress his cheek. "Don't go, Andrew. Spend the night with me."

JUST LIKE THAT, ALL OF his honorable intentions and steely resolve went out the window. He captured Summer's mouth in a kiss before she could change her mind. But now that the decision had been made, she seemed as eager to get to it as he was.

Their kiss morphed from hurried to fierce. They pushed and pulled at each other's clothes until he was naked and she wore only tiny red bikini panties and the strappy red high heels. Her body was long and lean, with a tapered waist, and thighs toned from riding. From her navel gleamed a tiny gold ring. Her luxurious hair hung over each shoulder, covering her breasts. She was such a vision, Andrew was hard as a stone from wanting her.

She was drinking him in, too. She reached forward to trail her finger down his chest to his stomach. "I always fantasized about you," she murmured. "I always thought you were the most handsome man I'd ever seen."

A smile curved his mouth. "What about now?"

Her gaze and hand lowered before she made eye contact again. "Now, I *know* you're the most handsome man I've ever seen."

Andrew groaned at her soft, velvety touch. His erection surged in her hand. He pulled her close and finally, after days of wondering what it would feel like, he sank his hands into the depths of her golden hair.

It was like spun silk—sumptuous and fluid in his fingers. He wrapped his hand around the back of her neck and pulled her mouth to his for a deep, languid kiss. He wanted to devour her, could feel a tide of desire rising in him like he'd never felt before. He pushed aside her hair and laved her breasts until her dark pink nipples beaded in his mouth. Every sigh, every gasp she uttered fueled his passion. He felt drunk on her, almost disoriented by her ministrations on his sex. Never before had he almost forgotten a condom, never before had he felt so desperate to give and take pleasure. When he held his body over Summer's, cradled between her thighs, her hair fanned around her like a gossamer veil, he was struck with a primal urgency to drive his body into hers. When he thrust into her at last, he felt as if he was falling.

She was a verbal lover, candid about what she liked. He found her pleasure points and worked them until she broke in his arms. Seeing her trembling in climax propelled him over the edge. He burst inside her with an intensity that bordered on pain, then fell forward, burying his face in her encompassing hair. She smelled like fresh air and sunshine and all the good things of country living.

Things he thought he'd gotten out of his system, things he'd left behind to follow his dreams in New York.

When his heartbeat slowed, Andrew rolled over and pulled Summer onto his chest. She sighed in his ear and curled her body into his. His body pulsed in recovery while his mind clicked with revelation. Making love to Summer had taken him to a new physical plane. Their chemistry was unbelievable.

Truly, it had to be a fluke.

The only remedy, he decided as he rolled her onto her back and kissed her hard, was to do it again....

ANDREW SLIPPED OUT OF her bed before dawn. He dressed quietly while staring at Summer's sleeping figure tangled in the sheets. The way her glorious mane of hair swirled around her nude body made her look like a mythical creature. His body ached from their ardent lovemaking, and his mind reeled from the implications. The fact that he didn't want to leave alarmed him—and hastened his exit.

When he closed the door behind him, he paused in the hallway to drag his hand down his face. His plan had been to get in and out of Tiny as quickly as possible.

He hadn't counted on this...this...*complication.*

9

THE NEXT MORNING when Summer stepped out into the hallway to meet Andrew for breakfast, she had to grip her purse to keep from reaching out to touch him. Her body still tingled from his lovemaking—sex with him had been better than she'd ever allowed herself to imagine. Even now, her body was flush with desire, and her heart was flush with...love?

It must be love, she decided when he smiled at her. She'd never felt this way before—shaky, as if she were teetering on a precipice...on one side was sheer happiness and the other, sheer heartache. Surely Andrew had felt their cataclysmic emotional connection.

He winked and angled his head. "Are we good?"

Her lips parted in surprise. His casual indifference stung, but Summer adopted her best impression of a modern woman the morning after a meaningless hookup. "Sure."

She reminded herself that she'd wanted to seduce him. She had no right to expect anything more from the one-night stand. But after spending a night in his arms, feeling his heart beat beneath her cheek, she couldn't help but fantasize about the possibilities of a happily ever after.

"Ready?" he asked.

She nodded. "I'm…starving."

By the time they reached the restaurant, her heart rate had stabilized and she was breathing normally. The change in the hotel dining room mirrored the change in their interaction from last night to this morning—the roses and wine had been replaced by carnations and orange juice. Their light conversation centered around her job and the things he had left to do around his father's property.

Once, when their hands brushed reaching for a saltshaker, their gazes locked and she thought she saw a flash of desire in his light brown eyes, but it passed. On the drive home, he was relatively silent except for the calls he made and received regarding his job. Because his phone was connected to the dashboard monitor, she got to listen in. The range of discussions was impressive and Andrew's opinion was obviously sought after—it all sounded very exciting.

And far removed from her small existence in Tiny, which was now only a few miles away. Their time in Nashville was already starting to feel like a dream.

Andrew's phone rang. The name "Charles Basker" flashed on the dashboard monitor.

"I wonder what Charles wants," Andrew murmured.

"Probably to discuss the aftermath," Summer joked.

He hit a button and spoke into the hands-free microphone. "Hey, Charles."

"Andrew, glad I caught you. I have news."

"I'm listening. Summer is here, too."

"Good. It turns out that when the segment for Mane Squeeze ran yesterday, regional phone grids were down because of the storm—land lines and mobile networks, too."

"We noticed our own phone networks were down," Andrew said. "Do you think that's why we didn't get many orders?"

"I know it is. Our switchboard has been flooded with calls all morning from people wanting the 'stuff that the blonde with the gorgeous hair was using.'"

Summer exchanged a glance with Andrew. Excitement bubbled in her chest, although Andrew's expression was more cautious.

"How many calls?" he asked.

"So far, we have orders for eight thousand units."

Summer gasped. Eight thousand?

"And the orders are still rolling in," Charles added.

Andrew's hands tightened on the steering wheel and he gave a little laugh. "Charles, I wasn't expecting this kind of response. I don't know if we can have that much product ready in six weeks."

"I hear you, but you have to decide now whether you're going to take your father's product to the next level. I took the liberty of making a couple of phone calls—Prince Manufacturing is interested in distributing and so is Hollister."

Summer's eyes widened. They were two of the largest consumer-goods companies in the country.

"And with your advertising contacts," the man continued, "this stuff could become a sensation."

Andrew pulled a hand over his mouth, clearly affected. "Thanks for the heads-up, man."

"No matter what you decide, that spokesperson of yours is pure gold, man. Whatever you do, don't let her go."

Andrew turned his head to look at her. Summer blushed. But when he cut his gaze back to the road, she had the feeling he wasn't pleased with his friend's advice.

"I'll get back to you as soon as I sort things out," Andrew

said. He disconnected the call and was quiet. He turned on his signal to take the interstate exit for the road to Tiny.

She chattered excitedly about what this would mean for Mane Squeeze, and for a horse-rescue center.

Andrew didn't respond. Instead, he seemed preoccupied with their surroundings, casting critical glances at shabby homes and muddy pastures that lined the rural road leading into Tiny. His irritation was palpable.

"You don't seem pleased," she ventured.

His jaw hardened. "I hadn't planned to devote so much time to this project."

She squinted. "Then why even go to the trouble of setting up the commercial?"

He averted his glance and realization dawned on her.

"You thought it would flop," she said. "You thought it would flop and that would be the end of it."

The tightening of his mouth confirmed her accusation.

She scoffed. "Do you believe now, at least, that Mane Squeeze could be successful?"

He sighed. "Not without a tremendous amount of work. And I have a career to get back to. I've already taken off too much time as it is."

"But this was your father's dream."

"But it's not *my* dream," he said tersely. "And my father didn't even see fit to share his dream with me. I'm sorry, Summer, if I don't care as much as you think I should."

Hurt stabbed her, because it seemed as if he was talking about more than just the hair conditioner. "But…you can't just pull the plug now."

"We'll fulfill the orders, of course. And if there's interest in the marketplace, we could offer the formula to the highest bidder."

Disappointment choked her. "This is your father's recipe," she managed to get out. "The decision is yours. I was only helping *him*."

He glanced at her hair. "From what Charles said, you could probably make a pretty penny as the spokesperson if someone buys the formula."

Summer's heart shriveled. He was distancing himself from the project, distancing himself from her.

He turned down the road toward her house. What a difference twenty-four hours made. When he'd picked her up yesterday, she had been buoyant with optimism. Now as he pulled into her driveway, she turned her head. "I was wrong about you, Andrew."

He put the car into Park. "What's that supposed to mean?"

"I assumed you still held the values we were both raised on—knowing what's important in life, such as preserving the land and the good work of your father."

His jaw hardened.

"Instead," she continued, "you're bearing a grudge against Barber because he didn't share every aspect of his life with you. Did you ever stop to think you weren't very sharing, either?"

Instead of answering, he reached down to hit a button that popped the latch on the trunk. "I'll get your suitcase."

"Don't bother," she said, opening the door. "I was doing fine before you came back to town, Andrew MacMillan, and I'll be fine when you leave."

She climbed out of the car and closed the door, then walked around to pull her overnight bag from the trunk. She slammed the lid with more force than necessary and strode toward her home without looking back.

10

OVER THE NEXT FEW DAYS, Andrew threw himself into the laundry list of things that needed to be completed. Repairs to the house and property were finally done, and Tessa was in discussion with a representative from the State Park for the parcel of land. Over the phone he negotiated a deal with a small manufacturer to produce enough of the hair conditioner to fill the orders from the home shopping channel. And he secured an agent to approach both Prince and Hollister about purchasing the Mane Squeeze formula, although he knew it could take months—maybe longer—to finalize a deal. After viewing the clip from the successful segment Summer had done for the hair conditioner, the agent mentioned the deal would be sweeter if he could offer her up as a spokesperson to the winning bidder.

Andrew had told the agent he would let Summer know.

Not that he'd seen her lately, except from afar. Every day after work she came by to feed and exercise the horses. He knew the moment she arrived because Truman leaped to his feet and barked until Andrew let him out, only to return an hour or so later to scratch at the door, whining and depressed.

Andrew caught sight of her a couple of times in worn jeans and that battered cowboy hat, but resisted the pull of her, which was harder now that he had firsthand knowledge of the pleasure of her company...and her body.

He knew Summer had feelings for him, but she was operating on a school-girl crush and the romantic notions of a woman who hadn't seen the world and didn't want to. Her life was here in Tiny with the land and the horses, a place he didn't want to be. This had been his father's life. It would never be his.

He glanced at the urn of ashes on the mantel, still frustrated about what to do with them. It was so like his father to keep this last part of himself from Andrew, too, to have his ashes entailed away with the land that he'd loved more than he'd loved his son.

Andrew ground his jaw. This was one decision he could make on his own...and in his own time frame. His father had refused to visit him when he was alive, but now, like it or not, he would spend some time in the place Andrew had chosen to call home.

So he didn't feel guilty when he placed the urn in a box of his father's personal items on the floorboard of the passenger side of his car the next day when he packed to leave. He took one last look at the freshly painted house and neat yard and thought his mother would at least be pleased that he'd gotten it back in shape for the new owner. He had left the sale of the property in Tessa's capable hands. Red had also promised to keep an eye on things.

Andrew swallowed hard, fighting emotion and nostalgia, knowing it was natural to have pangs about selling one's child-hood home. But his life awaited him in New York.

So he whistled for Truman to jump into the passenger seat, then climbed behind the wheel and drove away, telling himself the gnawing in his gut would subside. Some of his apprehension, he knew, was due to the fact that he was stopping to say goodbye to Summer.

It was Sunday morning, and he hoped to catch her before she left for church. Truman loped alongside as he walked to her front door. He rang the doorbell and waited. It was a sunny spring morning, with a crisp breeze blowing. From this vantage point, he could see her vegetable garden in the distance, studded with hardy plants that could be nurtured through mild winters. He squinted at the gossamer sheen on areas of bare dirt—probably a layer of insulating cloth.

The door opened and Summer stood there, dressed in a pretty skirt and blouse, her hair held back from her face with a scarf. When Andrew couldn't seem to find his voice, Truman said hello for them. She looked down and scratched the dog's happy head. Then she looked back up.

"Hello, Andrew."

"Hi," he offered. "I just wanted to say goodbye."

She looked past him to his car sitting in the driveway, then back to him. "I heard you were leaving today."

"You heard?"

"You know how word travels around here. So…you're going back to New York?"

"That's right. Home."

Her mouth tightened. "Do you want me to keep Truman?"

"No, I've decided to take him back with me."

"I'm not sure he'll like being cooped up in an apartment all day."

"It's a condo," he corrected. "And it's not so bad. I live near some really nice parks."

She nodded in concession. "I'll keep an eye on the horses. I'm going to put an ad in the newspaper to try to find homes for them."

"Use this," he said, withdrawing a check from his pocket.

She held up her hand. "No, I couldn't—"

"It's the projected proceeds for orders from the home shopping channel. Actually, it's not much after taking out start-up costs for the manufacturing plant, but I want you to use it to take care of the horses as long as you can." He extended the check. "Please…take it."

She pressed her lips together, but relented. "Thank you."

"The agent who's selling the formula agreed to represent you if you'd be willing to be the spokesperson for whatever company buys it. It might require some travel, but the money would probably be good."

She gave him a sad smile. "I don't think that's possible now."

"Because you're still mad at me for selling my father's formula?"

"No." She lifted her hand to remove her scarf.

Andrew gaped. Her hair wasn't pulled back…it was *gone*. Most of it, anyway. "You cut your hair." His voice sounded accusatory even to his own ears.

She touched the pixie-short locks and gave a little laugh. "Yes." She nodded toward her vegetable garden. "The birds have it now."

The thought of her beautiful mane of hair being scattered over dirt and left for the birds made him sick to his stomach. "But… why?"

She shrugged. "Time to let go of old habits. Don't you like it?"

Once the original shock wore off, he realized the absence of her voluminous hair threw her fine-boned face into relief. Her cheekbones were high, her nose shapely. Her neck was long and elegant, and the short bangs set off her cornflower-blue eyes. She was as stunning as any runway model and still the sexiest woman he'd ever seen. "Yes…I do like it."

Their eyes met. Snatches of the night they'd spent in the hotel rose in his mind and his hands itched to reach for her, to kiss this beautiful woman with the gamine haircut and lie down with her.

She looked away, breaking the spell. "Anyway, as you can see, no one's going to be asking me to endorse Mane Squeeze."

She'd cut her hair purposefully because she didn't want to be associated with the product if it was no longer connected to Barber. Andrew nodded. "Fair enough."

Summer cleared her throat. "I saw Tessa in town the other day. She said she's close to making a deal with the State Park for your dad's farm."

"That's right."

"Will you be back when that happens?"

"No. The paperwork can be handled remotely."

She nodded, and seemed to exhale. In relief?

A loud meowing noise sounded behind her, then her butterscotch-colored cat came into view. The Persian tossed insults at Truman until the dog's ears and shoulders drooped.

"Shush, Gabby," Summer said, then smiled at Andrew. "She's actually going to miss him, I think."

Gabby denied Summer's claim with a yowl, then turned her back on Truman and walked away, her tail swishing.

Truman looked up at Andrew and whimpered.

"I think that's our cue to get going," Andrew said to the dog.

"So I guess I won't see you again," Summer said. Her voice was light, but her expression was unreadable.

"Probably not," he agreed.

"Well, then…safe travels." She leaned forward to give him a brief, platonic hug. She released him quickly, then gestured to her hair with a wry smile. "No chance of me getting caught on you again."

While he digested that statement, she crouched down and hugged Truman to her. "Goodbye, boy. I'll miss you every day."

Truman barked and licked her face. Smart dog.

Andrew wanted to say something—it's been nice, I'm sorry, good luck—but everything that came to mind sounded shallow and patronizing. As Summer had said before, she'd been fine before he arrived and would be fine after he left.

Instead, he simply lifted his hand in a wave and walked back to his car. He felt her recriminating gaze on him throughout. She thought he'd turned his back on his upbringing, on his father's wishes. He'd let her down.

Andrew told himself it didn't matter, and put the car in Drive. He drove slowly on the roads winding back out of Tiny for a final look at the place where he'd felt so confined as a young man. It was a pretty town, with a safe, insular community, and the people were kind.

But he didn't belong here anymore.

As he drove past the retail area, he idly scanned the shop marquees and blinked in surprise because they heralded, "So long, Andrew!" "Come back soon, Andrew!" and similar sentiments every few feet.

Andrew swallowed a lump in his throat. From the box of his father's things, Barber's ashes mocked him. *You won't get a personal welcome back to Manhattan.*

True enough, he admitted. In fact, not a single person in the dense city had probably noticed he was gone.

Truman looked at him, and Andrew reached over to scratch his neck. "Don't worry—you'll like it there, I promise. No pesky females to torment you."

Truman barked in agreement, then lay down in the seat, settling in for the ride, his paw resting on the urn.

11

ANDREW PINCHED THE BRIDGE of his nose in frustration. "Just go, Truman, for heaven's sake."

Truman glanced around the park at other dogs who were crouching obediently to "go" for their owners, then looked up

at Andrew and whined in confusion. Then he spotted a squir-
rel in a tree and lunged. Andrew held the leash, with Truman
straining at the other end. "Stay…stay, boy! Remember how to
'stay'?"

Apparently not, since the dog began to bark incessantly, and
when Andrew reprimanded him, he lifted his muzzle and howled
as if his heart was breaking. The other people and pets in the
dog park stared at the full-out canine meltdown. Andrew half
tugged, half carried the traumatized dog back to his condo. Truman promptly dropped next to the fireplace where Barber's ashes
sat on the mantel.

Andrew surveyed the homesick dog with a sigh. A week into
city living, Truman was not adjusting well to concrete, traffic
and leashes. The dog had worn himself out. His eyes were closed
and his chest heaved with slumberous breaths.

He was, Andrew thought, probably dreaming of wide-open
fields and a certain Persian cat he liked to chase. Not that Andrew could criticize—his own dreams the past few nights had
been haunted by a place where birds' nests were woven from
strands of silken blond hair.

Just the thought of Summer made his chest ache…not to mention other parts of his body. He'd returned to work in his corner
office on the fortieth floor of a building with a tony address, but
moved through the days like an automaton. He'd caught himself
staring out his window on more than one occasion. This afternoon he'd watched the landscapers on the ground far below and
envied their freedom.

And somehow, the valentine that Summer had given him all
those years ago had wound up in his briefcase. He found himself
pulling it out at the oddest times, when his mind should've been
on serious matters and instead chuckled over the horse cartoon
and her "I think you are awesome" message written in girlish
cursive.

Now he glanced over his living room and marveled once
again over the similar arrangement of his father's furniture and
his own. He walked over to the mantel and adjusted the urn to

center the engraved design. His hand tingled, almost as if his father were speaking to him.

Go home.

Andrew stood there infused with wonder. In a flash of enlightenment, his mind opened…and received. In a torrent of raw emotion, he surrendered to the knot of agony in his chest. Summer was right. He'd been focused on all the wrong things.

He loved her. He wanted to be with her, even if it meant living in Tiny. Together they could market his father's formula, and make a life together. His mind raced as the possibilities unfolded. He yanked up his phone and called Tessa Hadley. With no preamble, he told her to cancel the sale of the farm.

"I'm sorry, Andrew, but the papers were signed four days ago—the transaction has already gone through. You got your asking price, I thought you were pleased with the deal."

His heart sank. "I am…I was. Will you call the representative and tell them I'll buy it back for ten thousand more than the State Park paid for it?"

She reluctantly agreed, and called back in a few minutes. "I'm sorry, Andrew, but the buyer isn't willing to sell the property back to you at any price."

He closed his eyes. What had he done? "Okay, Tessa, thanks."

He disconnected the call. The crushing weight of failure pulled on his shoulders. He'd let his father down. He'd let himself down.

He would give the proceeds of the sale of the formula to Summer for her horse-rescue program. At least he could feel good about that. But a sale could be months in the making and meanwhile, he knew she was scrambling to relocate the ten horses in her care.

Needing to feel close to his father, he pulled out the box of personal items he'd removed from Barber's desk. Most of them harkened back to Barber MacMillan's veterinarian days—appointment books, photos and journals. Andrew poured himself a drink and settled down to read the leather-bound diaries, hoping to gain some insight into his father.

The stories were amazing. Andrew was drawn in to his father's world of animal patients and their owners, of a thousand mundane details of living in Tiny that somehow his father spun into absorbing gems. He often mentioned his beloved wife. But most remarkable to Andrew were the entries about himself—his father had raved about his son's talents and intellect and divulged that he feared he would lose him because "he is too big for this place."

And when Andrew had left, his father was bereft. Until that moment, Andrew hadn't realized how much Barber had missed him. The holiday visits that Andrew had found so frustrating, Barber described as joyous. He'd been despondent every time Andrew had driven away.

Andrew wiped his eyes and kept reading until the wee hours. His father mentioned Summer in many of the entries, what a sweet, beautiful person she was and how he hoped she'd find a good man to love and take care of her. He also mentioned the conditioning formula he was secretly developing, how Red was getting suspicious about the money he was spending on his clandestine project and how he was considering telling Andrew about it. He was afraid his son would think he was a fool.

When Andrew closed the last diary, a folded piece of paper fell out. He picked it up and realized it was the hair conditioning recipe, the same one that Summer had shown him in the binder she maintained.

Except on this paper, next to the amount of water required for a batch of Mane Squeeze, his father had written, "I realize now the secret ingredient in the formula isn't the aloe and evening primrose oil, but water from the cave spring. I believe it has something to do with the limestone that filters the water. Horses that eat limestone-fed grass in Kentucky and Tennessee have stronger bones, so it follows that the mineral-rich water would make human hair stronger, too."

Dazed, Andrew touched his forehead. Water from the cave spring was the secret ingredient? And maybe limestone made it special…or maybe it was something else in the depths of the warm spring. Not that it mattered. Without access to the water to test and use in the recipe, the formula was of no use to anyone.

He pushed to his feet and walked to the mantel with a heavy heart. His father had been right about so many things…if he'd only listened. He only had himself to blame for losing the farm, the formula and Summer. But there was one thing he could do for his father—he could spread Barber's ashes over the land he'd loved.

He picked up the urn. Truman stirred, then lifted his head. "Come on, boy," Andrew said. "Let's take a ride."

12

FUELED BY ADRENALINE and a clear head, Andrew drove through the night to arrive in Tiny just after dawn. The roads were buzzing with school buses and farm trucks…it was the picture of Americana. Truman became more animated as his surroundings became more familiar. When they drove past Summer's house, he barked excitedly.

"If she doesn't want me, maybe she'll still take you," Andrew offered.

As he drove onto his father's property, it occurred to him that the State Park might have already put up fences or posted a security guard on the property, but to his relief, there were no barriers. He climbed out, cradling the urn. Truman was ecstatic to be back home and bounded away happily, making tracks in the frost-laden grass.

It was a cool morning, with a stiff breeze blowing. His light jacket felt good as he walked past the stables and headed out into the fields. He turned in the direction of the tallest rise on the farm, a pretty little hillock not far from the cave spring. Andrew climbed to the top and turned to survey the MacMillan property, deeply grieved that he'd been so short-sighted as to sell it, and not just because of the cave spring.

His family's sweat and tears were in this land. He opened the urn and slowly upended it on a breeze that carried the ashes away in a mesmerizing, swirling pattern. Truman chased the dust, as if he knew what it represented. Andrew lowered the empty urn, satisfied. Now his father's ashes were part of the land, as well.

"I'm sorry, Dad," he whispered, "for getting it all wrong."

After a few moments of silence, Andrew retraced his steps toward the house, feeling at peace for the first time in a long time…except about one thing: Summer. After he'd ruined things so thoroughly, would she even talk to him?

As he approached the stables, he heard a horse whinnying as if in distress, and loud banging noises. He hurried toward the stable and found Sallie, the last horse Summer had rescued, wild in her stall, kicking and keening.

Andrew balked. He wasn't good with the big beasts, not like his father, not like Summer. He was tense around them, and the horses seemed to pick up on it. In hindsight, he realized it was probably because he resented the time and attention his father paid to the animals. Whatever the reason, he was uncomfortable around them, and they were uncomfortable around him.

But if he didn't do something to calm the old horse, she was going to hurt herself, or incite the other horses to injury. Indeed, they were all pacing and braying. Only Max seemed unruffled.

Andrew pulled a blanket from the wall and advanced to the mare's stall with caution. He didn't want to spook her further. "Easy," he murmured. "Easy, old girl." Her ears twitched and she paused for a few seconds, snorting and huffing, her breath white clouds in the cool morning air.

He opened her stall door, but that set her off again. She reared and kicked, her eyes rolling wildly.

He pulled back to escape flying hooves.

SUMMER WAS STROLLING toward the stables when she heard a horse neighing, in trouble. She set off on a run, lost her hat and kept going. She rounded the corner and came up short.

Andrew was in Sallie's stall, his big arms around her neck, murmuring into her ear. "Easy, girl…easy. That's it…quiet, calm…easy."

Her heart catapulted to her throat.

He looked up and smiled.

"What are you doing here?" she whispered. He looked travel worn and his jaw was dark with a half day's worth of beard. She'd lain awake every night since he'd left hoping, wishing he'd come back, but knowing it was impossible. Yet, here he was, dressed in dusty jeans and boots, as if he were back to stay.…

He lifted a handful of corn for Sallie to nibble, still rubbing her neck. When the corn was gone, he slowly backed out of the stall and closed the door. "I came back to spread my father's ashes on the farm, like he wanted."

She didn't have the right to be so disappointed at his reason for returning. She was glad he had respected Barber's wishes. "That's nice."

Truman came bounding up and ran around her knees with abandon. His coat was covered with burrs.

"Oh, and Truman hated the city," Andrew added. "I don't suppose you'd still be willing to take him in?"

Summer smiled. "Gabby will complain, but she'll come around eventually." Did he have any idea how much he was torturing her by standing an arm's length in front of her?

Andrew shifted from foot to foot. "Would you be willing to take me in, too?"

Summer squinted. Surely she'd misunderstood him. "What did you say?"

He stepped toward her and lifted his hand to her cheek. "Would you be willing to take me in, too? I've decided I hate the city, too, because you're not there."

Her heart began to pound in her chest. "But your job…"

"I'll reinvent myself."

"You could market your father's formula," she suggested excitedly.

He winced. "There's a wrinkle—suffice it to say I messed up royally. Turns out the secret ingredient in the formula is the cave-spring water."

Summer gasped. "How do you know?"

"I found it in my father's diary…after I authorized the sale of the place to the State Park." He looked pained. "You're right— I was focused on all the wrong things and wound up losing the things that were the most important." He caressed her cheek. "Unless you're willing to give a stupid man another chance."

Summer's heart filled with hope, but she didn't want to assume anything. She needed to know how Andrew felt about her. She lifted her chin. "Why should I?"

He sighed. "Because I love you desperately…and I can't live without you."

Her heart expanded and overflowed with joy. Emotion clogged her throat. She put her arms around his neck and brought his face close to hers. "I love you, too, so much. But you should know— I just sold my house."

He pulled back. "But you love that place."

"But I love this place more."

His eyes flew wide. "This place?"

She nodded. "I worked out a trade with Tessa—my place for this one, she gets two commissions."

A smile curled Andrew's mouth. "And I get you?"

Summer nodded and pulled his mouth to hers for a deep, promising kiss. When she drew back, she fingered her shorn locks. "Be honest—do you like my hair? I've been thinking about letting it grow again."

"I love it," he murmured. "But since you have control of the secret formula, you can do whatever you want." He nuzzled her neck. "Short hair or long, woman, you've got me all tangled up. For good."

* * * * *

LESLIE KELLY

Sleeping with a Beauty

To Caitlin, Lauren & Megan…thanks for all those
wonderful nights, listening to bedtime stories.

Prologue

ONCE UPON A TIME, *in the kingdom of Seaside, in the world of Elatyria, a beautiful princess was born. This princess always smiled, sang like an angel and was adored by all.*

But one day, she fell under a spell cast by an evil fairy and was cursed to sleep forever. Her heartbroken parents had themselves and their court cursed, too, hoping someday their daughter would awaken and they would be reunited.

Years passed. Then decades. Finally, a century or two.

The castle—perched high on a cliff above the sea—fell into ruin. Under a spell cast by the wicked fairy, the waters became rough and wild. Any ships daring to trespass were dashed against the jagged rocks. There was but one small pathway to the castle, known by only a few, and a thick hedge of thorns protected it.

Soon, those who knew the real story died off. Whispers of the sleeping beauty turned into myth and the people of Seaside drifted away, forgetting there had ever been a royal family.

The years marched on, relentless and unforgiving. The castle and the people in it lay in shadowy silence. The gleam of their jewel-encrusted gowns faded and their gold plates grew tarnished. Dust settled over the chests full of diamonds and rubies until they were useful only as nests for mice. Time had swallowed the royal court, and it appeared destined to sleep for all eternity.

Then, one day, a handsome prince from a faraway land heard about the sleeping princess. Determined to find her and make

*her his bride, he sailed the wild seas, scaled the high cliffs, en-
dured the sharp thorns. Some say he battled a dragon (which is
a bit silly, really, since all Elatyrians know dragons have very
sensitive skin and can't live near the salty-aired sea).*

*His trials strengthened his resolve and the prince fought his
way into the castle. He ignored the slumbering royals, strode
past the tables piled with gold and kicked jewels away. Then,
in a room in the tallest tower, he found the sleeping princess.*

*Overwhelmed by her beauty, the prince kissed her. The curse
was broken, the sleeping maiden awakened by love's first kiss.*

*As the prince carried his bride out of the castle, her sweet
tears of joy fell upon each person and they, too, awakened to the
bright dawn of a new age. Wanting to leave the dark memories
of their long sleep behind, the royal court didn't waste a minute
packing up the castle. They simply followed the happy couple to
the prince's kingdom, where they all lived happily ever after.*

But, uh, this story isn't actually about them.
It's about the castle. And the jewels. The gold.
All that treasure.
And the people who wanted to find it.

1

SHE'D FOUND IT.

After all these years, all the study, all the effort—from guards
bribed, to towers climbed, to trolls evaded—Ashlynn Scott had
finally discovered the location of the most mysterious ruin in all
of Elatyria. And soon—maybe tomorrow—she would reach it.

Creeping through the thick forest in the dead of night, she
clutched her small leather satchel even more tightly against her

side. Inside it was a yellowed, fragile piece of parchment, jagged around the edges, faded with age. And priceless.

To anyone else, it might look like an illegible old drawing. But Ashlynn knew better. The decrepit, faded page, which she'd found in a place far, *far* from her beloved home here in Elatyria, matched two other pieces already in her possession. When those pieces were fitted together, she had no doubt they would make up three-quarters of an ancient map—the three most important quarters. The ones that would show the way to what would be the discovery of her life.

Coming across Cinderella's lost slipper had been a bit of luck, more than anything else. And her job of excavating the site of the cottage of the original seven dwarves had merely built on what someone else had started; Ashlynn hadn't actually located it. Though, she had found the poisoned comb that crazy witch had used on her stepdaughter before her successful trick with the bad apple.

But *this* was the big one. The find that would put Ashlynn Scott's name right up there with her own late father's, as one of the preeminent historians of the age. It would cement in everyone's minds—including her own—that she'd deserved to take over for him as lead historian at the most revered museum in all of Elatyria. Despite her age and her sex.

"Sleeping Beauty's castle," she whispered.

It was the stuff of legend: a deserted palace filled with treasure, but, more importantly, with the history of a lost kingdom. Many doubted it existed, believing a story so fantastical had to be myth. They'd scoffed at her late father, ridiculed him for being sure the castle would one day be located.

Now, Ashlynn could prove her father right…vindicate them both. Because the map wasn't a myth. It was real. And she had it.

Well, most of it.

"As much as I need," she muttered. "It *has* to be enough."

The new piece showed the exact location of the castle and part of the long, treacherous path that led to it. Yes, the path itself wound off the page, onto that elusive fourth quarter. But she had the most important parts: the beginning and the end.

Ashlynn had discovered the first piece of the map inside the lining of an ancient dress, folded into a tiny square, fragile and dry. She'd been curating a museum exhibit on the lost kingdom of Seaside, which now existed only in history books, its lands having been gobbled up by its neighbors centuries ago. The dress had come into her hands by accident—the map along with it.

With the support of the Grand Elatyria Museum and its patron, Queen Penelope of Riverdale, Ashlynn had made it her mission to find the rest of the map. She'd searched every record, spoken to the last few descendants of the Seasidians. She'd traveled the lands, scoured great libraries, studied old texts. Finally, she'd found another piece hidden behind an old painting.

The search for the third quarter had taken even longer. It had also taken her somewhere far away. She'd had to visit a land called Pennsylvania, in the world called Earth, which existed just beyond Elatyria's borders. It hadn't been her first trip— Ashlynn's father had taken her to a town known as Chicago as a child. But this time, she'd had to go by herself.

I wish you could be here. Regret stabbed her as she thought of how much her father would have loved this quest. He'd also be very worried about her going on it alone. The theft of antiquities was rampant in Elatyria, and the two of them had been targets of thieves before. Now that he was gone, she had very few people she could trust…and over on Earth, absolutely none.

But now she felt safer than she had in weeks, because she was *home.* The night was deep, the mossy ground spongy and soft beneath her feet, the air moist and rich with verdant soil. She'd missed this clean, heady scent during her weeks in that *other* place, where every breath was full of machine-made fumes.

The nearest border crossing between the two worlds could only be accessed during the full moon. There were a few larger crossings that could be traversed at any time, but none was close enough to her home. So, restricted by the cycle of the moon, she'd been stuck over on Earth for many long, lonely days.

Now she was back in Elatyria and was so overjoyed she felt

like hugging the nearest tree. She wouldn't, of course. She was no longer over *there,* where trees couldn't hug back. And she didn't care to be crushed by the enthusiastic embrace of a gnarled oak.

Behind her, an owl hooted, another night animal howled.

And a twig snapped.

Her joy fading, Ashlynn froze. Listened. *Silence.*

But that didn't mean nobody was there.

With stealthy purpose, she quickened her pace, clinging to shadows, alert for any movement. The starry sky provided light to guide her, but also made her too-easily visible to any pursuer.

Perhaps she was overreacting. Maybe that step had been the tread of a doe, or the scurry of an anxious-to-get-home gnome.

But she feared it hadn't been. She was being followed. She knew that. She'd known it for weeks before she'd left Elatyria. Whoever it was might have been at the border, patient and determined, waiting for her to return when the moon waxed full.

She also knew *why* she was being followed.

Someone else was after the map…and the mysterious castle to which it led. That someone knew Ashlynn was hot on the trail.

Spying the shapes of buildings in the nearest village—Foxglen, through which she'd passed weeks ago when she'd left for Earth—she walked even faster. It wasn't Riverdale, where she lived, but there were people there. Plus, it boasted a small, clean inn and a less than clean but somewhat palatable tavern, with the dubious name of The Mare's End.

The tavern. She could actually spy its pitched roof from here, and breathed a sigh of relief. During the time she'd been gone, she'd had horrible visions of the place burning down or being shaken apart by a rampaging giant.

But no, there it stood in the distance, the tavern with the old, stone floor, which had a loose stone beneath the back table. Hopefully nobody was seated there, so she could sit, warm her chilled body, wrap her hands around a mug of mulled wine.

And retrieve the other two pieces of the map, which she'd hidden beneath that loose stone.

She still wasn't sure she'd made the right choice in stashing the pieces there. But a month ago, during the brief time the border was open, she had been forced to act quickly. To her surprise, she'd learned a new Antiquities Protection Bureau had set up inspection stations at the major crossings. They were checking all packages being taken from Elatyria to Earth. She couldn't have risked them finding the map pieces and misconstruing her intent. Of course she would never sell them to some eccentric collector, she was merely holding them to keep them safe. But how to explain that to hired hands who would see the map and likely seize it, no matter her protestations about who she was or what she did?

To go all the way home to Riverdale to store it with someone trustworthy would have delayed her trip by a full month—until the borders opened again with the next full moon. So, torn with indecision, she'd finally left them hidden in Foxglen, wrapped carefully in oilskin and hidden beneath the tavern's stone floor.

They're safe. They've got to be.

Anticipating that exciting moment when the three pieces would form a wonderful new picture—one which, she felt sure, would be enough to show her the way to the castle—Ashlynn stepped out of the forest, a stone's throw from the nearest cottage. Safety beckoned, as did comfort. Yet, the eerie feeling that she was being watched persisted.

She suddenly realized why.

He leaped out of thin air. A large man, lunging for her, silent and with undoubtedly deadly intent.

Before Ashlynn had time to react, or even make a sound, he wrapped a powerful arm around her waist, clamped a big hand over her mouth and dragged her back into the forest.

OF ALL THE JOBS Raine Fowler had ever taken, this had to be one of the worst. He'd survived poisoned darts in the tomb of an ancient king. He'd made it through the crash of a small plane in the Amazon. He'd been shot at while, um, liberating a Mayan artifact from a group of competitors. Hell, he'd even managed to survive after hooking up with the daughter of an overprotective billionaire who'd hired him to lead them on an archaeological safari.

But this? Having to play babysitter and follow some hardheaded chick into the next frigging world so he could try to keep her from getting herself killed? Crazy. Especially because the hardheaded chick was, at this moment, trying to chew off a few of his fingers. He winced when she got in one particularly good nip, instinctively pulling away. "Would you stop it?"

"Let me go!"

Her angry voice cut through the night and he slammed his hand back. "Quiet," he growled, his grip tight across her mouth.

A sexy mouth, he had to admit. It went well with the sexy rest of her. Hey, just because the woman was a royal pain didn't mean he hadn't stiffened his seams and needed to take a mental cold shower the first time he'd laid eyes on her. And just about every damn time since.

He'd first seen her nearly a month ago, in Philadelphia. He'd been contracted to find her, follow her and keep her out of trouble. He still wasn't entirely sure who the odd-looking old man who'd hired him was. But gold spent well in any world; these days, probably better on Earth—where he spent most of his time. And the stranger had been offering a lot of it.

But maybe not enough, he thought as she head-butted him, the back of her skull thunking on the bridge of his nose.

"Ow," he snapped, tightening his arm across her slim waist. "Lady, you're getting to be more trouble than you're worth. I should let them have you."

But he couldn't. He'd taken the contract, agreed to protect her from afar until she got safely home. And once Raine Fowler took an assignment, he finished it. Failure wasn't an option, not in his business where one bad job could mean another dozen potential ones dried up and disappeared.

He'd been an independent contractor—some might call him an adventurer, others might say tomb raider or even soldier of fortune—for a decade, having followed his uncle to South America when he was just eighteen. His uncle had been the best, and he'd taught Raine well. His number one rule? *Once you take the job, you see it through to the very end.* And he did. Always.

Besides, he'd only been paid half of his fee. The rest wouldn't cross his palm until she was safely home in Riverdale.

So he'd found her, studied her, learned all he could.

He knew she was beautiful, that was without doubt. And he knew she appealed to him on a deep, visceral level that he didn't like to acknowledge, considering she was, after all, his responsibility…whether she knew that, or not.

He also knew a brain lurked inside that sexy exterior. She was determined, persistent as a bloodhound. He knew she liked music but she couldn't sing for shit, knew she didn't care for pizza—bizarre—but had no problem scarfing canned ravioli—more bizarre. And he knew she had a thing for Disney movies—hence his knowledge of her singing abilities. (She sometimes went all Beauty-singing-to-the-Beast behind closed doors, through which he'd heard her.) Though, actually, that Disney thing made sense, given where she was from. Most Elatyrians were drawn to that stuff, if only so they could get all indignant about their history being fodder for an entire civilization's amusement.

One last thing he knew about Ashlynn Scott: someone was after her. Someone with enough money to hire serious muscle.

Thankfully, he'd moved faster than Miss Nippy-Teeth and had gotten to the village ahead of her. Which was why he'd been here to stop her from making the biggest mistake of her life—the mistake being the shortening of that life by a lot of years.

She continued to struggle. Twisting in his arms, she elbowed him in the gut, then kicked his shins. Though he had at least five inches in height on the woman, she had pointy elbows and wicked little feet. He was going to be bruised tomorrow.

"Two of them are waiting for you in the tavern, another's circling the village," he snarled. "He'll be coming around that corner in about thirty seconds. Now will you please stay still?"

She froze, twisting her head to stare up at him. The full moonlight brought out the deep, midnight-blue of her eyes and the utter mistrust on her face. She looked at him as though he was a cobra who'd offered to pluck out a splinter with his front teeth.

"I'm trying to help you," he mumbled, quickly shifting his gaze. He didn't particularly want to notice how blue those eyes were. Or think about how delicious those perfectly curved lips might taste. Or how silky her long, honey-brown hair felt, draping over his forearm.

Nor did he want to see just how much lovelier her heart-shaped face was up close…even if she did look ready to impale him on the nearest handy tree limb. He'd seen her on Earth, but never this close. Most of the time, he'd had to make do with listening to her through the walls of a cheap hotel room, his imagination filling in that which his senses hadn't yet beheld.

He knew now that his imagination hadn't come close to the real woman now pressed against his body. And Raine was a very imaginative guy. Especially when it came to the mysterious Ms. Ashlynn Scott of Riverdale.

Hearing the scrape of boots on cobblestone, Raine drew her down into a crouch and breathed a word into her ear. "Watch."

Right on schedule, a burly thug with a wicked knife strapped to his hip trudged around the nearest corner. Ashlynn stiffened. Even with his hand clapped over her mouth, she still managed to make a sound. "Mmph…."

Reckless woman. Raine couldn't tighten his hand any further and tried to think of another way to keep her from calling out. One immediately came to mind—he'd fantasized about that, too, during those long, quiet nights when he'd listened to her through the wall and tried to imagine what she wore to bed. And what she *didn't*. But he immediately discounted the idea of kissing her: he liked his lips and tongue too much and he'd lay money she would bite him if he tried it.

Instead, he rose, dragging her with him, and moved backward, pulling her deeper into the shadows. When they'd gained another few yards distance, he whispered, "He's a Hunter and you're his prey. Call for help and we're both in trouble."

She nodded once, then directed her attention toward the real threat—the Hunter. He looked entirely out of place in this bucolic village, the sneer on his face saying he was looking for a fight. Or looking to kill somebody soft and pretty. *Bastard.*

Said bastard paused before turning the corner, looking toward the trees. Though Raine was sure they couldn't be seen since they were well hidden in the shadows of the forest, he did feel his heart thud harder in his chest.

He didn't really fear the guy with the knife. He only wondered if he could take him out before the man's two friends emerged from the tavern. Three might prove a bit challenging, especially if the woman he was trying to protect decided to cut and run the second his back was turned. Then he'd just have to find her again. Here. Where he was out of his element. Sure, he had ties to Elatyria, but he was Earth-born and -bred and seldom took jobs on this side of the reality line.

The armed man hesitated. His head tilted back and he inhaled deeply, as if he could smell something—his prey? Raine briefly wondered if the thug was an animal in more than the figurative sense. But considering the moon was full, he discounted that worry. If the brute were wolfish, he'd be a lot hairier right now.

Then, with a frown, the knife-wielding Hunter turned and resumed his patrol. After a dozen steps, he turned past another building and headed away, down the next cobbled street, his footsteps finally disappearing into the night.

"Whew," he whispered. "Close one."

Funny, though—that thudding in Raine's chest didn't stop right away. In fact, as the woman he was holding sagged back in pure, visible relief, he'd have to say it sped up even more. Because, she was now pressed harder against him—her thighs meeting his, her curvy backside brushing his groin.

She felt good. Too good. He had hoped she wouldn't, had hoped his deep, immediate attraction to her wouldn't be a problem, considering he'd already decided she was a pain in his ass. From the moment he'd found her, he'd figured she was the kind of goody-goody he couldn't stand, all righteous and holier-than-thou, who would surely look down her nose at a guy like *him.*

She was the purist, the haughty researcher, the historian.

He was the renegade who wasn't allowed back in some countries, had people after him in his own and who had four words, *Raine Fowler: Odd Jobs,* printed on his calling card.

She'd call him an opportunistic scavenger.

He preferred to think of himself as a man of adventure.

But none of that mattered a damn right now. Because, this man of adventure was suddenly picturing the erotic adventures he'd like to have with the woman pressed so provocatively against him. He wished he hadn't let his thoughts travel down the werewolf path, because the way she was positioned, it would be far too easy to drop them both to their knees and take her from behind until they howled at the full moon overhead.

"Hell," he muttered, feeling his body react to his mind's imaginings—a far too frequent occurrence when it came to her.

"If I let you go, are you going to stay quiet?" he asked. He didn't entirely trust her, but figured he should release her before she noticed his reaction. Besides, it appeared the danger had passed, for now.

She nodded once. Raine lowered his hand and took a good-for-his-sanity step back. When she drew a shaky hand to her mouth, he wondered if he'd hurt her. Not that he was going to apologize—he had very likely just saved her life.

"I'm sorry, I wasn't trying to scream, I was just startled when I saw him."

"It's okay. He obviously didn't hear anything."

"Who is he?" she whispered, her breaths sounding choppy.

"Somebody who's been waiting here for you to come back across the border. Your description's all over the village. They're saying you came through a month ago."

She swore softly under her breath, as if both believing him and being immediately frustrated by the revelation.

"Now, how about we *don't* wait here for his two buddies to come out and help him look. Let's head back into the forest."

She hesitated, indecision written on her face. He might have just saved her, but she still didn't know him from Adam.

He stuck out his hand. "Raine Fowler."

She eyed his hand warily, then, as if it pained her to release her ten-fingered grip on the travel bag she carried, extended one of her own. "Ashlynn Scott."

"I know."

She yanked her hand away. "*How* do you know?" Then her gaze narrowed further. "And how did you know where to find me?"

"Sorry, lady, but I've seen sloths that move faster than you. I followed you across the border, then moved ahead of you and got here almost an hour ago. After doing some scouting, I backtracked to where I figured you'd be showing up."

"You were *following* me?"

"Yeah, lucky for you."

Hearing a loud laugh back in the village, he grabbed her elbow and half pushed, half led her back the way she'd come, seeking the sanctuary of the deep forest.

His move apparently caught her by surprise. She took several steps, then stopped suddenly. Raine bumped into her, his mouth landing against that thick hair, his leg slipping between hers from behind. Worst of all, his groin mashed against her sexy ass.

He wished he could say he was gentleman enough not to enjoy the hell out of it. Again. He was, however, gentleman enough not to take advantage of it. Again.

Well, maybe gentleman wasn't the right word—he was *smart* enough. This was the wrong place, the wrong time and the wrong woman. Though, something told him he was going to have a hard time remembering that, the longer he spent with her.

She swung around and planted her feet, apparently oblivious to the whole man/woman vibe that was seriously messing with his head. Well, to be more accurate, both his heads.

Get your big *head back in the game, man.*

"I'm not going any farther without an explanation."

"Can we at least walk as I explain? I'd prefer not to get gangbanged by a trio of brainless slabs of muscle tonight."

She glanced back toward the village, which wasn't far enough away to suit him. "Fine."

They walked. He explained. And tried not to bump into her again.

"Like I said, I got here early enough to scout things out," he said, keeping his voice low. "The locals say three strangers have been spreading the word that you'd be showing up tonight and have offered a reward to the first person who spots you and turns you on." Realizing what he'd said, he called himself a jackass, but hoped she hadn't spent enough time on Earth to learn all the lingo. "*In.* Turns you in."

"How did they…"

Her gaze shifted up where, between the thick canopy of trees, glimmers of moonlight were visible. The moon was enormous over here—a clear sign the border was open.

Seeing that brilliant sky, Raine wondered, not for the first time, if Elatyria's plane of reality, which seemed just one or two degrees west of Earth's, was also a bit closer to the heavens. Sometimes, it seemed that way.

Then he remembered the downside of the place—little electricity, almost no indoor plumbing, no McDonald's, but lots of dragons, giants and scurvy. No. Definitely not heaven.

"So they knew I'd come tonight?"

"Yep—the very first night the border opened. You did just what they thought you'd do."

She shook her head. "Stupid. I should have known they'd wait for me here. I'd expected them to try for me in the borderlands."

He almost tripped. "You *knew* there was somebody after you?"

"Yes. I've seen that Hunter before."

The mind boggled. "And you still just…"

"I needed to go to Earth. Foxglen is a half day closer to the border than any other village. What was I supposed to do?"

"Not leaving a trail two lost kids could follow without the benefit of breadcrumbs would have been a good start."

He thought he might have heard her emit a tiny chuckle, but probably had imagined it.

"I didn't think they'd strike until they thought I had all four…"

"All four what?"

"You're saying you don't know?"

"I *don't*."

"But you do know my name, huh? How do I know you're not one of them? This could be a scheme to get me to trust you."

Raine put his hands up, palms out. "Hey, you want to find out for yourself who's a good guy and who's a bad one, go right ahead. But, uh, just so you know, I didn't get paid enough to put my life on the line. I'm not bailing you out twice."

A lie. He might not have been paid enough to risk his life, but he'd do it anyway. *Always finish the job.* Plus, he didn't like big thugs who picked on defenseless women.

The throbbing in his hand made him clarify that thought—*almost* defenseless women, with sharp teeth. God, something was seriously wrong with him that he found that so damned sexy.

Her brow scrunched. "Paid? You mean…"

"Yeah. Somebody hired me to watch over you."

"Who?"

"Frankly, lady, that's what I'd like to know. Just who are you, and what, exactly, are you up to?"

Still sounding skeptical, she asked, "You want me to believe you don't know why someone would be hunting me, or why someone else would hire you to protect me?"

"I haven't the slightest clue."

"I don't believe you."

"I've been called a liar before." He shrugged. "Considering I just saved your ass, though, maybe you ought to cut me a break."

She sucked in a surprised breath. "You're from over *there*."

He knew what she meant. Most people here didn't talk about Earth, just as most people on Earth didn't talk about Elatyria. Considering he had roots in both worlds, he didn't see the need to be coy about it. "I've been tracking you since Philadelphia."

Her eyes widened more as she stared searchingly at his face. Her beautiful lips parted, her breaths audibly moving over them.

Then, with a gasp, she looked away, long lashes sweeping over her eyes. "I remember you," she whispered, more to herself than to him.

He gaped, shocked that she'd seen him. "Seriously?" He must be losing his touch.

"You were at the store right across the street from the motel, buying a big box of chocolate candy for your…what is that holiday called? Your valentine?"

He sighed heavily. "My mom." Given this case, he'd nearly forgotten the holiday was this week and had run out super early one morning to get a few gifts. He'd *thought* Ashlynn was still sound asleep in her hotel room. Apparently not. Shit.

Interesting that she'd remember him. More interesting that she wouldn't meet his eye. Hmm.

"How long have you been following me?"

"Long enough to know you're in some kind of trouble."

"That's ridiculous," she proclaimed, even as her arms tightened around the leather satchel she always carried, which was about the size and shape of a laptop case. It didn't take a genius to know there was something in that bag she was desperate to protect and that it wasn't a laptop, since Elatyria had that whole "no electricity" thing to deal with. While he wasn't one to nose into other people's business, if her precious cargo was making her a target for hired thugs, he'd like to know what it was. Especially because, as her temporary bodyguard, he was in the line of fire, too.

"Well, thank you for your assistance," she said. "And for warning me about the Hunters. But now that I'm aware of the situation, I really don't need your help anymore. I'll wait until darkest night to go back to the village."

He barked a laugh. "You're not going to Foxglen."

"You can't tell me what to do."

He stopped and faced her. "I was hired to protect you."

"I didn't ask for your protection," she snapped.

"No, you didn't, but here I am. So why don't you stop arguing and tell me what this is all about?"

He moved in close. She quivered as he invaded her space.

Raine took advantage of her distraction. Without hesitating, he reached out and grabbed the satchel from her. "Then you can fill me in on what's in this bag."

2

ASHLYNN MIGHT BE BOOKISH and she might have spent much of her life in classrooms and museums, but she was no coward. Thinking only of the piece of map, tucked securely inside her bag, she lunged at the annoyingly attractive stranger. Her hands fisted, she also lifted a knee sharply, aiming for his groin.

"Oof," he yelped when her knee came close to its target.

"Give me that," she snapped.

The man was too tall for her. In spite of being in pain, he lifted the bag out of reach and spun away. When Ashlynn swung a fist at him, he caught it in his much bigger hand. "Hit me one more time, lady, and I'm going to forget I'm a gentleman."

"Nobody would mistake *you* for a gentleman!"

"Insults, huh? Guess you really don't want this back."

She ground her teeth in frustration. Then, remembering what he'd said, she glared at him. "You say you were hired to protect me?"

He nodded warily, as if not trusting her now that she wasn't trying to attack. "Yeah."

"I don't think *protection* includes stealing my property."

"I don't think whatever's in this bag *is* your property."

She flushed a little. Because, while she had the best intentions and wanted to use the map to find the castle for its archeological benefits, she hadn't exactly bought and paid for it—just the book inside which it had been carefully hidden. She'd found it, recognized it and bought it, without letting the seller know exactly what it was he was selling.

As if some underage clerk in a dusty old store would have even understood if you'd told him. Of course he wouldn't, no more than most others on Earth would. They believed her world was a fantasyland made up of fairy dust, talking frogs and moonbeams. They had no idea fairy dust was toxic if ingested, talking frogs were often possessed by the evil spirits of dead witches, and full moonbeams brought out the beast in many locals.

But this man, this irritatingly sexy man—who she'd seen once, buying that silly heart-shaped box, and then had the strangest dreams about for the next two nights—would recognize it. He'd know it was important. And he might refuse to give it back.

Or, stealing it might have been his objective all along.

There was one way to find out, even if it was risky. "I say it is my property. If you want to stop me from taking it back you're going to have to hurt me. Which doesn't go very well with that 'protection' job you claim to have undertaken."

"I could stop you without hurting you," he said, his eyes gleaming in the faint shafts of moonlight. "Or, at the very least, distract you enough that you wouldn't care anymore."

The hint of a smile on his sexy mouth and the thorough stare he raked down her body told her where his thoughts had gone. Ashlynn had to swallow hard, feeling that stare as if it was a touch. Like one of the many touches he'd given her during her long, heated dreams—the most sensual she'd ever experienced.

"Don't even think about it," she whispered.

He inched closer, though the satchel remained behind his back. She would have to step close to that rock-hard body and reach around him to try to get it. *It's not going to happen.*

"I can't not think about it. I've lived next door to you for weeks. Listening to you roll over in that creaky motel bed. Hearing you try to sing in the shower."

She gasped when she realized he'd been right there, beneath her nose, and but for that one visit to the store, she had never even noticed him.

He lifted a hand to her hair. "Smelling your scent in the air as I walked ten steps behind you."

Ashlynn trembled. Tried to breathe, but found it difficult. But not because she felt threatened—she didn't fear physical assault from this man. If that had been his intent, he'd had his chance when he'd had her hunched to the ground, at his mercy. No, this assault would be purely sensual. Provocative.

Possibly irresistible.

It had been a long time since a man had sent a rush of heat through her, making her feel slightly dizzy, weak in the knees. He'd done it on first sight. Now, close up, he was truly causing her world to spin beneath her feet.

"Don't come any closer," she ordered when he eliminated another inch of space between them.

"What's in the bag?" he whispered.

She swallowed, hard. "That's none of your business."

"Then I guess you won't be getting it back anytime soon," he said, his smile almost pleasant. "Unless you want to *take* it."

He sounded confident that she wouldn't, as if he could seduce her right out of her property. Damn him.

Was he right? She did feel so strange, so unlike herself. Unsure. *It's because you know he's dangerous.*

Maybe. Or it could be because he was so incredibly sure of himself. Or because he'd possibly just saved her life.

Or because he was so unbelievably handsome.

Mind-numbingly so, with dark blue eyes made almost purple by the night. She hadn't seen his eyes on that previous occasion and had been imagining them brown. But no, they were like the richest shade of royal velvet.

They were striking against his thick, jet-black hair, which hung a little long, almost brushing his shoulders. His strong, squared jaw hinted at determination, while the faint stubble on it invited thoughts of lazy mornings and the rasp of skin on skin. And his wide mouth, which held a hint of a smile, was the kind women longed to taste on sight—soft, sexy, wry and inviting.

Damn.

She closed her eyes and shook her head, wondering if the rich air was affecting her. It certainly wasn't like her to start picturing illicit touches and caresses with a stranger.

Moonlit madness. And the lingering effects of dreams she should never have had. That was all. She was back in Elatyria, where everything seemed magical, mystical. Not like Earth, so dull, blunt and immediate. Here, fantasy and reality merged and swirled together. A brigand who stole from her could almost seem like the hero she'd fantasized about since she was a child hearing her father's stories of fair maids and the noble men who rode to their rescue. Here, a paid adventurer—possibly a thief—could suddenly seem like the man of her dreams.

Well, all right, he *was* the man of her dreams. But only in the literal sense.

She opened her eyes, seeing the way his mouth had opened as he drew a slow, steady breath across his lips. His eyes gleamed with wickedness and his big, hard body was dressed in clothes more suited to a pirate than a prince.

That should have been enough to end her mental wondering. Instead, it heightened it. Because, to her, pirates had always been ever so much more interesting than boring Prince Charmings.

The long stare continued. His eyes hunted her face for a clue to what she was thinking. But there was no way she would reveal it. Finally, though, she focused only on her quest, on how hard she'd worked and how far she'd come. No way was some sexy rogue going to deter her from finishing what she'd started.

She stiffened her jaw, determined not to show the thoughts he'd inspired with his casual, sensual threat. Then, unsure whether she was driven more by anger or desperation, she bit out the words, "Give. Me. My. Bag."

Her tone, or perhaps her unflinching expression, apparently convinced him. He finally lowered the satchel and let her take it. "You win."

She sighed in relief. She'd done it, convinced him she was unaffected by him, that he couldn't charm his way into revealing her secrets. *Maybe he wasn't convinced. Maybe it's all a trick.*

"I can't force you to trust me. Though, you could give me the benefit of the doubt since I just saved your life."

Her life. Could someone really be prepared to kill her for a few torn pieces of parchment? No, of course not for the parchment. For the castle to which those torn pieces of parchment led. And what was, supposedly, in that castle.

Legend said the Sleeping Beauty's family had been so anxious to leave the castle that they'd left behind their treasures. It sounded silly, but if they really had been asleep for centuries, they might have believed everything around them was touched by the dark curse that had left them there to rot. That was one theory, anyway. Another theory was that it was not true, that they would have taken an hour or two to pack up the good stuff.

Frankly, Ashlynn subscribed to the latter idea. It seemed incongruous to her that any ancient kings—notorious gold grubbers as they were—would have left something precious behind.

But whether she believed it or not, men had killed for less than a castle full of treasure. *And they might kill you just for the chance to find out it's there.*

"Okay, princess, we should cover a little more ground."

She fell into step beside him. "I'm no princess."

Flexing his hand, which was reddened from her bite, he replied, "No, I guess you're not. Princesses don't fight dirty."

She snorted. "*Nobody* fights dirtier than a princess in a world where they outnumber the princes two to one."

"Why is that?"

"Because stupid princes are always trying to find a way to prove their manhood, so they go out and try to slay dragons or capture hydras and get themselves chomped into tiny bits."

A hint of a smile appeared on his lips. "I meant, why were you willing to fight so hard when you could end up getting hurt?"

"You wouldn't have hurt me," she insisted.

"No, I wouldn't have. How'd you figure it out?"

"Intuition, I suppose."

"That and I'm slightly less intimidating than the knife-wielding wonder-thug back in the village?"

She chuckled. If he were like most men she knew, he would be acting sulky or angry that she'd managed to get her bag back without telling him anything. Instead, he seemed good-humored. "Well, at least you're cleaner than he was."

"Wow. Thanks."

"And you don't have a black eye and blackened teeth."

"His teeth weren't black. That was just a big giant hole where they used to be."

"What did his two companions look like?" she asked.

"During your Disney-movie marathon on Earth, did you happen to catch Alice In Wonderland?"

She sneered. "I did. Ridiculous. As if the Queen of Hearts's courtiers were giant-size playing cards!"

"Did you happen to notice Tweedle Dum and Tweedle Dee?"

"You mean that's what the other two men looked like?" That didn't sound too threatening.

"Not exactly. More like Tweedle Dum and Tweedle Dee's mom had sex with a giant and produced Tweedle Dangerous and Tweedle Deadly. They're each at least seven feet tall with big bodies, tiny heads and lots of scars. They have mean scowls but soft voices, which, in my world, means that like Alice, they've been popping some 'eat me and you'll grow' pills."

"Oh, dear," she murmured.

"Speaking of Disney movies and Earth, what exactly were you doing over there for so long, anyway?"

"Looking for something."

"In every bookstore in Philadelphia, yeah, I know."

"How do...oh, right. You were following me." She wrinkled her nose, surprised she'd been oblivious to his shadowing. Then again, she had been in another world. Everything had felt strange and unusual, so maybe that was why the presence of a secret bodyguard hadn't stuck out.

"What was it you were looking for?"

"That's classified."

He chuckled. "You watched some spy movies while you were there, didn't you?"

She couldn't deny it. "That James Bond, he's a scary man, isn't he?"

"You went to a Bond flick?"

"There was a—what do you call it?—a movie marathon? It was on the television at the hotel once when I had nothing to do."

He hesitated, then asked, "You do know those movies are fictional, don't you? I mean, you didn't really think one guy went from looking like Sean to Roger to Timothy to Pierce to Daniel…but was always the same man, right?"

She waved a hand. "Don't be ridiculous. Of course I know that. But considering your people have fictionalized so much about my world, who's to say Mr. Bond doesn't exist on yet another plane of reality that neither of us knows about? Personally, I hope there's one where that little boy wizard lives. I quite enjoyed those books during my recent stay."

He paused midstep. "Touché. I never thought of that."

Pleased that he didn't immediately tell her she was wrong, like one of her colleagues had when she'd dared to suggest there might be more than two worlds, she smiled and continued. "He could be utterly real and might very well watch movies in his world about men walking on the moon and think they're the most ridiculous thing he's ever seen." Then she thought about it, tapped her fingertip on her mouth and added, "Of course, that's also what most people here think."

"Hey, don't sweat it. A lot of people on Earth think that, too. They're called conspiracy theorists," he said with a grin.

She liked that grin. Liked his laugh. Liked that they were walking through the forest in the darkness of night, utter strangers—well, at least, he was a stranger to her—yet she was actually enjoying herself.

She could like this man. A lot. Which would normally be a good thing. But when combined with the heated attraction she'd felt for him at first sight, was probably a bad one instead.

"Now back to what you were looking for…."

Or, maybe she couldn't like him. He was far too persistent.

"Does it have something to do with a book?"

Figuring he wasn't going to let up unless she gave him something, she admitted, "I was researching two brothers named Grimm. They visited Elatyria centuries ago and caused all sorts of mayhem."

"Uh, yeah," he drawled. "I've heard of them."

"It was bad enough for them to share Elatyria's history as make-believe stories on Earth, but they also created mischief *here*."

Including terrifying children with ridiculous tales of an evil time called the Inquisition.

That was one bad part of visiting Earth. She could have happily gone through her whole life without discovering that those Inquisition stories were true. And people thought the ancient practice of sacrificing virgins to dragons was barbaric? Yeesh.

She shook off the images she'd seen in an Earthen textbook, focusing on the success of her trip. Now, she felt nothing but gratitude toward the Grimms. She suspected it was one of them who'd hidden the map piece between the lining of one of their own books, where she had discovered it.

"By the way, how do you know so much about Elatyria?" she asked. "Obviously you've been here before."

He reached out and swept a jagged branch out of their way. "My parents were from here."

That surprised her. "Really? And they...emigrated?"

"Yeah. They were from different villages and were told who they had to marry, all that stuff. So they ran away together."

Interesting. What would it be like, she wondered, to love someone so much you'd move to another world to be with them?

"You doing okay? I know you've been walking all day."

She glanced at the sky, gauging the passage of time. "I'm fine. And I think we've gone far enough, don't you?"

"How far's far enough?"

"Far enough that we're safe to wait here until those three Hunters drink too much ale and fall into such a deep sleep that they won't notice me sneaking back into the village."

"Maybe I didn't make myself clear," he said, stopping. His chin was thrust out and his brow pulled down, all evidence of good humor gone. "We're not going back to that village. We're heading the other way—toward Riverdale. You'll get home, I'll get paid, and we can say sayonara."

Ashlynn tried not to feel a twinge of sadness that he so easily talked of saying…whatever the word was that he'd said, which she assumed meant farewell. But she forced the sensation away, angry at herself for getting distracted by his easy manner and friendly charm. Not to mention his appearance.

"You hear me, princess?"

"Stop calling me 'princess.' I'm a historian."

"You hear me, historian?"

"I heard you." Spying a big, graceful white pine, Ashlynn walked to it, then lowered herself to the soft cushion of fallen needles below. It would do for a bed. It couldn't be any worse than that creaky, lumpy one she'd slept in for the last thirty nights. Had she been a real princess, she would have been black-and-blue after sleeping on that thing. She didn't imagine it had any peas beneath it—it felt more like boulders.

"What are you doing?"

"I'm taking a rest." She lay down on her side, hugging her bag close. "I'll sleep for a while, then head back to the village in a few hours."

"But I just said…"

"I heard you. Still, I *am* going back there." Knowing he wouldn't let it go, she explained, "I left something there when I passed through last month, something I need very badly. And I intend to go get it."

His mouth dropped open. "You're crazy."

"No. Just determined. Now you can go, with my thanks. Your warning came in time and I appreciate it. But there's nothing you can say that will stop me from going back to Foxglen."

He thrust a hand through his thick, black hair, frustration rolling off him. As if he just wasn't used to anyone—any woman—refusing to do whatever he desired.

You might not be refusing if he desired something else.

She pushed that thought away. This man might have been friendly and protective, but he was still a stranger. And, judging by his readiness to say goodbye, a disinterested one.

Expecting him to leave, she was shocked to see him drop onto another pile of needles, muttering a curse. "Look, lady. I don't get the rest of my money unless you get safely home. So, if you're going back to that village, I'm going to have to go, too."

She opened her mouth to refuse, not liking that some unknown entity had hired this man to take care of her. Was it someone from the museum? Or perhaps someone sent by Queen Penelope, who had shown great support for the arts, history and science since reclaiming her family's throne?

"This man who paid you, what was he like?"

"Old. Long gray beard, but well dressed."

A face appeared in her mind. "This man, did he sneeze a lot?"

Raine chuckled. "Yeah, he went through a half-dozen handkerchiefs during our single conversation."

That cinched it. Uncle Edgar, her father's closest friend—Ashlynn's own godfather—was one of the few who knew about her quest. He'd wanted to be her escort, but his health wouldn't allow it. He'd obviously still found a way to get to Earth and make sure she was looked after. "I know who it was."

"Care to fill me in?"

"A dear old family friend who knows what I'm working on and was worried."

That was very nice of him. But, as much as she appreciated the thoughtfulness, that didn't mean she was happy about having this man, Raine, second-guessing her every move. She'd been raised to be independent, to think for herself, not to be one of those silly females who needed a man for every little thing.

Though, she suspected it wasn't a *little* thing she needed from this man. In fact, she imagined it was a *big* thing. A *very* big one, given how big and masculine he was everywhere else.

Stop it. He's not interested. That was very obvious.

She, on the other hand, *was* interested. She had been from first sight and was growing more so by the minute. He might be pushy and bossy, but he was also intelligent, self-confident and had a sense of humor. She liked that. She saw it often in males from Earth, but not so much here, where men were too busy being rugged and tough to ever just laugh at life. Or at themselves.

Yes, she thought she might be able to enjoy her time with Raine Fowler. As long as he didn't try to stop her from doing what she needed to do, she might actually be glad he'd come into her life so suddenly.

Not that she was about to let him know that.

"If I let you come with me, you'll have to do as I say," she insisted.

He snorted. "Snowball's chance. Hell. Ever heard of them?"

"I mean it, or no deal. I'll sneak away while you sleep."

"I can go for days without sleep, princess."

"Stop calling me that," she snapped. "Most princesses are giddy, vapid, foolish and vain. Focused only on their own beauty rather than the well-being of anyone in their kingdoms, longing only for the attention of a handsome man. I am not like them!"

Without hesitating, he replied, "Well, you do have one thing in common with them, historian. You are beautiful."

She froze, shocked at how much the compliment pleased her. He'd said it as casually as he'd say the night was cool or the ground hard; something that was accepted, understood. Men had told her she was beautiful, but only when they were holding her hand, looking deeply into her eyes…and trying to get under her skirts or into her priceless collections. Never just because they believed it.

But he sounded as though he did. Which made something inside her go soft and warm. Maybe she wasn't the only one feeling this strange connection, wondering what it might be like to touch, to taste, to…

"You're not going back tonight."

So much for soft and warm. The man was an ass. "Yes, I…"

"Because they'll be on guard all night long," he said, as if she hadn't spoken. "If we go, it'll have to be early in the morning when, hopefully, they'll have figured you for a no-show until the next moonrise. Their guard should be down. Hopefully they'll be taking shifts and two of them will be sleeping."

He made a good point. "That means you agree to my terms?"

He rolled over onto his side to face her, leaning on his elbow, which made his shirt bunch and strain against the thick, flexing muscles of his arm. *Mercy.*

"You say you have to get something. Fine. We'll get it. But if you want to get out of this alive, you have to do it my way."

She nibbled her lip, thinking it over.

"Otherwise, I'll make a racket as soon as you get there so there's no chance of you slipping in unnoticed."

"But you won't interfere, beyond ensuring we're not caught?"

"Not as long as you follow my instructions."

"And you won't be nosy about what it is I'm getting?"

He rolled onto his back, lacing his fingers together and resting his head on his hands. "Can't say I won't be curious."

"You can be curious," she said. "But your job is to make sure I come out alive, not to stick your nose into what I'm doing. Deal?"

"Deal." Seeming almost irritated with himself for agreeing, Raine punched at the ground to try to make himself more comfortable. "Stupid tree root," he muttered.

Bad move. Because, without warning, a large branch swooped from above him and swatted him with a face full of pine needles.

Ashlynn tried unsuccessfully to hide a smile.

"Damn this crazy place. Trees shouldn't have feelings!"

"Just imagine what she'd do if I spilled the beans about Christmas," she said, sotto voce.

The man's eyes widened at the thought of the reaction *that* story would inspire in this grove of evergreens.

"'Night," she said with a cheeky grin.

"Witch," he muttered, sounding amused.

Chuckling, she rolled onto her side, not facing him. She did not want to fall asleep with the image of those purple-blue eyes and that too-handsome face in her mind. Determined not to think of him at all, she inhaled another deep breath of the sweet, cool air of her home world and hoped for dreams of a mysterious castle and the secrets of a long-lost civilization.

And not about the very sexy, slightly infuriating man resting a few feet away.

3

RAINE SELDOM SLEPT MORE than six hours a night, so he was awake well before dawn. It took him a few moments to recall where he was. Gazing up at the innocent-looking branches of a pine tree, and remembering how not-so-innocent the conifer really was, he rolled out from under it and glanced across the clearing.

Ashlynn was still there, curled up on her side, now facing him. Her long lashes were dark and spiky against her face, and he knew that, even if he'd met her by accident back on Earth, he would have recognized her as Elatyrian. She had the creamy-smooth skin of someone raised in a place where there was no pollution, no smog, nothing to dull that shining natural beauty.

She shifted a little, frowning in her sleep. But despite the movement, she never released her death grip on the damned bag, which was pressed against her body.

Don't think about that body.

That was easier said than done, considering her clothes had shifted in the night. He caught a glimpse of bare skin, then sucked in a breath and turned his head to look up at the dark sky peeking through the canopy of trees. He actually managed to look straight up for a good ten seconds.

To hell with it. He might try to be gentlemanly, but any guy with a set of hormone-producing balls would look again.

He looked.

Ashlynn wore a loose peasant skirt that had ridden high on one bent leg. Her leather sandals were sturdy, but still managed to look sexy as sin, with laces that wound from her ankle all the way to her knee. Her lacy white blouse had pulled loose from the skirt, enough to reveal an inch or two of tempting middle— a perfect spot to place his hands when cupping her hips.

The blouse had slipped, too. No, she wasn't flashing him, but the scooped neckline now revealed the top curves of those perfect breasts, which rose gently with each steady breath.

Shit. Time to think about something else. Not about how that leg would feel twisted between his. Or whether the spot behind her knee was as sensitive as he imagined. Or whether her skin smelled as sweet and flowery as her hair.

Or how her breasts would feel in his hands, how her nipples would taste on his tongue, how it would feel to roll on top of her and slide into that soft, warm body.

Cool it, jackass. She's a job. Nothing else.

A job that could land him in a world of hurt later. Or, now that they'd slept for several hours, sooner.

He still couldn't believe he'd agreed to take her back to the village. It was like agreeing to escort a Christian to the lion pit—she could be chewed to bits.

He could think of only one way to get them in and out. And since he didn't have an invisibility cloak at his disposal, they needed to be *so* obvious that they'd be rendered invisible anyway. Which meant Ashlynn needed to cover up those perfect breasts and those stunning legs. Not just from his own lustful view, but also from the sight of anyone else who would look at her and see the lovely young woman being sought by three thugs.

He knew of only one disguise that might accomplish it.

She'll hate it.

Which made it that much more attractive, considering she was making him do something he so didn't want to do.

"Paybacks are hell, princess," he whispered.

With sunrise at least two hours away, he rose and slipped away from their campsite, making his way toward a cottage deep in the forest. He'd met the occupants before. The owner was a shady character who always had a bit of everything for sale.

As expected, the man had something that would work. Luckily, he didn't haggle too much, so that by the time the sun rose, Raine had made it back to their makeshift camp. Just in time to see Ashlynn sitting up and stretching out the kinks of the night before. One stretch pulled her blouse higher, widening that tempting bit of skin and revealing the curve of one hip. The other reversed things. Both messed with his head.

He cleared his throat as he approached. "Morning."

She started, as if she'd forgotten he was with her last night. "Why didn't you wake me up?"

"I had an errand to run."

"I didn't mean to sleep this long."

"It's the air. It's drugging after being on Earth for a while."

She rose to her feet, pushing her hair back and twisting it out of the way. The dampness of the night air had put a few curls around her face, and one hung down her neck, dipping into a fishhook that hung right at her cleavage.

He swallowed. Looked away. He did not want to be the fish caught on that hook. At least, not while there were men stalking her and he had to keep her determined butt safe from them.

"The change in air quality didn't seem to affect you," she said with a yawn.

"I travel back and forth a lot."

"Why is that?"

He walked into the clearing, offering her a flask of water he'd refilled from a stream. "It's part of my business."

She took the flask. "And what business would that be?"

"Let's just say I am a man who deals with things. I find them. I protect them."

"You take them?"

"Sometimes."

She quickly bent and picked up her satchel.

"Get over it, historian. I'm not interested in what's in your bag. You're all I'm interested in right now."

"Because I'm the 'thing' in question for this job?"

"Pretty much."

"Lovely."

"You asked." Tossing a bundle of cloth at her feet, he added, "Speaking of protecting you, put that on."

She glanced down, her eyes widening as she caught sight of the rough woolen dress, dirty and stained. "Excuse me?"

"If you want me to take you back to Foxglen, you've got to blend in."

Picking up the bundle, she shook out the dress, which was several sizes too big and just about the ugliest thing he'd ever seen. Crusted with grease, dirt and some rust-colored spots that must be dried blood, the dress looked as though it had last been worn by Lizzie Borden attending a family brunch.

The trader's wife apparently had mad skills in butchering.

"I'm not wearing this."

He reached into the large bag he'd carried back from the trader's shack. "Sure you are. And these." He tossed her a heavy pair of wooden clogs, then dropped a wrinkled, smelly bandana on top of it. "Oh, and hide your hair, too."

"You're crazy."

"If you want me to cover your ass so you can get whatever it is you so need from that village, you'll do it. The villagers are looking for a pretty young woman, not a dirty farm wench."

Her jaw dropped. "*Wench?* Did you just call me a wench?"

He nodded, then, knowing she'd have to stop protesting sooner or later, began to strip out of his own shirt. He didn't have to change quite as much, considering nobody was looking for him. But it wouldn't do to show up in the, er, wench's company, looking as if he'd just stepped out of a Levi's commercial. Not that many people here knew what Levi's were. Or commercials.

"Be sure to rub some dirt on your face," he said, glancing over. Surprisingly, he caught her staring at him, her eyes almost as wide-open as her mouth.

Whoa. The woman was suddenly very easy to read. There

was lust in those deep blue eyes. Pure want. The way she licked her lips, the slow inhalations that made her chest rise and fall, said she'd been knocked pretty hard by sexual awareness.

Well, hell, join the club, lady. It's about time you got here.

Raine didn't move, shocked and incredibly turned on by how obvious she was about her interest. It was probably as obvious as he'd been this morning while she'd slept. He only wondered what they were going to do about it.

"Well?" he asked, the word loaded, though he wasn't entirely sure what he was asking. *Are you going to get dressed? Are you going to get un*dressed? *Are you going to touch me with your hands the way you are with your eyes?*

She jerked her attention off his chest and spun around, scooping up the ugly shoes and bandana. "I need some privacy."

He chuckled. "Looks like I do, too."

She muttered something under her breath before disappearing into the brush. Raine enjoyed the moment, knowing full well that with Ashlynn, it wasn't always easy to get the last word.

When she returned a few minutes later, Raine didn't just chuckle, he laughed out loud.

"Make one more sound and I take this off."

Hmm. That could be interesting. Especially because, even in the ugly, sacklike dress, with her beautiful hair hidden away, she was lovely. Far too lovely to go unnoticed.

He frowned. "Wait." Rummaging through his things, he came up with a leather belt. He handed it to her, along with some clothes and said, "Stuff these down your dress so you look matronly."

She did, and the end result was moderately better. Or worse, as the case may be.

"Don't forget the dirt on your face," he ordered, even as he bent to retrieve some to rub on his own. The clothes he'd bought from the trader for himself were as hideous as hers, and the damp soil made them even worse. For good measure, he rubbed a handful into his hair and smeared it on his face and forearms.

Ashlynn did the same, until the two of them looked as though they'd just fallen off the back of a turnip truck. Literally.

"Ready?"

"Ready," she told him. "Once we get there, I need to go to the Mare's End. It should only take a few minutes."

"Is someone at the tavern holding something for you?" he asked, skeptical, remembering what the owner and employees of the place were like. Not particularly trustworthy.

She shook her head, but didn't explain further.

Raine's curiosity was piqued, but as they moved back through the forest toward Foxglen, that curiosity segued into tension. This could go so wrong. How could anyone look at her and not see the beautiful woman under the dirt and the lumpy clothes?

He tried to distract himself—and her—by asking her about her life here in Elatyria. From the sound of it, she'd had a storybook childhood—right down to the death of a mother, the love of an adoring father and a brief stint with a wicked stepmother. Fortunately, things like divorce had made their way over here and that marriage had ended a year after it had begun. One thing was sure: she and her father had been incredibly close until his recent death, which obviously still grieved her.

The small talk didn't distract him. In fact, the closer they got to the village, the more the weight of what they were doing settled onto him. He'd been hired to protect her, but even if he hadn't been, he'd do it anyway. Ashlynn's was a life worth protecting. No matter what the cost.

That realization surprised him, as he usually didn't value anybody's skin as much as he valued his own. But it was true. He suddenly knew he'd do anything—risk anything—to keep her safe. He hadn't evaluated it, hadn't planned it. But having lived beside her, listened to her, studied her, followed her and now interacted with her, he knew Ashlynn Scott was *very* special.

"You're sure you want to do this?" he asked when they neared the end of the forest. "Maybe I could get this thing for you."

She squared her shoulders in determination. "I can do it."

"Still don't trust me, huh?"

"Not with this."

"But you do with your life? That's screwed-up logic, lady."

"Some people would say the item I'm going to retrieve is worth more than my life."

"Well *some people* need to be whacked with a stupid stick."

She blinked, looking up at him, curious. "Are there such things in your world?"

He grinned. "Sure. They're called baseball bats."

Though she still appeared puzzled, he had no time to explain. Because they had arrived.

The village was buzzing with activity—lots of people coming in to market this morning—and the time would never be better to slip in. Hopefully they'd blend in with the crowd and be out in an hour, never having been noticed.

"You ready?"

She took a deep breath, then nodded. But she couldn't hide the slight tremor on her pretty, albeit dirty, mouth. And though Raine wasn't the touchy-feely type, he couldn't help reaching out for her hand and squeezing it. "You're going to be okay. I promise."

She managed a tremulous smile. "Thank you."

Her expression was trusting. And right then, Raine acknowledged that there was nothing he wouldn't do to keep his promise. Absolutely nothing. He would keep her safe, if it was the very last thing he did.

Silent understanding flashed between them. Then, together, their hands still locked as if they were just a bored, overweight, middle-aged, filthy farm couple, they walked into Foxglen.

It was working.

To Ashlynn's surprise, she and Raine weren't immediately chased out of the village for being so filthy. In fact, compared to some of the people they saw—not to mention the pungent odors of their clothes—they looked pretty good. Even she had a hard time reconciling Raine's ragged, dingy appearance with the golden-skinned god she'd glimpsed while he'd changed.

She hadn't meant to stare. When he'd caught her, she'd wanted to sink into the ground. But not much could have made her look away from those incredibly broad shoulders, the thick arms flexing with muscle, all that warm, supple skin. She wasn't used to seeing such brawny, muscular men on Earth, which seemed filled with guys in suits who rode buses and trains to office jobs and never worked outside a day in their life. Raine was different. Apparently, his job finding, protecting and taking things kept him very active, indeed.

"You okay?" he asked as they moved through the crowd.

"So far, so good."

She only hoped it stayed that way, that they continued to blend. For now, they drew no second glances, no questioning stares. They also saw no one who looked like the hired muscle she'd spotted from the woods last night.

"Do you think they gave up and left?" she asked as they reached the main square.

Raine, who'd paused to buy a few pieces of fruit, shook his head. He handed her an apple, murmuring, "Don't be too obvious, but check out the baker's shop. Tweedle Dumbass is leaning against the side of it. I'd guess the other two are sleeping."

She glanced and saw the man, almost tripping as she realized just how huge—and frightening—he looked. She edged a little closer to Raine, glad he was by her side, no matter how much he'd annoyed her by insisting on it.

A moment later, when they stopped at another booth to purchase a wedge of cheese, she overheard a conversation that confirmed what Raine had told her.

"No sign of 'er yet, I 'ear," said an old woman, who was busily chopping up hunks of meat and lacing them on skewers.

"You t'ink she'll come tonight?" asked another. "I could use that re-ward money, that's for sure!"

"I 'spect so. Them Hunters seem right sure of themselves."

Ashlynn felt the blood drain from her face. Apparently noticing her reaction, Raine slid his arm through hers and casually led her away, as though they had just come for a leisurely market stroll with everyone else from the surrounding farms. Once they were out of earshot, he murmured, "I'd really like to get out of here, so let's do this."

She edged toward the tavern. "Give me five minutes."

"You're the boss."

Before she walked away, he put a hand on her arm. His fingers sizzled against her skin. She couldn't help wondering what it would be like to be touched by him with no barrier between them. No dirt. No map. No danger.

No clothes.

All of the above would be her choice. It was madness, perhaps, but Ashlynn wanted that to happen. The attraction was undeniable. The danger and excitement of what they were doing had only built the desperate need inside her. And once this was over, once he was no longer sticking around because he'd been paid to watch her, she hoped she'd have a chance to do something about it.

"Be careful," he urged.

Ashlynn nodded once, then walked toward the tavern. Squaring her shoulders, she stepped into the shadowy interior, pausing inside to allow her eyes to adjust to the dim lighting. The place looked just as she remembered: same dust-covered pictures on the walls, same dirty floor, same bored-looking serving girl.

It will be okay. As they would say on Earth, easy-peasy.

Then she glanced toward the rear corner—*her* table—and felt her stomach roll. Because, not only was it occupied, the two men sitting at it were familiar. One of them was the Hunter from last night. The other, well, she'd call him Tweedle Destroyer…a bookend to the thug patrolling outside.

Ashlynn's feet turned into lead. She remained near the doorway, panic hitting her hard. But she shoved it away, thinking about what she must look like to them—just another farm wife come to market. Not Ashlynn Scott, premier historian and curator for the Grand Elatyria Museum.

One of them glanced over. Her pulse raced as she wondered if her disguise would hold up. Fortunately, his piercing gaze didn't linger. After a quick sum-up, he looked away. She took a moment to breathe deeply, then slipped back out the door.

Raine was right outside. "What's wrong?"

"They're both in there."

"Hell." He grabbed her arm and pulled her around the side of the building. "Okay, that's it, we can't do this."

"You don't understand, I *have* to."

Maybe if the thugs hadn't been sitting *right there,* at a table directly over the stone where she'd hidden the map, she'd think about leaving and waiting for things to cool off. But how could she? For all she knew, they may already have found the oilskin-wrapped package. Maybe they had the two quarters in their possession and were waiting for her to come back with the third. They could know the exact spot she needed to check, might be guarding that spot like two cats hovering over a piece of cheese left to tempt a mouse.

Still, this mouse couldn't leave. Not without knowing if all was lost. "If we could just draw them out for a few minutes…"

He frowned, raking a hand through his hair, which even the dirt couldn't make less attractive. "Minutes? You're sure?"

She saw by his expression that he had an idea. "If you get them to leave, I could be in and out in under two minutes."

He muttered something under his breath, then said, "All right, you win."

"What are you going to…"

"Never mind. Just stay here. After you see them come running out, you wait thirty seconds, make sure they're totally out of sight, then hurry in."

He turned to leave.

"Raine," she said, grabbing his arm, "thank you."

A crooked smile appeared on his handsome, dirty face. "What can I say? I'm a sucker for a challenge. I just hope this is worth it."

4

THERE WAS NO WAY IN HELL this was going to be worth it.

In fact, as Raine entered the tavern and saw the two scarred men seated in the back corner, he questioned not only the plan, but also his own sanity. Fighting back when you had no choice was one thing. Leaping into the snake pit and saying "Bite me" was quite another.

He swallowed down the urge to turn around. Trying not to be obvious, he studied the layout of the place, checked the escape routes—one behind him, a window on the opposite side—and gauged his chances of making it out of here without a broken limb.

He'd give himself one in five. Not bad odds...but they would only be met if he pulled this off without a single hitch.

Walking slowly, like a weary, timid farmer, he skirted the scarred, empty tables. He studied the men as he approached, getting a more complete picture than he had last evening.

One of them looked terrifying, the other merely frightening. Both bore scars that told tales of previous battles. The Hunter he'd seen last night wore a knife on his hip, another one strapped to his arm. Too bad he was the merely frightening one.

If this were a Disney movie, the two of them would start singing a showstopper about how they were really nice guys, just misunderstood. *But this sure ain't a Disney movie.*

"Hey, handsome, want a pint?" the serving girl asked.

It took Raine a second to realize she was speaking to him. Given his costume, he'd have figured only a blind person would call him handsome. Of course, next to the only other patrons in the place, he probably looked like George Clooney. But they *all* probably smelled like Porky Pig.

"Not yet," he said.

She simpered and flounced away, heading behind the bar. *Good.* Nobody close enough to get hurt if furniture started flying. Well, other than him, of course.

Historian, this better be worth it.

Finally, he reached the giants' table. They didn't notice him at first. They were too busy discussing a large sheet of parchment on the table. It was yellowed, jagged and looked like a map.

Raine liked maps. Especially ones that led to interesting objects. So he couldn't resist peering over the whole thing.

"Want your nosy nose cut off?" one of the men growled.

Trying to remember to be meek and subservient, he snatched the dirty cap off his head. "Begging your pardon," he said. "Are you the ones offerin' the reward?"

The smaller of the giganatrons shot up. "You saw the bitch?"

What Raine saw was *red,* but still managed to stay cool. If he punched the walking wall, he'd have to fight them both. While that might be satisfying, if he survived it, he probably wouldn't be in much condition to protect Ashlynn from goon number three.

"I think I saw 'er down by the livery stable."

The other man rose, too. "Alone?"

"Aye."

The men exchanged a glance.

"My reward?" he asked, trying to sound needy.

"Wait here. If it's her, you'll get what's coming to ya."

Raine had seen enough movies to know *that* was never a good line to hear. If he really were here turning in some poor woman, he'd be booking it the minute these two turned their backs.

Oh, wait. He *was* going to be booking it the minute these two turned their backs.

They turned their backs. "Don't go anywhere," one said.

He watched as one man scooped up the map and shoved it into his pocket and the other unsheathed his knife. After they left, Raine counted to thirty, hoping Ashlynn would do as he'd told her—wait until they were out of sight before moving.

She came in when he hit thirty-one. Heading for the door, he walked past her, muttering, "I'll be outside. If I see them coming back, I'll signal, and you get out of here."

"Understood."

He walked outside and began scanning for the enemy. His thudding heartbeat counted off every second. Each thud provided another moment for her pursuers to return. But true to her word, Ashlynn was back out in a minute.

She flashed a smile, patting her bag as if it contained her long-lost kidney. Whatever she'd come for must now be safely tucked inside it with her other treasures. "Let's go."

He grabbed her hand and headed down the street. Having sent two of the guards in the opposite direction, he only prayed they'd gotten the third one. Especially because they had to pass right by the corner where they'd last seen him.

"How'd you get them to leave?" she asked.

"Sold you out."

She chuckled. "Did they pay you?"

"Nah. They were too busy racing after you. I thought they were going to leave without their weapons or their treasure map."

Ashlynn suddenly stopped in the middle of the marketplace. A man carrying a goat, who'd been walking behind her, almost ran into her, and his goat tried to nibble on Ashlynn's dirty hair.

"Watch it, wench!"

Ashlynn ignored *that* guy calling her a wench, and stared up at Raine, whispering, "Treasure map?"

"Yeah." Taking her arm, he added, "Can we talk about this after we get away from the bad guys who've put a price on your head?"

She nodded, but even through the dirt, he could see the color had left her cheeks. Ashlynn remained quiet as they hurried through town, then broke across the wide field toward the forest.

Though he knew he shouldn't let it, his curiosity got the better of him. Halfway across the field, Raine risked a look back. Seeing all three of the thugs huddled together in the middle of the town square put an extra bit of spring in his step.

"God, please don't let them look this way," he muttered.

Luckily for them, the men didn't. A few more strides and they reached the woods. Another few and the trees swallowed them up. "Whew," he said. "We did it."

She smiled a bright, happy smile that stopped his heart for a second. But they weren't in the clear yet. They kept walking, needing to get as far away from the village as they could before the Hunters began looking for the farmer who'd given them the bad tip. Each step brought them closer to safety and, after an hour, he finally began to relax.

Eventually, even the need to gain some distance couldn't prevent him from tugging at the ugly, filthy clothes he was wearing. He took off the cap and swung it away like a Frisbee, then the shirt, dropping it between one stride and the next.

"Wait," she said, stopping. She unfastened the belt, letting his bundled clothes fall to the ground.

Raine grabbed his own shirt out of the pile while she shimmied out of the dress. He'd held his breath until he saw she'd worn her own clothes underneath. Smart—he wished he'd done the same thing so he could have had something between his skin and that shirt.

"I might have to burn these. The smell's never going to come out," she admitted, gazing down ruefully at her clothes, then at her sacred satchel. "Fortunately, I have spare clothes to wear."

The magical mystery bag obviously had lots of pockets.

Saying nothing, Ashlynn kicked off the ugly clogs. Then she pulled her blouse free of her waistband and pushed the skirt down off her hips to the ground, revealing those amazing legs. Her blouse was long enough to cover her bottom…but she quickly took care of that problem, pulling it up and taking it off, too.

Whoa. And whoa. *And whoa.*

She wore what would probably be considered modest underwear—no Victoria's Secret stuff here, more like Wal-Mart three-pack specials. But oh, God, did she wear it well. The plain, cotton boy's-shorts-type panties were obscenely sexy, hugging her hips and making a thing of art out of her ass. And the simple white bra covered everything it was supposed to, yet still revealed the most luscious curves he'd ever seen in his life.

She was perfect, every inch of her, from top to bottom. And even though her face and arms were dirty and her hair a tangled mess, he wanted her with a hunger that bordered on desperation. Adventure, danger, excitement—they always revved his engines. Having shared the adventure with her, a woman unlike any he'd ever known, just upped the ante. And now, the sight of her perfect, nearly naked body had slammed the pedal down and gotten his every juice flowing.

"Raine?"

He stared into her face, helpless to hide what he'd been thinking. And saw an answering gleam that told him he wasn't alone in this. She felt it, too. Maybe she, too, had been feeling it for a long time.

This wasn't the time, or the place. But something in him refused to keep walking without giving in to it, just a little.

Without a word, he opened the flask at his hip, poured some

water onto his shirt, then approached her. She said nothing, just lifted her face to him as he used the wet fabric to wipe away the grime. Gradually, he uncovered the beautiful features below—those high cheeks, delicately curved brows, that succulent mouth.

His touch lingered, the brush of her soft skin against his fingers as sensual as anything he'd ever felt.

That unblinking stare as she watched him revealed what she was feeling. So did the soft stroke of her hand against his bare stomach. He didn't even know if she was aware of it, but she'd reached out to touch him as he washed her face. Her hand glided across his abs with a lightness that drove him slightly mad.

He slowly lowered his hand. She took the flask and the shirt. Wetting another spot, she reached up to repay the favor. Or just draw out the erotic tension. He couldn't be sure which.

She washed him as deliberately as he'd washed her. Each touch sent the tension up, especially when she brushed a wet fingertip across his lips. Raine couldn't recall whether there had been any dirt there, but frankly, he didn't care.

He groaned, nipping lightly at her finger.

"Raine?"

One word. Just his name, and a question at that. But he understood.

He bent to her and brushed his lips against hers. A breath, then their mouths came together, warm and sultry, lips parting, tongues tangling. Maybe it was because of the sense of adventure or the beautiful morning or just the incredible attraction they'd been feeling since day one—his day one being much longer ago than hers—but the kiss was perfect. Hot and hungry, new and exciting.

He dropped his hands to Ashlynn's hips and tugged her close, loving that soft skin. He needed to feel her nearly naked body pressed against him like he needed sunshine and adventure and the very air in his lungs. Unable to stop himself, he slid his hands down, beneath the seam of her panties, tracing a path on the perfect curves of her ass, tugging her up a little higher so she could better fit the hard angles of his body.

She gasped against his lips, obviously feeling his rock-hard cock pressing against her thighs, and the temperature went up a hundred degrees. The slow build went into warp drive, the intensity ratcheting up as if they'd been building up to this with an hour's worth of kisses.

Her arms snaked around his neck and she tugged him even closer, tilting her head, thrusting her tongue ever deeper into his mouth. As if unable to help herself, she raised a leg, wrapping it around his and angling more intimately against his groin. Raine lifted her by the waist, groaning in satisfaction as she wrapped both legs around his hips, letting him hold her.

The kiss deepened, and the hunger mounted. He knew it was crazy, knew they weren't far enough from the village—two days' walk probably wouldn't be far enough. But he couldn't stop, and she didn't seem inclined to make him.

"Please," she groaned.

"You're sure?"

"Oh, yes."

Hearing the feminine certainty in her voice, he gave up any thoughts of resisting. All his doubts evaporated, his control snapped. He backed her up against the nearest tree, bracing her so he could free one hand.

There was lots he wanted to do with that hand. He started by tugging one bra strap down, freeing her breast to the morning air and his covetous attention. *Beautiful.* He plumped it, stroked her hard little nipple, watched her shiver in delight as he played her body like an instrument.

Knowing he'd get back to this point when they had more time, he reached down, tearing her panties away with one hard jerk. Ashlynn moaned, tangling her fingers in his hair, rubbing herself against him as if desperate for his most intimate touch. Even through his jeans he could feel the heat of her; she was so wet he could smell the intoxicating sweetness of her arousal.

Raine wanted to do so much, so damn much. He longed to taste her breasts, suckle her until she cried, but the intensity of it was killing him. Mostly, he just wanted to give her what she most seemed to want—a wild, frenzied coupling up against a tree.

He plunged his tongue in her mouth, even as he slid his hand between her legs and tested the wetness there.

Drenched. Ready. Hot. *Oh, God, yes.*

"Please," she whimpered, pressing against his hand, wanting more. He didn't hesitate, plunging a finger into her tight channel, and was rewarded with a cry of delight. He found her clit with his thumb, toying with it even as he gave her another finger and stroked hard, fast, deep.

She moaned with delight, and so did he, loving the way she felt in his hand, loving her smell and the sounds she made and the expression on her beautiful face.

But it wasn't enough. Not for either of them.

Saying nothing, Raine reached for his jeans, quickly unbuttoning and unzipping. He grabbed a condom out of his pocket, lifted the packet to his mouth and tore it open with his teeth, then shoved his jeans down his hips. Ashlynn sighed with pleasure when she saw his hard cock jutting toward her. Her hand shook as she brushed her fingertips down the length of him, all cool, soft skin against hot, hard need.

"I've been dreaming about this," she admitted.

"Truly?"

She nodded. "After I saw you, that first day in the store, you filled my dreams."

His chest swelled. "That's only fair, considering after the first time I saw you, you've been filling my fantasies."

She sighed with pleasure at his admission. "Raine, I want you so much I think I'm going to die if I can't have you inside me."

"I've gone to too much damn trouble protecting you to let you die now," he muttered as he rolled the condom into place.

He grabbed her hips, tilting her toward him and plunged hard, fast, deep. She let out a little scream, which he caught with a kiss, swallowing her cries of delight.

No more words. No thought. No time. Just hunger, need and excitement. She was tight, welcoming and hot, and he let himself be consumed by her, sucked into her, body and soul. He lost who he was and where he was and everything except the need to plunge deep into pleasure, pull out, then plunge again.

They were both panting, thrusting, crying out. She took every stroke, the dig of her nails in his back demanding even more.

"Can you come this way?" he asked her between gasps.

"I don't care if I can or not, it feels too good to stop."

"I care," he insisted.

Giving her no warning, he pulled out of her and dropped to his knees on the ground. He grabbed one of her thighs and hooked it over his shoulder. Taking one pleasurable moment to look at her pretty curls and those pink, plump lips, he buried his face in her wet sex.

She positively purred.

His tongue found her clit and flicked it hungrily, as though he hadn't eaten in days. He gained almost as much pleasure from this as he did from being inside her…and, judging by her cries and the sudden stiffening of her body as she climaxed, so did she.

"*Now* we can finish," he muttered, straightening and going right back to what he'd been doing before.

"Oh, yes," she cried as he thrust into her again.

There was no stopping things this time. Nature and instinct took over. His brain wasn't even part of the equation anymore. His body strove for release, pounding and driving until, finally, he attained it. He came in a hot rush, sure he'd never felt so good. And then, spent, he wrapped her legs around his waist and sat down on the ground, holding her as the two of them slowly left the stolen moment of hot sex and primitive passion and returned to the here and now.

5

THOUGH WHAT ASHLYNN most wanted to do was spend the day naked in Raine's strong arms, she knew she couldn't. They'd taken a terrible chance stopping for as long as they had. As sanity returned, they both acknowledged it with a few last kisses.

They gathered their clothes in silence. She wasn't sure whether he was deep in thought or merely needed the rest after that amazing show of endurance. Mercy, she didn't think she'd ever get over what the man had just done to her. Certainly no man had ever done anything like it before. Oh, she'd been no virgin, but never had she felt so utterly, completely *taken*.

It had been magnificent. Unforgettable. And she would never—no matter what happened, no matter how long she lived—regret it.

"You okay?" he asked, watching as she pulled her bra into place. He touched her shoulder, frowning. "You're scratched up."

"Tree bark," she said. Then, lowering her voice, added, "Thank goodness that tree didn't mind being used as a bed."

He cupped her face in his hand and bent to brush a soft kiss on her lips. "Believe me, beautiful, when I make love to you in a bed, you won't end up with any scratches."

"Maybe I like scratches," she said, her voice throaty.

He swallowed visibly. "You like it rough, wild?"

"I do now." Thinking of all the ways she'd like to have sex with him, she leaned in close, then stood on tiptoe to nibble on his earlobe. "I saw some interesting movies on the late-night cable station in that motel room."

He closed his eyes, made a helpless sound and pressed against her, as if unable to help it. She could feel through his jeans that he was already getting hard again, and half regretted taunting him when they needed to leave. But some wicked inner spirit made her add, "I'd like to try some of the things I saw."

"Like?"

"Maybe yours will be the back scratched up this time."

He laughed. "Believe me, it was." He turned, showing her the scratches on his back—marks she'd put on his body while he pleasured her.

She didn't apologize. He'd driven her out of her mind, she'd been helpless. Nor did he look as though he minded. "I meant scratched by a tree or the ground. I'd like to be on top of you, to ride you…how do they call it, cowgirl style?"

"Lord have mercy," he said with a groan.

But she wasn't finished. "I think I'd also like to be on my knees and have you come into me from behind."

He rubbed his mouth. "I was thinking about that last night."

"Truly?"

"Oh, yeah," he admitted. "So, I take it we aren't going to get to missionary position anytime soon?"

"What's that?" she asked, unfamiliar with the term.

He laughed softly, then gently stroked the small of her back, his fingertips sizzling against her skin. "It's when we're in a soft bed, and I lay you on your back. I worship every inch of your body, touching you, tasting you for hours."

She liked the sound of this.

"Then I move on top of you, between your parted thighs and slide into you slowly, making love to you all night long."

Ashlynn fanned herself with her hand. The position sounded familiar and was, in fact, how she'd always had sex before. But the way he described it made it sound *much* more interesting.

She didn't know how long this was going to last—if Raine Fowler was going to be in her life long enough to do all the things they'd talked about. But, oh, she hoped so. Not only because of how good it would be. But because, since she'd met him, Ashlynn felt more alive than she had in years. Vibrant and excited, aroused and, despite the circumstances, happy.

She could become addicted to this man.

"Okay, historian," he said, sounding rueful. "Much as I'd like to stay and help you experiment, we'd better hit the road before those goons pull out their magical map and find us."

The map. Gods, she'd forgotten all about the map. She had been thinking of nothing else during their escape from Foxglen, then he'd touched her and nothing else had mattered. "Tell me about this map."

He shrugged. "It was old."

She tensed, wondering if it was even possible. "How old?"

"It was on antique-looking parchment, pretty faded."

"Were the edges smooth or jagged?"

"Two were jagged, like it had been torn in two places. It almost looked like the corner of a bigger map."

Feeling her strength drain, she sunk to her knees, acting as if she'd done it to reach into her bag for clean clothes. "Do you remember any details about the map? Could you describe it?"

"Probably. I got a good look."

She rose and slipped into a pair of loose-fitting pants and a top, wondering if he could hear the thumping of her heart. So the thugs had the last piece of the map—she had already decided it probably didn't matter, that she could find the castle without it. But if Raine had seen it enough to remember any details....

"Tell me."

Raine opened his mouth, as if to answer, then closed it. "How about you tell me why you want to know so badly?"

Something in her rebelled at answering. Ashlynn had been on this quest alone for a long time. She'd wanted it that way, knowing the prize she sought could bring out the worst in people. She'd seen priceless artifacts stolen from the museum, knew there were those who tended to get a little crazy when gold was at stake. She just wasn't used to trusting new people.

"Can I really trust you?" she whispered, talking more to herself than to him.

He flinched. "Jeez, you are some piece of work."

She held out a hand. "I'm sorry, I didn't mean it that way."

"Considering I've saved your life and you just let me bang your brains out up against a tree, I'd hope you'd trust me by now."

"I do. It's just…this is a sensitive subject." Steeling her will, she reached into her satchel and withdrew the packet. She opened it carefully, revealing the folded map inside.

He gaped. "Did you steal that from them? Are you crazy?"

"No, it's mine. I hid it in the tavern last month."

She lifted the page to reveal the second sheet beneath, then said, "The third one's in my bag, too, tucked inside a book."

"Let me guess. You found it in a bookshop in Philadelphia."

She nodded.

"This map was your quest…the reason you went to Earth. And you now have three quarters of it?"

"Exactly. And it sounds like those men have the last piece."

"It looked just like yours," he admitted. "So that's why they're after you? They want to put the whole map together?"

"Yes."

"They didn't look like the type who would offer to buy it."

Oh, no doubt about it. They probably intended to take it from her, using whatever force was necessary.

"It must lead to something pretty important."

"It does."

He didn't ask the question; she heard it anyway. Ashlynn was left to rely on her instincts that had told her from *almost* their first meeting that she could trust this man. And she did trust Raine. He might have a bit of larceny in him, but she knew he wouldn't try to take this map from her if she told him the truth.

Taking a leap of faith, she carefully unfolded a piece of the map—the piece that showed the castle, naming it in elaborate, if faded, script. "This is what it leads to."

He stared at it, his brow scrunching as he tried to make out the words. Then it hit him and his jaw dropped. "You're serious?"

"Extremely."

"Sleeping Beauty, the story—you're saying it's *true?*"

"Aren't all the other ones true, in one form or another?"

"Well, yeah, but, I mean, even over here that story has always sounded like a fairy tale."

"The lost kingdom of Seaside is not a fairy tale." She elaborated, quickly schooling him on the subject, which she'd studied for years. She concluded, "Everything I've learned, every instinct I have, tells me this map is authentic. And that it leads to the castle where the lost royals of Seaside lived."

He swept a hand through his hair, looking unconvinced.

"If you've heard the story whispered about, here in Elatyria, you must know what they say about this castle."

He nodded slowly, a gleam appearing in those purplish eyes. "That it's filled with jewels and gold. Do you believe it?"

"No."

"But you're going to try to find this place, anyway?"

"Yes. The treasure I seek isn't measured in carats or ounces. An entire civilization's history is what I'm after. I've dreamed about discovering Seaside my whole life—the way people on your world long to find the lost city of Atlantis."

"I've always kind of figured Atlantis was over here," he admitted. "That somebody just got their stories crossed."

"Me, too."

He looked away, staring out into the forest. Raine was silent for a long moment, evaluating, considering the options. As if her revelation had changed everything.

Well, it had. For both of them. She knew Raine was determined to protect her. She even suspected he was no longer doing it just for money. So it wasn't as if she could continue her quest without him—he would insist on seeing her back to her home in Riverdale.

Now, with his knowledge of the fourth quarter of the map, and the fact that she'd opened herself up to him the way she never had with anyone, there seemed to be only one option.

"So, Raine Fowler, finder of many things. Do you want to join me?"

"Join you?"

"Will you help me find Sleeping Beauty's castle?"

Their stares locked. The excitement she felt was mirrored in his expression. And he answered with no hesitation.

"Yes, Ashlynn Scott. I will definitely help you."

RAINE HAD WANTED ASHLYNN from the minute he'd seen her. He'd desired her, admired her. Lusted after her. And *had* her.

But as they set out on their quest, he realized how truly remarkable she was. They walked for hours without rest. Stopped in villages only long enough to buy food, then kept going. They slept on the ground, with nothing but each other for warmth— oh, they definitely kept each other warm, especially trying out all those positions she'd learned on late-night cable TV.

Throughout it all, she never complained. Strong, relentless, she matched him stride for stride, her enthusiasm when they would spot a familiar landmark from the map absolutely contagious.

The map. He hadn't totally wrapped his head around it. Still, he had no doubt that the men who were after her had the fourth quarter of it. When he sketched out everything he remembered, the lines matched perfectly with those that trailed off the edge of hers.

They soon realized how fortunate it was that he'd seen it. Because if Ashlynn had gone with her original plan, to find the castle using just her three pieces, she would have failed. There was one very tricky crossroads—shown only on the quarter she *didn't* possess—that would have tripped her up. So, despite having come in late on this venture, Raine felt they were equal partners. He had brought something to the table, too.

As for what they'd find when they got there, he honestly didn't know. Part of him worried they'd find nothing, that the whole thing was an ancient prank…some mass-produced map sold in joke shops many centuries ago.

Another part—the instinct that served him so well when he was on the hunt for what others said was unattainable—told him they were on the path to something magnificent. In his mind, that meant gold and jewels. In hers, it meant a remarkable archeological site. He hoped they were both right.

It was late afternoon when they reached a lake that, in America, would probably be full of toxic runoff or sewage. This one didn't look as green and fresh as most others he'd seen in Elatyria, but it was water. It should at least wash off sweat.

Reaching into his pack, he pulled out a bar of coarse soap he'd bought in the last village. That seemed like forever ago. They'd walked for nearly two days since then, not seeing a soul, or a cottage, or a single plowed field. The landscape had grown more rough, thick trees giving way to skeletal stumps, and the temperature felt as if it had gone up fifty degrees.

"Want to take a dip?" he asked, gesturing toward the small body of still water. "Wash off some of the dust?"

"Absolutely."

He extended the soap toward her upraised hand, but instead of taking it, she slowly dropped that hand to her side. Ashlynn was looking past him, staring rapt at something in the distance. Her mouth slowly fell open.

"Ash? What is it?" he asked, swinging around, his heart pounding. Had the thugs caught up with them? He'd thought more than once in recent days that someone was following them.

Nobody was there, but he didn't let his guard down. This was no longer about getting paid, or finishing a job. It was about protecting Ashlynn.

Because he was falling for her. Big time.

Every hour they spent together drove that certainty harder into his mind...and his heart. Raine had never paid much attention to that particular organ before, but since the other day when he'd wiped off her dirty face with his shirt and finally tasted that beautiful mouth, he'd known Ashlynn Scott was someone he could care about. Every minute they'd spent together since had pushed her just a little deeper into his life.

He didn't know how he was going to say goodbye when this was all over. And a big part of him hoped he wouldn't have to. Hey, people had relationships across the U.S. He knew a guy from New York whose wife commuted out to L.A. every week. So why not an Earth to Elatyria relationship?

Relationship? Get real, dude.

But he was being real. Maybe for the first time in his life.

"Am I really seeing that?" she asked, sounding dazed.

"Seeing what?"

"Look at that hillside."

He followed her stare, seeing the rocky outline of a hill in the distance. The day had grown cloudy, the air moist, and he couldn't make it out very well at first. Then a breeze shifted some of the clouds, and he saw what she was talking about.

"It's a dragon," she whispered.

It didn't take much imagination to see what she meant. The rocks and ground had arranged themselves into a shape that resembled a dragon, head back, wings unfurled. If it had remained cloudy, or if they'd gotten much closer before seeing it, they probably wouldn't have been able to make out the resemblance at all. Right now, though, it was obvious.

Ashlynn grabbed the satchel, yanking it open and retrieving the map pieces. She quickly leafed through them until she found the one she wanted. He knew what she was looking for even before she unfolded the thing and tapped her finger on an image.

"The Dragon's Lair," he said, his excitement growing.

"I always thought it was figurative—everyone knows dragons don't live near the sea."

He rolled his eyes. "Oh, sure. Everybody knows that."

"So, I assumed whoever this mapmaker was had intended to make the trip look as dangerous as possible, to discourage those with bad intentions from trying to find the castle."

Hmm. Bad intentions. What, he wondered, did that mean?

He didn't have any bad intentions. He just wanted a few fistfuls of diamonds and rubies. Maybe a gold mug to carry them in.

He wasn't a tomb raider, though some people thought otherwise. He didn't have to be. Raine knew full well that the rules here were similar to the ones on Earth. A ten-percent finder's fee was pretty standard. Should he and Ashlynn discover this mystical lost site, they would be rewarded by every monarch in her world, even if it contained no riches at all.

Besides, deep down, he really wanted her to succeed. Wanted her dream to come true. Ashlynn deserved to find her castle and do all her archeology and history stuff.

"If that's really the dragon on the map, then the entrance to the secret pathway is right through its mouth," she said.

Meaning all they had to do was climb that hill, walk into the black cave that served as the creature's mouth, face whatever came after it…and hope they didn't get chomped on by any real fangs. Dragon's, or otherwise. *Piece o' cake.*

His desire for a bath suddenly outweighed by his sense of adventure, he dropped the soap into his bag, slung it over his shoulder and reached for her hand. "Ready?"

"More than you can possibly imagine!"

They smiled at each other and, though his feet were almost tapping in impatience, Raine couldn't resist sliding his hands into her hair and tipping her head back. "I'm happy for you," he said before dropping his mouth onto hers.

As the kiss ended, she looked up at him, her eyes dreamy and soft. "Thanks. And, Raine? I'm happy you're with me."

"Me, too." He winked, then dropped an arm across her shoulders. "Now let's go slay that dragon."

6

IT WAS A DAMN GOOD THING Raine was with her.

Not because of any dragons—there had been none. Though, when they'd passed through the cave that led to the path, Ashlynn would swear she'd seen a few glittery objects that might have been scales from some ancient, long-dead creature.

The real issue was the sneaky twist in the path. If she'd been alone, she might not have noticed it. And since it appeared to double back the way they'd come, she almost certainly wouldn't have turned. Raine, however, was sure of what he'd seen on the other piece of the map. And, judging by the sea of thorny brush they had to hack their way through, she knew he was right. The hedge was just how the legends had described it—secretive and close, wicked and twisted. It would discourage anyone from traveling on, especially someone not sure they were going the right away.

"You doing okay?" he asked as he used a hunting knife he'd produced from his pack to cut their way through.

She carefully plucked a branch out of the way, her fingers

already bloodied from the dozens she'd already moved. "I'm fine."

"Luckily, it's getting thicker," he said.

She snorted. "Luckily?"

"That means we're getting close. It's always worse right before you break through. Remind me to tell you about the pendulum that swung down about an inch from my face once."

Despite the circumstances, she had to smile. Raine had told her many stories as they'd traveled. Tales of his adventures, his near misses, his successes. Each had thrilled her, charmed her, opened a door to a lifestyle she'd never conceived of. She studied history, looked at artifacts, carefully uncovered them at precise dig sites, then put them on display.

Raine actually fought for them. He'd strode through jungles, explored ancient temples. He'd battled angry natives and dishonest bureaucrats and had emerged triumphant at times, beaten at others.

While she'd been studying life, he'd been out there—to use an Earthen expression—grabbing it by the balls.

It was exciting. Thrilling. Just like Raine. He excited and thrilled her down to her toes. More, though, during the past few days, he'd surprised her with his tenderness. He'd been kind and playful, sexy and steady, daring and protective. The kind of man she'd dreamed of finding, in the outward package she'd never have expected.

He was the man she'd been waiting for all of her life. And every step they drew closer to the end of their quest was another step closer to his departure from her life.

Ashlynn had never felt so torn. This wasn't the first time she'd thought about how much she dreaded the thought of him going back to where he belonged. But it was the first time she realized just how soon that moment could come.

"Stay right behind me," he ordered. "It's getting darker."

Definitely darker. The hedge had gone from a daunting chest-high barrier to a nearly impassable over-the-head one. The twisted shrubs had folded over on themselves, forming a canopy that blocked out the sky. Inside the dark, treacherous tunnel Raine created with every slash of his knife, the air was stale and thick. Unpleasant. And the farther they went, the closer the wicked plants came, until it was impossible to move without brushing against one. Usually painfully.

This vicious barrier could not have come naturally. Someone had put it here. Which meant there was something worth guarding at the other end of it.

Ashlynn cursed the fact that she hadn't brought home a pair of those sneakers people in his world wore. Her sandals were sturdy and comfortable, but she'd taken more than one thorn to the toe. "Ouch!" she muttered as a wicked, needle-sharp point scraped across her calf.

She should have brought home some jeans, too. Next time, she needed to make a list of things to bring back from Earth. Unfortunately, her number-one obsession—a confection called Chunky Monkey, which, she had been very relieved to learn, did not contain any real monkeys—would probably melt in the borderlands. But potato chips definitely would not.

Huh, funny that she was thinking about her next trip to Earth. When she'd arrived home last week, she had thought she'd never go back. Yet, every day she spent here at home reminded her of something she had liked back there.

One big reminder? Raine Fowler, the man carefully holding another razor-sharp branch away so she could maneuver around it.

She couldn't let him go without a backward glance. More, she *wouldn't*. She just hadn't figured out how to tell him that yet.

"Thanks." She didn't meet his eyes, not sure what he'd see in hers. Probably too much.

"Not a problem," he told her, though she knew by the drops of blood dripping from his fingertips that it was a problem. But he hadn't voiced a single complaint. It seemed his sense of adventure outweighed any physical discomfort.

She loved that sense of adventure. Loved being part of it.

For the past several days, Ashlynn had allowed herself to live like he did. To think only of the here and now, this moment, their journey and the thrill of the chase. Raine had no other expectations, no other obligations, and could come and go as he pleased. And so, that's how she'd felt, too.

It had been incredibly appealing, living this way, with *him*. Part of her wasn't sure how she would ever give it up. Honestly, as much as she wanted to find this castle, and to document the history within its ancient walls, a tiny part of her wished they'd just have to keep on looking.

"Hell," he said with a groan, lifting a hand to his face.

Ashlynn touched his shoulder and made him turn around to face her. He'd taken a thorn to the forehead and blood freely dripped down his brow. "This is crazy," she said. "You could have been blinded! We should go back."

He wiped the blood off with the back of his arm. "Hey, no pain, no gain. And we're almost through the worst of it."

"Yeah, right."

"I mean it," he said, shifting to the side so she could see past him into the dark tunnel ahead.

It took a second, but she quickly realized what he meant. It looked lighter about ten paces ahead of them, as if the hedge thinned out beyond. If it were thin enough to admit light, perhaps there was fresher air up there, too. And there might be an end to their trial by thorn.

"Stay with me, historian," he said, his voice thrumming with excitement.

Her heart sped up, her breaths grew shallow, because of both the bad quality of the air and the excitement washing through her. There was no escaping his contagious enthusiasm. "I'm not going anywhere."

She inched behind him. Wiping sweat and dirt and blood off her face, she helped where she could. Though, mainly, she only watched, seeing the way his thick shoulders and broad back flexed beneath his shirt as he hacked at the unforgiving barrier.

Mercy, he was beautiful—a picture of masculine strength and agility.

"Do you see?" he asked, his breaths hoarse.

"It's lighter," she replied. "The air…"

"Definitely moving."

They kept their voices low, as if they both knew they were about to reach the end of the line. And were equally as nervous about what they would find.

"You ready?" he asked, glancing over his shoulder at her.

She drew in a deep breath, tasting freshness, coolness and a hint of salt. *The sea.* Then she nodded.

Raine reached back and took her hand as they moved on. The shrubs were not only thinning overhead—revealing a bit of bright sky with a few puffy clouds—they were also spreading out, drawing back, leaving enough room for them to stand abreast.

"We break through together," he said.

Hand in hand.

Excitement roared through her. Yes, she was worried about what might happen between her and Raine later, once they'd found what they were seeking. But for now, all the hopes, the dreams, the planning...everything was coming to fruition. She was about to find out if she—and her father—had been right about the most famous legend in all the worlds.

Raine extended the long knife, cut away a few more branches. They stepped, side by side, until they reached one last barrier— tall and imposing, thick and impossible to see through.

Knowing in her soul that they'd come to the end, Ashlynn reached out, unable to resist tugging at the branches with her bare hands. She ignored the thorns, didn't feel any pain. Raine did the same, sheathing his knife, and the two of them dug and pulled and clawed their way through the last few feet of hedge.

At last, a hole. No more shrub, no more thorns. Light poured in, bathing their faces. Together they took one more step, pushing through as if they were being born out of a long, dark passage.

And emerged to witness the most glorious sight Ashlynn had ever beheld in her life.

WELL, IT SURE WASN'T much to look at.

Sleeping Beauty's castle—if this was, indeed, hers—looked

like a lot of ruins he'd seen over the years. Gray and huge, with collapsed walls, thick vines growing over everything and trees that had sprouted up inside roofless parts of the structure.

Interesting—and probably to Ashlynn, fascinating. But he'd been expecting the wow factor. Though King Midas hadn't had anything to do with Sleeping Beauty—at least, as far as he knew—he'd almost pictured this place being covered with gold leaf. He'd envisioned a Disney score swelling up when they stepped out of the hedge and some talking animal to greet him.

Squawk.

A bird flew out of the ruin, swooping overhead and dropping another kind of welcome altogether. Right on his shoe.

"Hell," he muttered.

She wasn't even listening. A quick glance told him Ashlynn was totally, completely enraptured by what she saw.

"It's magnificent," she whispered. A visible shiver ran through her. "I keep asking myself if I'm dreaming!"

Raine couldn't help smiling, glad for her. Maybe his expectations had been too high. The place was pretty damned cool, dipped in gold or not. "So, ready to go in?"

Her hand trembling, she reached for his. "I'm *so* ready."

"Let me lead the way, okay? There are probably rotted floors, unstable walls. We've got to take it slow and easy."

"Understood."

One more thing he liked about Ashlynn—she had so much common sense.

Maybe it was because of that common sense, and because he had her to look after, but Raine didn't barrel right in as he might have done if he'd been alone. He carefully evaluated every step they took, watching for hidden dangers. But as they drew farther into the castle—and began to realize there was much more to see inside than the outside had led them to believe—his own caution began to give way to wonder.

"My God," he whispered as they pushed open a nearly rotten doorway to enter what had once been the great hall.

"Unbelievable," she replied, equally as overwhelmed.

The outside might have looked like a ruin from some European country. But inside—well, this was pure Elatyria. Pure fairy tale. Because, as if the powerful magic of the world itself wouldn't allow the true destruction of anything pure and beautiful, the interior was remarkably intact. Yes, some walls had fallen, some roofs had caved in. But many still stood solid and proud, as they had centuries ago when the last occupants had departed.

The graceful marble columns were dirty, yes, but still gleamed with soft beauty. On the walls, rotted tapestries couldn't detract from the hand-painted murals that depicted chivalrous scenes of knights and dragons and ladies. Furniture made of stout oak, and perhaps the heart of the most powerful beanstalks, remained in place, covered in dust but mostly unbroken.

"The thrones," she whispered.

He followed her stare, seeing a raised dais with two intricately carved chairs. Still plush and covered with red velvet, they looked as though their occupants had just arisen and stepped away for a moment.

Both drawn to different things in the cavernous room, they separated, Ashlynn moving to study the paintings on the farthest wall, Raine to examine the thrones more carefully. He told himself he was looking for jewels embedded in the wood, having pictured this moment in his mind ever since he'd heard about this place.

But he suddenly realized something. Even before he'd reached the dais and examined the thrones, he knew that, even if there were stones to rival the Hope Diamond studding every corner, he wouldn't dig them out. This place almost seemed like sacred ground. A feeling of reverence he'd never experienced at another site washed over him. He wouldn't desecrate it, not for all the jewels in Seaside's lost kingdom.

Now, a handful of them lying on the floor? That would be another story. Fortunately, there was a lot of castle left to explore. And the more they found, the bigger that ten percent finder's fee would become.

"Raine, look at this!" Ashlynn called, sounding excited.

He strode across the richly veined marble floor, to her. She was pointing to a series of paintings, smaller and less ornate than the floor-to-ceiling ones that graced much of the hall.

"The whole story is here," she told him, her voice actually shaking.

She pointed to each picture in turn, and he saw what she meant. They began with an image of a beautiful family of three—the king, queen and beautiful little girl. Then storm clouds, a dark fairy, a spindle. A sleeping maiden, the grieving parents, a royal court falling into slumber.

God, it's all true?

With everything else he knew about Elatyria, he shouldn't have been so surprised. But, hell, this was pretty major stuff. It would take some time to process.

"Someone stayed behind to tell the tale," she told him as she moved down the wall to the last sequence of paintings. "Mercy, this alone is a priceless treasure—the mystery of the disappearance of the entire royal court is explained right here!"

He stared at the images, trying to see whatever it was she saw. It took a long moment, then the truth started to dawn. The painting showed the happy Beauty—awake—and in the arms of a handsome man who stood on the bow of a ship. The royals were gathered behind them on the decks, celebrating as the ship literally sailed off the edge of the sea into a dark blue abyss.

A blue abyss with some odd shapes—like landmasses.

Familiar landmasses.

Very familiar ones.

"Holy shit, it's Earth," he said, everything making sense.

The handsome Prince Charming who rescued the beauty was from Earth, and he took her and all the rest of them back with him. Raine knew enough about Elatyria to know its geography didn't match Earth's. And there was no disguising those familiar shapes—from Africa to Europe and Asia, right down to North America and the tiny tail of Florida. It appeared the Elatyrians had known more about Earth's geography than Earthlings had.

She laughed and clapped her hands. "Yes! That's why they disappeared forever, leaving no trace, no descendants...except for the person who painted this mural and possibly drew the map."

And that's why the legend had become one of the most long-abiding, popular stories in *both* worlds.

Raine closed his eyes, shocked into silence. For years he'd called himself a finder of things. Of treasures. But today, he felt like the finder of a deep, irrevocable truth. And he at last understood what *real* treasure was.

This game Ashlynn played—searching for truth and clarity amidst the deepest mystery—was powerful. More thrilling than any he'd ever known.

He reached for her, drawing her into his arms. She looked up at him, her eyes gleaming with excitement and pleasure.

"I'm so happy for you," he told her, a little overwhelmed at the seriousness of the moment. Although this had started as an adventure, it had ended with a discovery that truly shook him.

"Thank you. This is a dream come true," she replied. Then she wrapped her arms around his neck, tugging him down for a long, warm kiss.

He held her tight, plunging his tongue against hers as if needing to memorize the taste of her, almost desperate to make the moment last. Right in the middle of the kiss, he realized why.

Her dream had come true. They'd found her Holy Grail.

But now her real job was about to begin. She would be tied to this place, throwing herself into her work for probably decades.

She didn't need him anymore. In fact, there would almost certainly be no place in her life for an adventurer with a less-than-sterling reputation. She was back to being the proper, respected historian. What could she possibly want with a guy who, minutes ago, had been considering digging jewels out of an ancient throne with his knife?

They were mismatched, completely wrong for each other. The romantic interlude was over. Now it was time for both of them to get back to reality—a reality that didn't include them.

They couldn't be together. Not in her world. Not in his.
He was going to have to let her go.

7
___

ASHLYNN SENSED RAINE's near-desperation as he kissed her, and
wondered what he was thinking. Possibly he was just slightly
overwhelmed, like she was. Happy. Excited.

Not saying goodbye. Please, don't let him be saying goodbye.

But somehow, deep down, she knew he was. She didn't know
why, but she sensed the change in him.

Maybe it was because they'd come to the end of the adventure. They'd discovered the big prize, and Raine—a "finder"—
had never said he was one who liked to stick around once he'd
found something. Be it an artifact, a historical site…or a woman.

When they finally drew apart, she managed a tremulous
smile, willing her heart to stop pounding and her imagination
to stop going places she didn't want it to go. They'd just arrived.
There was no way Raine was going to walk away now. He'd stay
for a while, she knew it. And hopefully, during that time, she'd
find a way to convince him to stay a little longer. Or else she
could talk him into taking her with him when he left.

That was insane, considering there was so much to do here.
But Ashlynn knew that if she let him just walk out of her life,
she'd regret it until the end of her days.

She'd found her great prize, finished her father's work.

Now she was ready to live.

"Raine…"

"You do know there's one thing I'm dying to see, right?"

She swallowed, not sure whether to be glad or not that he'd

interrupted what might have been an embarrassing confession. What if she'd said "I love you" and he said nothing in return? Worse, what if her admission made him leave?

"Ash?" he prompted, apparently noticing her silence. "Are you thinking what I'm thinking?"

She doubted it. Then, quickly bringing her mind back into the game, as they said in his world, she made herself focus on the here and now. On the excitement she'd felt just a few moments before. And she realized she knew what he was talking about. There was much to see, much to explore, but one secret place screamed to be discovered.

He stepped away and took her hand. "Let's go find..."

"Her bed?"

"Absolutely, beauty. Let's go find the place where she slept."

If there was one thing that could get her mind off the sudden tangle of emotions she felt at the very thought of losing Raine, it was finding that one last, mystical spot.

So they spent the rest of the day exploring the castle, looking for Sleeping Beauty's bedchamber. It proved a little more difficult than Ashlynn had hoped. The castle was enormous, with winding tunnels—some blocked with debris—staircases that rose into chamber after chamber, hidden rooms behind what had once been secret doors. Eventually, once Raine was convinced the place was sound enough that she wouldn't fall through a floor and break her neck, they split up so they could cover more ground. That left her alone with her thoughts—which welled up to taunt her with what-ifs again.

It also meant she was alone when she found the chamber.

It was not, as legends said, in the topmost tower. Instead, the beauty's room appeared to be a regular one at the end of a corridor on the third floor. Nothing to mark it on the outside, and it wasn't terribly large.

But she'd found the right one. She knew it.

Because, as soon as she entered, she saw the way the room caught the afternoon light, which poured in from window openings overlooking the cliffs and the blue sea far, far below. The room glowed gold, and standing directly in a strong sunbeam was a huge, raised bed, draped with pink satin. Soft, shimmery bed curtains shielded some of it from view. Ashlynn found herself tiptoeing toward it, almost afraid of making a sound lest she awaken the ghost of the lady who'd been trapped in this room for so very long.

"Here you slept," she whispered when she reached the bed and saw the huge headboard, into which had been carved a few words, in an ancient language. *In sleep, her beauty never fades.*

Tears pricked her eyelids, and she had to close them for a moment, completely overwhelmed. This was the culmination of her life's work—and her father's. It was also, however, the legend of her dreams, the fairy tale of her childhood. The story to end all stories, in all the worlds.

And it had happened here. Right here.

It was almost too much to take in. She simply had to stand there, in silence, absorbing the moment.

She did so, for what seemed like a long time, then Ashlynn became aware of a strange sensation. The room held a strong, almost magnetic aura. She hadn't noticed it at first, being too excited, but now felt as though she were being held in place by irresistible forces.

She reached out her hand, feeling almost compelled to brush it against the ancient covering on the bed. To her surprise, she found it fresh and soft. No dust arose from the satin—which should have been rotten and nearly gone after all these years. But it wasn't. It appeared entirely intact.

Enchanted.

The room had to have been enchanted by whatever good sorceress had helped the king and queen remain with their daughter throughout her long sleep. This bed had been made to last for years—centuries—staying as fresh and soft as the girl who'd slept on it.

She suspected it was the enchantment that pulled her now. At least, something did. Something made her lift her leg, slide a knee onto the bed—*soft, downy.* Even though the pragmatic historian's voice in her head screamed at her to not even consider doing such a thing, she was unable to resist climbing up onto the mattress, sure she'd never felt a more beautifully comforting fabric against her bare calves.

"Just for a moment," she told herself. "Just once." Then she'd go back to being the cold, analytical researcher. But for just this one second in time, she'd let the remnants of magic take her.

She lay down upon the bed, though she didn't rest her head on the pillow, having enough presence of mind to hope she might find a strand of golden hair on it later. Lacing her hands together over her waist, she closed her eyes and tried to imagine the past. To picture this young girl being awakened by the kiss of a handsome man she'd never met.

The fantasy seemed so real. She could almost hear his footsteps crossing the stone floor, feel the weight of his body as he knelt on the bed beside her.

Then he kissed her. Warm, soft lips pressed against her own. They felt real. *Very* real.

Because they were.

She froze for a second before realizing Raine must have found her, must have been drawn by the magic and had joined in her impromptu reenactment. Smiling, she reached up to wrap her arms around him and slowly opened her eyes.

To see the face of a complete stranger.

"Oh, my God!" she shrieked, pushing him away. She rolled out from under him, crossing the bed and leaping off the other side. Shaking, she stared in shock at the handsome, elegantly dressed man who watched her, his eyes gleaming, his sensuous mouth curved in a smile. "Who are you?"

"I've come to rescue you, my beauty," he said with a courtly bow.

She gawked at him. "I don't need to be rescued."

"But my kiss awakened you..."

"No, I assure you, I was wide awake."

He shook his head and tsked, getting off the bed and coming around toward her. "But only because my kiss broke the spell."

"There was no spell," she snapped. "I'm not a sleeping beauty."

"Oh, but you are a beauty." Another step, slow and deliberate, as though he was stalking her.

"I'm *not* interested."

"Your kiss says otherwise."

When he got to within a foot, she threw a hand up, palm out, to stop him. "No means no, mister."

"Prince Philip of the Dry Lands," he clarified.

Her mouth dropped. Prince Philip? The most eligible bachelor from the southern kingdoms? The one princesses competed for at some ridiculous annual tournament, trying to catch his eye by virtue of their great dancing, singing and harp playing? The one who had run through a string of willing women almost since he was old enough to hold a scepter?

This encounter had just gone from bizarre straight into crazy.

"Let go of me, you bastard! Ashlynn!" a voice yelled.

"Raine!" She turned to dash toward the door, knowing he was in trouble. This conceited prince, who'd apparently read too many stories and decided to act one out, must have brought some hired help. She suddenly had a thought about who that help might be.

Oh, please, don't let it be the Tweedles.

She didn't make it two steps before the prince stopped her, grabbing her arm. "Wait, don't you understand? You're my destiny, my princess, my bride."

"No, I'm not," she insisted through gritted teeth as she tried to yank away. "I'm not a princess, I'm a researcher. I just got here a couple of hours ago."

"I know that," he said, smiling as if she were a child and patting her hand. "But it doesn't matter. I knew this magical place would show me my destiny. Entering this chamber, seeing you on that bed, bathed in sunlight, well, I just knew. You were meant for me. We'll be married at once."

"Look," she said, her desperation growing, "I'm just not that into you."

"But…but…every girl wants to marry me!"

"Dude, get over yourself," she said, slipping into Earthese, which seemed appropriate at the moment. "You are not all that and a bag of chips. Now let me go before I show you how un-ladylike I can be!"

He gaped, shocked into letting her go. Ashlynn leaped toward the door, but before she could exit, two moving mountains came in. Her worst fears were confirmed—these were the men who'd been after her in the village. Worse, they were dragging a furiously struggling Raine behind them, and the third goon brought up the rear to block any attempt at escape.

"Ash…"

"Let him go," she demanded, reaching for the closest Hunter and trying to pull his arm away. It was like trying to move a tree trunk.

"Release him," the prince said, his voice still a little strained, as if he hadn't quite gotten over being rejected.

The men glared, but did as they were ordered, letting Raine go. Ashlynn threw herself into his arms, hugging him close to make sure he was okay. He held her tight for a second, then pushed her behind him, shielding her with his big, strong body.

"Who the hell are you and what do you want?"

One of the Hunters moved to strike him, but the prince waved an imperious hand. "I am Prince Philip. And what I want…" He cast a glance between Raine and Ashlynn, who continued to cling to the man she'd fallen so madly in love with. The prince shook his head, as if both disappointed and disbelieving. "Well, what I want appears to have already been taken. Am I to assume you have already claimed the beauty?"

"You're damn right I have," Raine said, his chest and arms tightening, the muscles flexing beneath his sweat-slickened skin. The way he said it—as if daring the prince to even think about making a move toward Ashlynn—sent a little shiver through her. Both of happiness—because he spoke like a man who had no intention of letting her go, ever—and of concern. Because it wasn't a prince Raine would have to fight…it was his hired goons.

"Pity."

"Yeah, it would have been more of a pity if I hadn't been there to keep those thugs of yours from getting their hands on her!"

The prince frowned, eyeing his men. The trio wouldn't meet

his eye, all looking toward the floor. "They were merely supposed to follow her, discreetly."

Ashlynn snorted and rolled her eyes.

"They put a price on her head that had an entire village ready to drag her in, dead or alive. And if she came alive, they seemed ready to happily take care of that," Raine snarled.

This time, the prince didn't look annoyed—his frown darkened into visible anger. The goons looked at him, then at one another, and, moving as if pulled by the same puppet strings, swung around and hurried out of the chamber.

"They won't get far," the prince assured them. "I have loyal troops right outside, and the rest of my entire royal guard is waiting at the entrance to the thorny path. The only other exit is over the cliff." He tapped his fingertip on his mouth. "Hmm. I wonder which way they'll choose to depart?"

Ashlynn found herself rooting for the cliff. Although, from what she'd heard about Prince Philip's royal guard, their swords might be a good enough reception for the Hunters, too.

Prince Philip walked over and took Ashlynn's hand, bowing over it. "Please accept my deepest apologies. I heard you were looking for this place, about which I have dreamed since I was a boy. I meant only to follow you, not to ever put you in harm's way. I suspect those men decided to try to take the map and find the treasure for themselves. You do believe me, don't you?"

She did. Though, if his guys had slit her throat, that wouldn't have been much comfort. Still, one didn't say that to royalty. She curtsied instead, murmuring, "I do, and your apology is gratefully accepted, Your Highness."

He seemed pleased that she'd finally remembered protocol. Of course, he could hold his breath until the crack of doom and wouldn't get that same title out of Raine's mouth.

"Now I should go," the prince said. "May I be the first to offer you both my congratulations. Miss Scott, you have surely given our world a great gift." Then he looked at Raine. "And you, it appears, have been given an even greater one."

With that, he strode toward the door.

"Wait, that's *it?*" Raine asked.

The prince paused and looked over his shoulder. "Of course."

"You weren't after the castle?"

The man shrugged and lifted his mouth in a half smile. "I have plenty of castles. I was trying to find my destiny." His expression warmed noticeably as he stared into Ashlynn's eyes. "It wasn't a total loss, my fair lady. I will remember that kiss we shared until my dying day."

Another slight bow, and the man departed, leaving Ashlynn and Raine alone in Sleeping Beauty's bedchamber.

Once he was gone, Ashlynn drew in a deep sigh of relief, thinking about the bizarre turn of events over the last thirty minutes. She hated to even think about what she might have done had the prince turned out to be a more petulant sort. And she was very thankful he had a bunch of soldiers waiting to take care of his henchmen.

Raine appeared deep in thought, too. He was silent for a long moment, as if also absorbing what had just happened. Then, finally, he turned to face her.

His expression confused her. He didn't look relieved that they didn't have competition over their incredible find. There was no sign of that sexy smile, that laid-back confidence. Instead, a dark frown creased his handsome face.

She didn't understand why...until he crossed his arms over his broad chest, stared at her—hard—and asked in a steely voice, *"What kiss?"*

SHE'D KISSED SOME RICH, snotty prince? Seriously? He'd been out in the corridor, fighting his way through three mountains of meat to make sure she was okay, and she'd been making out with royalty? And, judging by the look on that prince's face, doing it pretty damn well?

"Oh, don't be silly," she insisted, trying to laugh it off.

Raine wasn't laughing. "You kissed him."

"Technically, he kissed me."

"So you just, what, let him stumble and fall onto your lips?"

"For your information, I shoved him off me and rolled away."

Oh, this just got better and better. He glowered at her, wondering where the hell this jealousy was coming from, since he'd certainly never experienced it with anyone before. "You were *lying down* and you kissed him?"

"It wasn't like that…"

"What was it like, then? If I hadn't been dragged in here by the goon squad, what would have happened?"

She moved closer, until they were toe-to-toe, and poked at him with an index finger. "Dig the wax out of your ears, Earth man! *He* kissed *me.* I was lying there in that bed, picturing *you* coming and kissing me, sweeping me up onto your horse and taking me to live happily ever after in your kingdom. Only, I opened my eyes and realized it was a spoiled prince with a reputation as a man whore instead!"

Raine froze, hearing what she said…what she was really saying. "You…"

"Yes," she snapped, obviously angry. "I was fantasizing about you. About me. About you *and* me."

"Together," he whispered.

She nodded slowly. "Together."

"Where?"

She inched closer, sliding her leg against his, then reaching up and touching his face. She gently stroked his jaw, which throbbed from one of the lucky punches a Hunter had landed. Then, rising up onto tiptoe, she pressed her lips there, kissing away the hurt. Her voice as soft as her touch, she whispered, "Anywhere you want."

Raine lifted a hand to her face, brushed his rough thumb against her cheek, amazed that such softness could cover such strength. Amazed by every little thing he knew about this woman. And all the things he had yet to discover.

It would take a long time, he suspected. Perhaps even a lifetime.

"You're mine now," he told her, meaning every word. "The prince all but decreed it."

"Yours?" She tossed her head and smiled back. "That's a very Elatyrian attitude for an Earthling. I thought you American men were all sensitive souls, gentle and understanding."

"My blood's pure Elatyrian, remember?" he told her. He slid his hands into her thick hair, cupping her head, drawing her close. "Besides, I'm gentle. I'm understanding," he whispered. "I mean, I didn't chase that prince down and beat the crap out of him for daring to kiss you."

"I think you meant to say you have a strong desire to live," she said, her tone wry.

He chuckled, then moved his mouth toward hers, needing to feel her, possess her, claim her. Now and forever.

She rose to meet his lips and they kissed slowly, with deep tenderness and deeper pleasure. The heat that was always between them rose, but this time, something else came with it. A depth of emotion he'd never felt until he'd met her. It filled him, settling into all the curious hollows of his heart that had led him to explore dangerous places and seek out new experiences. All that wonder, that curiosity, that sense of adventure, was now completely wrapped up in *her*.

The kiss slowly ended, but while their lips were still close, still sharing breath, they whispered the truth of it.

"I love you, Raine."

"And I love you, Ash."

He loved her, and he would stay by her side in her world and in his. As long as they were together, he didn't give a damn where he lived. Making her happy would be his quest for the rest of his days. Besides, he could get used to this truth-finding, mystery-solving life. The high of being the one to solve the riddle was every bit as good as how he felt when he was handed a reward for a job well done.

She remained in his arms and they swayed slightly, as if dancing to some old melody still riding on the airwaves of this magical place. But it wasn't magic or enchantment that put the lightness in his heart and the happiness in his soul. That was entirely due to the woman in his arms.

"So, historian," he eventually murmured. "You've found the prize you've been seeking all your life. What are you going to do now?"

She hesitated a moment, then tilted her head back and looked up at him. Offering an impish smile, she replied, "I'm going to Disney World?"

Raine threw his head back and laughed.

"No, seriously," she said, "I've always wanted to and I just didn't have a chance on this past trip. Promise you'll take me there. Ooh, and I want to visit Venice—the city with all the canals? And Paris! That tower seems amazing. And I'd so dearly love to see El Dorado."

He gently stroked the small of her back. "Sorry, sweetheart, that one's fiction."

She twined her fingers in his hair and smiled up at him. "Maybe in your world. Maybe in mine. But, who knows, we might find it in a place just waiting to be discovered."

He nodded, liking that idea. No, loving that idea. Him and Ashlynn exploring all the worlds? Sounded like a perfect life for a man who found things. Especially now that he'd found the most important thing of all.

She rose to kiss him again. But before she could, Raine remembered one more thing he'd found. It had been right before he'd heard the hired thugs in the castle and had gone off to rescue her.

It had been most…intriguing.

"Oh, Ash?" he whispered against her cheek.

"Yes?"

"I think I've solved another part of the mystery."

"Mmm. Really?" As if uninterested in anything but him, she kissed his jaw, slid her soft tongue against the corner of his mouth, tempting him into more. So much more.

Their lips met and he lost himself to her again, knowing he could tell her the rest later.

After all, the treasure chamber had been sitting there for a thousand years.

The mountain of precious stones and piles of gold weren't going anywhere for the next few hours.

And he had enough treasure to explore right here.

* * * * *

MICHELLE ROWEN

Catch Me

To Brenda Chin...thanks for everything!

1

FIND YOUR TRUE LOVE at the Valentine Café.

The bright pink flyers tacked to telephone poles and walls in the neighborhood were definitely attention getters, no doubt about it.

But was it the truth? Or was it only advertising?

Ginger Redman had hoped for truth, but she'd been waiting for her date to show up for almost half an hour and there was no sign of him yet. She peered out of the window toward the dark street, mostly seeing the small but busy café behind her reflected in the glass, as well as a woman wearing a bit too much makeup. One who could really use a brush at the moment to tame her wild mane of red hair.

Who goes on a blind date on Valentine's Day anyway? she silently asked. *I mean, how pathetic is that?*

She let out a long, shaky breath. Good question. When she'd set it up, she'd just looked at it as nothing more than a Tuesday, not realizing the actual date. But it was a Tuesday with strings attached.

It was ten minutes past eight o'clock. She'd wait until eight-thirty and that was it. If her date hadn't shown by then, she'd buy—she glanced over at the counter and eyed the delicious-looking baked goods—half a dozen red velvet cupcakes with cream cheese frosting. She'd take the holiday-themed candy heart off the top of each one and smash it symbolically before consuming the tiny red cakes one after another. Of course, that would blow her attempt to eat healthy this week, but it would be totally worth it.

Five more minutes passed. She watched couples come and go from the café, holding hands and kissing, much sweeter than the sugary treats lining the shelves. It was starting to make her feel nauseous.

She glared at her reflection in the window again, depressed. She was thirty-two. *Thirty-two.* And utterly, totally single. Normally, this wasn't something that bothered her much, but on Valentine's Day it just seemed…lonely. Especially when one's date wasn't in any hurry to arrive.

She made a mental note to stop by the liquor store on the way back to her apartment and stock up. Red wine might go very nicely with those cupcakes.

Her phone vibrated and she grabbed it, figuring it was going to be her date apologizing for his tardiness. But no, it was another number. A familiar one that brought a smile to her lips.

She held the device to her ear. "Uh-huh?"

"Why don't you ever say hello to me like normal people do?" Stephen Fox asked.

"Too busy. I'm currently shoveling high-fat, sugared confectionaries into my mouth."

"That sounds kind of hot, actually."

"Yeah, so hot." She rolled her eyes and felt some of her tension ease. Stephen was somewhere out there, on a date of his own with some hot chick. Stephen tended to use phrases like "hot chick," but Ginger chose not to hold it against him. She'd planned to call him later to find out how his evening went and to unload about her own Mr. Perfect.

The Mr. Perfect who hadn't shown his face yet.

Stephen was the owner of Red Fox Publishing, a children's book company, and Ginger was one of three full-time editors on staff. He was also devastatingly attractive, a fact that Ginger tried to ignore as much as humanly possible. Since she'd started working for him a year ago, they'd become personal friends. It didn't take long before they realized that they shared the same sense of humor, the same taste in food and the same love of over-the-top action movies.

Too bad he'd never looked at her as more than a friend. She might be tempted. Instead, she reminded herself that he was Off-Limits. Just because they'd developed a friendship didn't mean he wasn't *also* her employer. Business and pleasure worked sometimes, but it all depended on the level of pleasure. Friends, yes. Lovers…no way.

She'd had a bad experience dating her manager at a small magazine she worked for just after college. Once their relationship took a nosedive, so did her regular paychecks. Before long, she found herself out of a job. A friendship was way easier to maintain than any sort of romance. Romances inevitably ended, but friendships could last forever. And fantastic jobs that also paid the bills were something to be handled with utmost care.

Besides, Stephen had made it very clear during a few of their many debates that he thought every romance had an expiry date, like milk or eggs. Based on her past experiences, she couldn't exactly say he was wrong.

"Don't forget," Stephen said over the phone. "Regardless of how exciting your Valentine's Day date is, we have that meeting with Jorgensen bright and early at nine at the office. His plane should have arrived an hour ago, in fact. I'll check in with him to make sure he hasn't killed anyone yet."

"Don't worry, I haven't forgotten."

How could she? Robert Jorgensen was a Very Important Author, a man whose books about a friendly blue monster who loved making lemonade and solving mysteries basically floated the entire operation and kept Ginger in red velvet cupcakes, not to mention rent money. He was also much more of a miserable bastard than his lighthearted books suggested.

She'd decided, after several unpleasant phone conversations with him as they discussed his books, that the man simply needed to get laid. However, she wasn't offering.

Now he was here in Toronto personally for a tour of the office, and they hoped to impress him. He hadn't yet accepted their latest contract offer. Sad to say, the future of Red Fox was currently hanging on his answer.

No pressure there.

"How's your date going?" Stephen asked.

"Oh…great." Ginger glanced across the empty table and ran her finger around the edge of her cold cup of coffee. "Just great. He's everything I thought he'd be."

"He's there right now?"

"He's getting a refill at the counter. I probably shouldn't talk much longer. It's rude, you know." She blinked. "What about your date? Isn't she giving you a lap dance or something?"

"Her talented tongue is in my ear as we speak. We're at Jack and Lucy's."

She raised her eyebrows. "Oh, the bar on Adelaide? You're just around the corner from me. I'm at the Valentine Café."

"That sounds ridiculously charming."

"It is. Happy Valentine's Day, Stephen."

"You, too."

She ended the call and looked bleakly at the screen of her phone. Again, her reflection stared back at her, accusing her of lying to someone she cared about.

"Well, what was I supposed to say?" she mumbled out loud. "Admit that I'd been stood up? With his opinions of internet dating, he'd never let me forget it."

Besides, if he was having an incredible night that would inevitably lead to mind-blowing sex, the least she could do is make it seem as if she had the same in store. Really, it only seemed fair.

STEPHEN FOX STUDIED the screen of his BlackBerry for a few long moments before he returned it to the pocket of his jeans.

Ginger had been lying to him. Her date hadn't shown up— the date she'd been talking about all damned week. This "Mr. Perfect" who had the potential to "change her life."

Online dating. What a stupid invention.

"Who was that?" The guy on the bar stool next to him asked before tossing back a shot of tequila.

"Just a friend." Stephen wasn't all that fond of that word. *Friend.* Just another *F* word.

Stupid blind date. On a stupid love-soaked holiday that was played up more for commercial value than anything real.

He flagged down the bartender to order another beer.

"You lie to your friends a lot?" the guy asked.

"What?"

"There's no girl with her tongue in your ear right now."

Stephen grabbed a handful of unshelled peanuts and launched one into his mouth. "The night's still young. Maybe I'm being optimistic."

"You totally saved me, you know that?" The guy leaned an elbow on the long, glossy wooden bar top and gave him a drunken grin. "That blind date could have been hell to get away from if I'd gone in there. I mean, what was I thinking?"

"It wouldn't have gone well. Like I told you, I saw her. She's..." Stephen grimaced as he forced the words out. "Well, let's just say, unless you're looking at having puppies instead of kids one day, she wasn't right for you."

"The picture she emailed me made her look really hot."

Stephen waved a hand dismissively. "It was probably from twenty years ago. Women do that all the time."

He was a liar. A horrible liar who was going to hell. But it was all for a good cause. Honestly, Ginger didn't want to date this guy, anyway. He was a total loser.

Just look at him, he thought. *Tall, built, handsome as a male model. Owns his own gym. Total loser.*

Yup. *Hell.* He was well on his way.

Stephen had shown up at the Valentine Café at the exact same time as Mr. Perfect, here, and spotted Ginger seated near the window. He'd seen the email about their date over her shoulder earlier that afternoon, so he knew when and where it was taking place. It had been a difficult task to lure this guy away before he saw her, but not as difficult as he'd originally thought.

Not that it had been a premeditated plan, or anything. He wasn't *that* cold. The thought that Ginger was at the café right now, waiting for this jerk to show, then feeling bad that she'd been stood up on Valentine's Day, didn't sit well with him at all.

Despite its commercial trappings, women *loved* Valentine's Day.

He was completely evil for doing this. However, his motivation was fairly solid.

The thought of Ginger being with any other man made his blood boil and his vision go red at the edges. It was the madness and the jealousy that made him do stupid, thoughtless things like this.

He'd met her a year ago, the day before she started working at Red Fox. Right here in this bar, Jack and Lucy's, in fact. Stephen had been getting over his last girlfriend, a woman who'd decided she wanted more adventure and excitement in her life so she cheated on him with three different men. In the same night.

Stephen had allowed himself to get as drunk as he'd ever been in his thirty-five years. So drunk that nothing else seemed to matter. So drunk that he was willing to do or say whatever he wanted to whomever he wanted without worrying about the consequences. And he'd done just that to a beautiful redhead whose long mane of hair had caught his drunken attention. A beer in each hand, he'd hit on her loudly and shamelessly.

Then he'd puked on her shoes.

Puked. On. Her. Shoes.

It wasn't until the next morning, when he'd dragged his hungover ass into work, that he'd met his newest editor, whom he'd hired over the phone since she'd lived in Calgary at the time. Ginger had thought the entire embarrassing (for him) situation was hilarious and told him to forget about it. He pretended that he had, then worked hard to show that he wasn't a lush who couldn't control himself. They became friends—good friends. Better friends than he'd ever been with a woman before. In his life.

Not a "friends with benefits" situation, either. A *platonic* friendship.

It was for the best. He didn't believe in true love. His parents had split when he was just a kid and it had hit him hard. And his most recent serious girlfriend's lack of interest in being even remotely faithful had left a bad taste in his mouth. And in his life.

Now he was dedicated to his job. Full stop. So, pursuing anything with Ginger felt unprofessional, given the fact he was her boss.

Of course, he wasn't made of stone. He had waited for some glimmer of attraction to show in her eyes during their many talks and late dinner meetings, but first impressions were lasting impressions. She would always think of him like a buddy capable of doing stupid things that made her laugh. That was all.

But despite his own "romance sucks" philosophy and swearing off serious relationships, he didn't feel like a buddy. And tonight, Valentine's Day, after he'd just destroyed her most recent chance at love—although, Mr. Perfect didn't seem, in Stephen's humble opinion, to be the right man for the job—he was on his third beer. Maybe he'd eventually puke on someone else's shoes tonight.

"So, who's the babe?" Mr. Perfect asked after a minute.

Stephen winced. "What do you mean?"

"The one you're thinking about." The guy leaned toward him. "I know what it's like to get hung up on a woman, dude. And you're pining for one right now."

"You think so, huh?"

"I know so."

Stephen shrugged. "She's not interested in me like that, so it doesn't really matter."

Mr. Perfect nodded sagely. "You're a good-looking guy. She probably could be. You just need to be more forceful. Sometimes when they say no, they really mean yes, you know what I mean? You just have to grab them and make them see that they want you. That's what I would have done with the babe tonight if she hadn't been a total dog." He stood up. "I still might. I mean, how bad could she be? I don't mind cougars."

Stephen held his arm out to stop the guy from leaving. "Not a good idea. You should go home. You're drunk."

And if Mr. Perfect made any more mention of "no means yes," Stephen thought he might add murder to his list of crimes tonight instead of general deceit and, making an educated guess for later, public drunkenness.

"Yeah, maybe you're right. So what about you? What about your babe?"

"Like I said—" Stephen flagged the bartender to bring him another beer ASAP "—she's not interested in me like that."

FORTY-FIVE MINUTES had elapsed.

Ginger could take a hint.

The Valentine Café officially knew nothing about romance, at least as far as Ginger was concerned, anyway. She considered writing a strongly worded letter to them to complain about their advertising campaign. It was lies, all lies.

I hate Valentine's Day.

Ginger swallowed past the lump in her throat and began to gather her things, dropped her phone back into her handbag and pulled her coat on.

"More coffee?" a white-haired lady asked just before she stood up.

"Oh, no. No, thank you."

The woman glanced at the empty seat across from her. "Romeo didn't show?"

Ginger tensed, wanting to deny it but deciding that it didn't really matter. "Afraid not. And his name was Brad."

"Then Brad wasn't the right Romeo for you."

"You're probably right." She grabbed her long, wavy hair and pulled it over her shoulder. "Your flyers are misleading."

"Flyers?"

"The ones that promise that this place can help a girl find her true love. I get that it's just a line, but…oh, I don't know. Forget it. It doesn't matter."

The woman's smile only grew warmer. "This…Brad. Did he give you any warning he wouldn't show up?"

Ginger thought about it. "Well, he was gorgeous and success-ful. I guess that was warning enough." She clutched the strap

of her bag that held a manuscript she was currently editing—
retellings of well-known fairy tales. It was one bright spot in
her week. She was loving every page of it. "Forget it, I'm just
feeling sorry for myself. It's this stupid day. It brings out the
worst in me. It just reminds me that I'm alone and, well, maybe
sometimes I don't want to be. Not all the time. It's so hard finding somebody really great."

"But not impossible."

Well, that was true. Her parents had married after knowing
each other exactly two days after they'd met. And thirty-five
years of marriage later, they were still madly in love. They'd
met on a blind date. Maybe that was why Ginger had been so
willing to give it a shot tonight.

They were on a Greek Islands cruise right now. Three weeks
of romance to celebrate their anniversary. Their *Valentine's Day*
anniversary.

Not everybody is lucky enough to find that kind of love, she
reminded herself. *Most people never do.*

The thought made her sad.

"It just feels like I have to do all the work," she said to the
old woman. "I need to look, I need to search and spend my time
and effort on finding someone. Just once, I wish my life was
like a…like a fairy tale. For men to want me without me having to do anything at all. I want them to fall under my spell so
I can finally figure out who is the perfect man for me without
people playing head games and everything being a struggle."
She suddenly laughed at how absurd she sounded. "Sorry, I'm
babbling. Too much caffeine, I guess."

The lady held up her finger. "Wait here just a moment, dear.
I think I have something that might help you."

She did? Unless she had a gorgeous single son hiding in the
kitchen, ready to fall madly in love with her, Ginger found that
extremely hard to believe.

The woman disappeared into the back room and returned a
minute later. "Eat this. It will make everything better."

Ginger looked down at the napkin she held. On it was a small gingerbread man. Icing was piped on him to make him look modern—with a suit, a tie and a smile on his gingerbread face.

"My perfect man," she said. "Totally edible."

"It's all yours."

She laughed. "A cookie's going to help me, you think? And how is it going to do that?"

The woman's smile held. "Eat it and let it work its special magic. It will give you exactly what you want. It will lead you to the perfect man for you before midnight tonight. I promise it will."

Midnight on Valentine's Day. This sounded like a fairy tale in the making.

Ginger laughed. If nothing else, the ridiculous statement had cheered her up. A magic cookie, huh? Sure, it was. Well, it wasn't a miracle or true love, but it *was* a free cookie.

"Thanks," she said, still smiling as she took a small bite from the shoulder, chewed it thoughtfully and swallowed. "Magic cookies are delicious. Who knew?"

"Sit," the woman said. "Have another coffee. I'll make it a decaf this time. You'll feel better in a minute."

It was surprising how good the gingerbread man was. Melt in the mouth, buttery—sweet, but not too sweet. Perfect. It might not really be magic, but it filled Ginger with a warm feeling inside, like the cookies her mom used to make when she was a little girl, fresh from the oven just in time for her to come home from school. They'd been warm and tasted exactly like love. It reminded Ginger of a time when things were simple and she could take life as it came, rather than trying to analyze everything first.

That was a good lesson to learn, that life doesn't have to be any more complicated than a cookie unless you let it. And Valentine's Day was just another day on the calendar, nothing more than a sneaky way to get through the coldest part of the year.

Maybe that's how the woman thought this cookie would work its magic. To remind Ginger not to take things so seriously.

"My goodness," a voice said to her left. "You're lovely."

Ginger blinked with surprise and looked up to her right. A

man stood there. He was fiftyish, with dark hair that was gray at the temples.

"Excuse me?"

"What's your name?"

"Uh…" She frowned. "It's Ginger."

"Ginger," he repeated slowly, as if appreciating the taste of each syllable. He gave her a warm smile and glanced down at the crumbs left over on her napkin from the cookie. "That's my favorite spice."

Sure, there was that. But she'd originally been named after the movie star on *Gilligan's Island.* Her father had been a big fan of the show and when his baby daughter had been born with a shock of red hair, she'd received the name of the stranded movie star.

"Why are you all alone?" the man asked. "You should be with someone who will treat you right, especially on a night like this. Let's go somewhere tonight. Anywhere you like."

Ginger stared at him blankly. "Is this a joke? Because, trust me, I'm not really in the mood. It's been a lousy evening."

"I'm not joking. I'm thinking dinner, dancing. It is Valentine's Day."

This was very true.

"Excuse me?" A woman in her fifties approached him with a sour look on her face. "What on earth are you doing?"

He glanced at her. "I'm asking Ginger to go to dinner with me."

"Yes, I can see that. My eyes and ears are working just fine, Larry." The woman then turned her glare on Ginger. "You need to stay away from my husband."

Ginger's brows shot up. "Your husband?"

"Larry—" her voice turned shrill "—we're leaving. Now."

Larry reluctantly did as his wife asked, casting a sad look at Ginger. "Maybe another time."

"Um…I doubt it."

Larry's wife took him by the arm tightly and directed him toward the door. He cast a last, regretful look over his shoulder before they left the café.

"That," Ginger said as the woman who'd given her the cookie returned with a pot of coffee to refresh her mug, "was bizarre."

She nodded. "Men can be unpredictable when it comes to romance."

"That wasn't romance. I didn't even know him."

The woman shrugged. "You did say you wanted your life to be like a fairy tale, right? Just like the one in your bag?"

How did the woman know what Ginger had in her bag? "Yes, but—"

"Sometimes wishes come true." She winked. "Enjoy the rest of your Valentine's Day, my dear."

Ginger watched her depart back behind the counter. It had been a very strange night. Maybe she'd forgo the cupcakes and head straight to the liquor store for something a bit stronger than red wine.

Out of curiosity, she pulled the manuscript out of her leather bag and stared at the next story she was set to edit: "The Gingerbread Man."

Well, that was definitely a fairy tale. However, it wasn't exactly one with princesses and princes, royal weddings and happy endings. It was more about a cookie who ran really fast when it realized everyone wanted to eat it.

She definitely hadn't wished for that. She'd wished for…what? She racked her brain. For men to show interest in her, for her to be the one to pick and choose who she wanted. Kind of like a less dramatic and more pleasant, real-life version of *The Bachelorette*. No gingerbread cookies need apply, other than the one she just ate, of course.

Her bag fell to the ground as she slid off her seat and got to her feet. Someone close by reached for it.

"Here," a young blond man said, holding her bag out to her, a wide smile stretching across his face. "You dropped this."

"Oh, thank you." She shoved the manuscript back inside.

"My pleasure. Really." He cupped her chin, then leaned forward and gently brushed his lips against hers.

"Hey!" She jumped back from him, shocked by the unexpected kiss. "What was that for?"

He frowned. "It's so strange, but I couldn't resist. Sorry."

"It's okay, just…don't do that again."

She glanced over her shoulder to see the man's wife, or girl-friend, glaring at her as though she was some sort of a man-stealing seductress. It was too bad, really. *This* one was really attractive. *And* a good kisser. Still, he wasn't acting rationally, and kissing strangers just wasn't her style.

Ginger slipped outside before she started to laugh hysterically. It was all so absurd. Two men, already with other women, had shown interest in her. Out of the blue. Maybe there was hope for her yet. Only—with someone available.

"That lady was right," she said under her breath. "I'd wished for more attention and I got it. Maybe that cookie *was* magic."

As if. Ginger might edit fairy tales, but she didn't necessarily believe in them. She might be a romantic, but she was a realistic one. What had happened with the two men had just been a fluke. She *had* taken extra time with her hair and makeup that evening. Maybe that was all it took to attract such attention.

Maybe next time she'd attract somebody *single*.

When her laughter finally faded, she dug into her bag and pulled out her phone, leaning against the brick wall next to the café's doors. She quickly called Stephen.

"Hello?" he answered. "See what I did there? I answered my phone with the common phrase 'hello.' None of this 'uh-huh' stuff."

"Very impressive."

"What's going on? Has Mr. Perfect proposed yet?"

"I'm afraid it wasn't a match made in heaven."

"Oh, no. I'm really sorry to hear that."

"You don't sound all that sorry." She frowned. "Are you drunk right now?"

"Not yet, but I'm working on it."

"Things aren't working out with the talented tongue?"

"The talented—? Oh, right. Her. Yeah, she's…gone. Hell, who needs her? I mean, how much sex can one man handle, especially on a Tuesday night? I'm a weary, old middle-aged man now, you know."

She couldn't help but grin. An attractive and sexy man, yes. An old one…definitely not. "Listen, you wouldn't believe what just happened to me."

"What?"

"This woman—I think she owns this café…well, she gave me a cookie—she called it a *magic* cookie. Anyway, I ate it and I've been hit on twice."

"A magic cookie?" he repeated dryly.

"I know, it sounds bizarre, but it sort of granted me my wish."

"You made a wish?"

She sighed. "I wished my life was a fairy tale when it came to men. For them to want me without me having to lift a single finger. So I could have the pick of whomever I wanted, easy as pie. Or…easy as *cookies*."

"Sounds delicious."

"Kind of like the Gingerbread Man, I guess. You know how everyone chased him because they all wanted to eat him?"

"So instead of the Gingerbread Man, it's *Ginger Redman* who's in danger of being chased and potentially devoured?"

She couldn't ignore the edge of humor in his voice. He wasn't taking this seriously. At all. "Pretty much."

There was a short silence. "So, you're saying that this wish of yours came true and now men are magically hitting on you. Welcome to reality as a gorgeous woman."

She ignored his sarcasm. "Problem is, both men were already with other women."

"Sounds like you should head directly home, order a pizza and stay far away from bad men with big appetites."

"I'm thinking you might be right."

"Off to bed with you, Ms. Redman. I insist. And I'll see you in the morning."

"Okay."

"And, Ginger…"

"Yeah?"

"I'm sorry about Mr. Perfect. But if he wasn't everything you hoped he'd be, then he didn't deserve you in the first place."

He sounded so sincere that it made a lump form in her throat. "Thanks."

Ginger ended the call and started walking. It was only a few blocks to her apartment, no more than a ten-minute trip.

It didn't take long, though, for her to realize that she had a bit of a problem. The two guys in the café? They were only the beginning.

She was being checked out by every man she passed. A few of them even whistled at her appreciatively.

Strange, very strange.

Another man fell into step with her after a block and a half.

"Happy Valentine's Day," he said with a big smile.

"Uh…thank you."

"Can I buy you a coffee? A drink?"

She swept her eyes over him. Tall, dark and definitely handsome. Plus, no wedding ring. "Thanks, but…I'm headed home. It's been a long day."

He nodded. "Okay, no problem. But here's my card…" He thrust a business card at her and she took it tentatively. He was a lawyer. "Call me anytime. I mean that."

She cleared her throat and tucked the card into her purse. "Yeah, uh, maybe. Thanks."

She continued walking. What the hell was going on?

Another wolf whistle caught her attention.

Unbelievable. She'd suddenly turned into the most irresistible woman in Toronto. For a moment she thought this might be a practical joke, but set up by whom? Nobody but Stephen and the woman in the café knew what she'd wished for.

She'd asked for her pick of any man she wanted.

A slow smile spread across her face. It couldn't possibly be real. But what if it was?

That would be kind of awesome.

"Ginger!" someone called to her. She turned to see a man tentatively approaching her. He was gorgeous—over six feet tall, built, with dark hair and light brown eyes.

It was Brad, her AWOL blind date. She'd seen a picture so she knew what he looked like.

"Brad," she said with surprise and more than a twinge of annoyance at being stood up at the café. "What happened to you earlier?"

"Wait a minute, you're not a dog," he said with confusion. "He told me you were a dog, but you—you're beautiful. Ginger, forgive me. I'm sorry I didn't show up."

Somebody had told him she was a dog? "Where were you?"

"At a bar, drinking. Sorry, I…I shouldn't have done what I did. I had no idea how beautiful you are.'

"Well, thanks, but…you did see my picture already. I sent it to you."

He shrugged. "Pictures can be manipulated. Who knows what's real anymore?"

Good question, actually.

"And now you want me to forgive you," she said slowly, cringing as a man walked past them and whistled at her again. She wasn't used to be noticed quite this much. It made her feel incredibly self-conscious.

"Yes, forgive me. Let me make it up to you. I'm…" He shook his head as if to try to clear it. "I'm feeling much different than I was before. You're something special, Ginger. I don't want to lose this chance with you."

Despite his very convincing words, there was something off in his eyes. A slightly glazed look and she didn't think it was only from a few drinks. It was as if he was under some sort of… spell.

Magic-cookie alert!

Her wish…this was more proof that it had come true. Brad had just done a one-eighty—one moment fleeing the scene and standing her up, the next apologizing and calling her beautiful. Not that it wasn't nice to hear, but…

This wasn't real.

The thought was like a blow. It had seemed so wonderful and full of possibility only a minute ago, but now she saw the reality. As much as she would like to believe that all these men had suddenly become attracted to her en masse, it simply wasn't the truth.

She'd be more disappointed if she actually cared about this guy standing in front of her. But she didn't. It was a bit of a relief to realize it, really.

Brad was very handsome, sure, but she wasn't interested—not anymore.

"Let's go somewhere and talk," he suggested.

"I don't think so. Happy Valentine's Day, Brad. I hope you find the right woman for you. But it's not going to be me."

Ginger turned and started walking away from him.

Tonight she had more men interested in her than she'd ever had in her entire life. And she didn't want any of them in return. She wanted the man she fell for to be madly in love with her in return—and not only because of a spell that would wear off at the stroke of midnight.

Another man whistled at her as she passed him at a bus stop.

This might turn out to be a long night.

It was official. Magic or not, Valentine's Day sucked.

2

MR. PERFECT WAS LONG GONE by now. What a jerk.

Maybe now he could stop obsessing about Ginger finding herself in the arms of the wrong man tonight—or any man, really. But especially if that man looked like a fitness model.

Ginger.

He hated that he was stuck in this bar all by himself, on a stupid holiday, thinking about her. Feeling jealous even though he had no right. And, the worst part was, just the thought of Ginger—her thick red hair, her beautiful curves, her long legs… and everything in between—made his cock painfully hard.

So much for trying to think of her as just a friend.

Stephen glared at his reflection in the mirrored wall behind the bar. "You could have any woman you want. She's not on the list. Remember that."

Stephen was tall and wasn't fat. He ran three miles a day and saw a personal trainer twice a week. He ate healthy most of the time. He rarely drank—except on certain Valentine's Days. The women he'd been with in the past hadn't had any complaints about dating one of Toronto's most eligible bachelors. Only that one ex-girlfriend had, to his knowledge, ever cheated on him. Publicly, shamelessly and often. So what if Stephen hadn't been "exciting" enough for her? When one's idea of exciting was group sex and jumping out of airplanes naked, he'd have to take a pass.

He owned his own business, now in its seventh year, and it was moderately successful, thank you very much. It would be better soon, at least once Jorgensen committed to the new contract. That was bankable talent right there.

Speaking of bankable talent, Stephen eyed his vibrating cell phone to see that Jorgensen himself was calling. He took a deep breath, let it out slowly, and then answered the call.

"Fox, here," he said, plugging his other ear so he could hear properly in the noisy bar.

"Fox, I'm not happy."

This wasn't particularly a surprise.

"I'm sorry to hear that. How was your flight?"

"Bumpy."

"Your hotel?"

"Adequate, at best. My view is blocked by that stupid tower."

"The CN Tower? It's a city landmark, not to mention a world wonder."

The famous author made an annoyed sound. "I can't stay here. I want to leave."

Stephen's grip on the phone increased. "No, no, no. Don't go. We want you here. We have a meeting tomorrow morning. You know, the one I flew you in for?"

"I want to meet tonight," the man said bluntly. "In my hotel suite. We'll settle everything so that I don't have to stay here any longer than necessary. I can't stand this town. Why aren't you in Manhattan?"

"I love Toronto," Stephen said, refusing to rise to any snobby author's bait.

"It's freezing cold here."

"It's freezing cold in Manhattan in February, too. It's not that far away." Stephen swallowed his annoyance along with another gulp of beer. He couldn't argue with Jorgensen, not now. The difficult author's backlist represented three-quarters of Red Fox's revenue. His new books could mean a true future for his business and a long-overdue opportunity for growth.

He had to keep reminding himself of that as he bit his tongue nearly to the point of drawing blood so he wouldn't say something he'd regret later.

"Are you coming or not?" Jorgensen said with annoyance.

"Yes, fine. I'm coming."

"Make sure to bring the redhead with you."

"You mean Ginger? Your editor?"

"That's the one. Half an hour, Fox. Don't be late."

The phone went dead and Stephen glared at it. "Yeah, Happy Valentine's Day to you, too, asshole."

It took him a little longer than he'd have liked to compose himself. Then he pulled out his phone to call Ginger and tell her they needed to be at the beck and call of the author of the Blue Monster Mysteries. Immediately.

He thumbed through his address book and hit the call button, then held his phone to his ear.

"Uh-huh?" she answered.

A smile tugged at his lips. "When are you ever going to answer with 'hello'?"

"Probably never."

"Are you home yet?" he asked.

"No, I'm randomly wandering the streets on my way there."

He heard something on her end of the line then. "Was that a whistle?"

She cleared her throat. "Yeah."

"Some guy just whistled at you?"

"I'm getting some…attention."

"You must look totally hot tonight." He grinned. "What are you wearing?"

"Don't be a smart-ass. I mean, I think I look good, but…this is…different. Remember that cookie I told you about?"

"The magic cookie."

"Right. Well, you can mock me if you want to, but I think it's real. It's making every guy I come across extremely interested in me. I'm trying to ignore it."

Good, he thought. The idea that men were hitting on Ginger didn't sit well with him at all. "I need you."

"Pardon me?"

He crossed his legs, ignoring his erection that had only become harder to ignore since he'd started talking to her. "I need to get together. Jorgensen's requested our meeting be moved up to tonight. And he wants to see you, too."

She sighed with frustration. It was a sound he was used to hearing from her when it came to the author. But tonight, the breathy sound shot right through him and made him even more painfully aroused.

Damn it. He didn't need this complication. He'd wanted to ignore his attraction to her, hoping it would lessen with time. But if anything, it had only increased with each day that passed.

He wasn't surprised that other men would want her—with or without any so-called magic in the mix. She was gorgeous: a beautiful face, with a cute little freckle just under her left eye that he found incredibly distracting during meetings; a gorgeous body that filled out blouses much too well, which was even more of a distraction; a generous and funny personality that always lightened his heart even on rough days when the numbers weren't looking good.

Damn. He wanted her.

But he didn't want to scare her off. She couldn't ever know how he really felt.

"How much have you had to drink?" she asked.

He eyed his car keys before shoving them back in his pocket.

After four and a half beers downed in less than an hour, getting behind the wheel probably wasn't a good idea. "Too much to drive."

"Fine. I know you're not too far from where I am. Meet me at the corner of Adelaide and John. We'll take the subway to get to Jorgensen."

"You're really okay with the meeting tonight? It's kind of inconvenient."

"I know how much it means to Red Fox…and to you. We'll get this jerk to sign the papers, Stephen. Promise."

"I hope you're right."

"We're a team, Stephen. Together we can accomplish anything."

He ended the call and looked at the screen. He had a picture of her to go with her phone number. He stared into her green eyes for just a moment before he tucked the phone into his pocket.

It looked as though he'd be spending Valentine's Day with Ginger after all. It would be easier to keep other men away from her if he was at her side.

Trying to remind himself that she was just a friend was getting more difficult when his body reacted to the very sound of her voice, the image of her both on his phone and in his head. He couldn't shake this feeling that there was magic in the air tonight when it came to Ginger Redman.

He decided to blame the beer.

GINGER HAD QUICKLY GROWN weary of the sound of men whistling at her. Now it just made the hair at the back of her neck stand up.

"She's so hot," a man said to his friend as she passed. "What's your name, sweetheart?"

"None of your business," she muttered.

"Oh, c'mon. No reason to be mean."

"Whatever you're feeling isn't real," she informed him. "It's because of a magic cookie."

That earned her a confused look. "A magic cookie?"

Exactly.

Another whistle from behind her made her shoulders tense

and she cast a look backward, just before slamming hard into a tall, firm body. It stopped her cold and knocked the breath out of her.

"Ouch." Stephen rubbed his shoulder before grabbing her arm. "Distracted much?"

She cringed, but she immediately relaxed at the sight of him. "You could say that."

His gaze swept over her. "I can see why men are falling all over you. That dress…" He inhaled sharply before his eyes snapped to hers. "It's…well, it's…"

"Expensive. Tight. And short." She grinned at him before looking down at the little black dress she'd recently purchased under her open coat. It hugged her body like a second skin while managing not to look trashy. "Worth every penny."

"And then some." He grabbed her hand. "Let's head for the subway."

"Sounds good."

Ginger's gaze moved over his body. He wore a white dress shirt from earlier at the office under his black leather coat, but he'd changed into dark blue jeans. Casual, for him. It looked good. Very good.

And his hand in hers—he didn't normally touch her. She hadn't even realized that before this moment. His skin was warm against hers in the cold night. It made her breath catch and she wasn't entirely sure why.

That wasn't true. She knew why. Seeing Brad earlier had only cemented it for her. She wasn't interested in him, she never had been. She was interested in Stephen.

And now she had resigned herself to spend Valentine's Day night with a man who just wanted to be friends.

They weeded through the people waiting for the next subway to come along. "See what I mean? The men down here—they're all checking me out."

"I noticed."

She bit her bottom lip hard. "I wished on that cookie and my wish came true."

"Cookies don't grant wishes, Ginger."

"This one did. I know it sounds crazy, but this all started happening—and you have to admit, this is not normal—after I made the wish and ate the cookie."

"Then maybe you should have been more careful about what you wished for."

She mock-glared at him. "Sure. *Now* you tell me."

"What's the problem, anyway? I'd have thought you'd be thrilled with the attention."

"Thrilled, huh?"

He nodded. "Women like attention from men."

"Nice. That's not sexist at all."

"It's the truth."

She shrugged. "It's just not natural. I guess I'll have to be patient and wait for the real thing. No magical shortcuts need apply." She looked up into his eyes. They were blue like the ocean. Sometimes clear, sometimes stormy. Right now they were stormy.

He raked a hand through his light brown hair that was a couple weeks overdue for a cut. His hand was tight on hers as the subway arrived, the doors opened, and they got on. The doors *whooshed* shut behind them.

"By the way," she said, "I thought I should remind you that Jorgensen is incredibly impossible and demanding. When he snaps his fingers, he expects to get whatever he wants. But if you give in, he'll keep doing it. I don't care who he is, you can't let him boss you around."

"I don't like it much, either, trust me."

Stephen was strong, confident and a fantastic businessman. But when it came to this author, all bets were off. She knew how much his books meant to Red Fox Publishing, but in a twisted way, she'd love to see Stephen tell the obnoxious man off one day.

"You really need to stand up to him." She frowned. "Hey, are you all right?"

There was a thin sheen of perspiration on his forehead as he stared out of the subway window as it started to move. There weren't too many other people in this car, but they remained standing anyway. She held tightly to the metal pole to keep steady as the station whizzed past them.

When he didn't answer other than increasing his grip on her hand, she grew concerned.

"Stephen," she prompted again. "What's wrong? You look a little…sick."

"Sick." He laughed quietly and raked his hair again. "Yeah, something like that. So this gingerbread cookie you ate—"

"Which was delicious, by the way. You really need to check out that café some time."

"I'm on it. But do you honestly think that it granted your wish to have men want you?"

She looked out of the window, reflecting on what happened. "The proof's in the eyes of every man I've passed since I left that café. It's like a tiny Cupid just shot them in the chest. I know it's hard to believe, but if I wanted to, I think I could have had any one of them."

"It's not that hard to believe."

There was something in his voice that made her gaze snap to him. "Stephen, what are you—?"

But she couldn't finish her sentence. The next second, he took her by her upper arms, pulled her against him and crushed his mouth against hers. She gasped with surprise against his lips.

Desire shot through her as she kissed him back. Hard.

What was this? He wasn't acting like himself at all. Stephen didn't grab her and kiss her. He…he kept his distance. He was friendly, but controlled and professional. He was…

Damn, he could kiss. Like, *really* kiss. Passionate, knee weakening, achingly hot. Forget desire…*lust* slammed into her, through her, deeper than she'd ever experienced before.

The cookie. It was a fleeting thought from a distance, but it quickly approached so she could see it closer.

The cookie's magic… Stephen had been affected by it, too. And because of that, he now wanted her. All because of a damn spell.

Not because he really did want her. Not like she wanted him—*had* wanted him for so long now…

She remembered the first time they ever met, a year ago at Jack and Lucy's when he'd been depressed over an ex-girlfriend who'd treated him badly, an ex-girlfriend that Ginger would now like to throttle for treating him badly. Stephen had gotten really, really drunk.

He'd been so appalled and embarrassed about his behavior—not like any other guy who would have laughed it off and not given it another thought—that she'd been utterly and completely charmed by him. She hadn't planned to hold it against him. Everybody had off nights and did things they regretted. Stephen, she'd later find, didn't have too many of those off nights.

His reaction had meant something to her. And that something had grown over the months to something much deeper than friendship.

Damn it, she thought. *Why do I have to pick the ones I can't have? Why couldn't I have been interested in Brad like this?*

Finally, Stephen broke off from her, pressing his hand against his mouth and giving her a look similar to the one he'd worn the morning he'd learned that the woman he'd acted like a drunken fool in front of would now be working very closely with him. Every day.

Shameful. Bashful. Shocked as hell.

It was like a lightning bolt right to her heart.

"Well," she said shakily. "That was unexpected."

"I don't know why I—" His gaze raked down the front of her, bringing heat to her skin wherever he looked. "I love you, Ginger. So much. You have no idea. You never have." He clamped a hand over his mouth for a moment. "Oh, hell. Why am I saying that out loud?"

She'd stopped breathing. *Love.* It was something he once told her he didn't believe in. It was only more proof that this wasn't real.

Stephen Fox didn't believe in love. And she hadn't believed in magic.

One of them was definitely proven wrong tonight. Too bad it was her.

He looked so mortified by the words coming out of his mouth that she couldn't help but laugh nervously.

"Don't worry, it's just the spell. I trust you. Just…pull yourself together. It'll wear off soon, by the stroke of midnight, the woman in the café told me." At least, she hoped it would. This was proving to be more difficult than she thought it would be. Random men showing interest in her was one thing…but Stephen?

Her knees weakened at the thought of the kiss they'd just shared. The man in the café had also taken her by surprise with a kiss, but that one hadn't been nearly as mind-blowing as this one.

Damn it. This was getting complicated.

"We need to talk to Jorgensen now." She forced herself to sound calm. "A lot rides on this meeting, right?"

"Right." He gripped the metal pole until his knuckles went white. "This is ridiculous. What is going on? Why am I feeling this way?"

"Magic. A magic cookie. Maybe that woman was a witch."

His frown was so deep it looked painful. "Witches don't exist. Neither does magic."

"You just told me you loved me," she reminded him. "What is that? Real or magic?"

He just stared at her. "I…did I really say that?"

"You did. And since I know you don't believe in love, that's impossible." She exhaled slowly, trying her best to stay in control of this situation. She looked up into his blue eyes. "But you want me right now, right?"

His eyes burned into hers. "Oh, yes."

She shivered. The need for him to touch her again pooled low in her body. "It's just a spell. It'll pass." Her confident expression wavered. "At least, that's what she said. I mean, the gingerbread cookie wasn't that big. Just…breathe. It's going to be okay."

For the next few minutes, he appeared to be waging an inner battle with himself. Finally, his expression began to look less tense.

"I'm better now," he said with a firm nod. "Totally in control of myself."

"Good." She tried not to sound too halfhearted. And she also tried not to touch him. That might make things worse—for both of them.

Unfortunately, right now she really *wanted* to touch him. That look in his eyes, that *heat*. It had slid right into her and it hadn't gone anywhere yet.

The cookie's magic, if that is what could be blamed for all of this, didn't seem to work both ways—at least, not before, anyway. She hadn't been interested in any of the men she'd come across tonight. But with Stephen, it was different.

The difference was obvious. She *already* wanted Stephen. Seeing that need reflected in his eyes, even if it was only because of the spell, meant she couldn't repress her own feelings as well as she normally did.

Her body couldn't resist, anyway. The need she felt for him twisted inside her, making her remember his lips and the taste of his tongue against hers as he possessed her mouth. She ached for the feel of his hand sliding down between her legs. Just the thought made her instantly wet.

Not helpful, Ginger's libido.

The last thing she needed was to fall completely for Stephen. It was bad enough to be stood up by a blind date, but it would be much worse to lose her heart to someone who only thought of her as a good friend.

Stephen was too important to her. She couldn't risk losing him over unprofessional behavior. Letting herself fall in love with her boss, even if that boss was her best friend, wasn't a good idea. Not now, not ever.

The subway came to a stop. She didn't look at him again as they got off the car, except to send a quick glance over her shoulder to ensure he was following her as the subway pulled away. They'd been the only ones to get off at this stop and were otherwise alone in this part of the station.

"Are you sure you're okay?" she asked tentatively.

His jaw was tight. "I kissed you."

"I know. You already apologized."

"I'm not sorry I did it."

She stopped walking and turned around, looking up into his troubled blue eyes. She knew he'd regret saying these things to her tomorrow. "Maybe I should go home. You can deal with Jorgensen yourself. Tell him you couldn't find me."

He shook his head. "Jorgensen wants what he wants."

"I know, but…he might be affected by this, too."

"We'll make it a short meeting. Besides, if you leave, I'd worry about you facing a gauntlet of marriage proposals on the way home. If I'm feeling like this, then I can't imagine what's going through the other men's minds. Scratch that, I can imagine. All too well. You might not be safe if you're not with me."

"The question is, am I safe *with* you?" she asked, holding his gaze.

It took him a moment to answer. "Of course you are."

She raised an eyebrow. "So you're my knight in shining armor right now?"

"An extremely horny knight in shining armor who is having a difficult time thinking about anything but ravishing you. But yeah, I guess I am."

She couldn't help but grin. "Ravishing me? I thought you published kids books, not romance novels."

"Maybe I need to think about broadening my publishing schedule." He swallowed hard. "Can you do me a favor, though?"

"Sure." She felt breathless suddenly.

"No eye contact."

"Who, with Jorgensen?"

"No, with me. The longer you look at me, the less able I am to control whatever this is."

Ginger's heart pounded hard in her chest at the thought of Stephen unable to control himself around her.

"I'm just having trouble believing this," she said. "You *want* me."

He looked at her sternly. "You're still looking in my eyes, Ginger."

"You have nice eyes."

"You're not making this easy for me."

She moved closer to him and pressed her hand against his chest to feel how fast his heart was beating. This was how she'd always fantasized he would look at her—this heat, this need. "You said yourself I'm safe with you. I trust you."

"You should never play with fire, even if it promises not to burn."

She wanted him. Right here and right now. The thought made her breath catch.

It would be so easy to forget everything, to let this happen. To throw caution and better judgment aside and to pull off his shirt and unzip his pants; to feel him against her. To guide him slowly inside her.

If he'd only stop looking at her as though he wanted to devour her, she might be able to restrain herself.

Nobody had *ever* looked at her with this much raw desire in their eyes. Not ex-boyfriends, not the other bespelled men tonight, not even the men in her most erotic fantasies.

Was she absolutely certain she felt safe with Stephen Fox?

Did she even want to feel safe with him?

"After this meeting is over…" He looked at her hand, which was slowly trailing downward, over his hard, ridged abdomen easily felt through his thin white shirt. His jacket was wide-open despite the chill of the night.

"Yes?"

"I'm going to take you as fast as I can—"

She held her breath, wanting to hear him say it. For him to say something naughty and uncontrollable. She might completely lose any inhibitions she had left then.

"—back to that goddamned café where we'll get some answers about how to break this spell. It can't wait till midnight."

Disappointment flowed through her, but it worked like a cold glass of water tossed in the general direction of her growing lust for him.

She pulled her hand away just as it had reached his leather belt. "Fine. Then let's get this meeting over with."

3

STEPHEN DIDN'T THINK it was all that professional to arrive at a business meeting with a raging hard-on, but there wasn't exactly much he could do about it at this point except try to hide it.

He forced himself to think about baseball, about cold showers, about anything nonsexual he could bring to mind, but nothing worked.

Instead he thought about the taste of Ginger's mouth, the feel of her warm hands sliding down the front of him and the whisper of desire he'd clearly seen in her green eyes that had made him more aroused than he'd ever been in his entire life.

What he normally felt for her, what he hid from the world and from her, was all on the surface now, as if he'd been turned inside out. It felt vulnerable, it felt uncontrollable, it felt…wild. Especially when he'd seen his own need reflected in her eyes.

He wasn't sure if it had been his imagination, but she'd kissed him back. He desperately wanted to feel her fingers slide down his stomach again and continue downward to wrap around his hard cock. To feel her lips and tongue take over as she sank to her knees in front of him and took him into his mouth…

A new subject to occupy his brain—not that much blood was flowing there at the moment—would be an excellent idea. He was a professional. So he would act professional, even under duress.

And this was definitely duress. Times a thousand.

Stephen didn't believe in magic, or at least he hadn't until tonight. He had believed in it back when he was just a kid. His father was a magician, doing card tricks and pulling flowers out of hats. Dressed up like a clown, he'd often been hired to be the entertainment at kids' birthday parties. It felt very real at the time, but now Stephen knew it wasn't. His father's disappearing act just before Stephen's tenth birthday had shattered any of Stephen's remaining belief in magic—or, upon witnessing his mother's heartbreak, in the possibility of true and everlasting love. His father had reappeared in Reno with another family a couple years later and made a few sheepish phone calls to his confused and hurt son to explain that it was all for the best.

Stephen had worked two part-time jobs while going to school to help his mother with the bills. He'd had absolutely no time to devote to a social life back then. What little time he did have for entertainment during his teens, he'd spent reading books— fantasies that helped him escape his regular life.

He'd written an essay about his love of books that landed him a scholarship, that helped earn him a degree, that helped get him an intern job at a publishing house where he learned the business from the ground up. It eventually gave him the courage to make a go of it on his own.

All from hard work and luck. Magic had nothing to do with it.

But this…what was happening with Ginger…this might make him believe in fairy dust again. Because this sure wasn't normal.

He'd told her he loved her. It had just spilled from his mouth as if it was something he was actually capable of feeling for anyone.

For Ginger. *Especially* for Ginger.

Just what was that Valentine Café all about, anyway?

Meeting with the author tonight had become an annoying gauntlet he needed to race through quickly before he could focus on what really mattered.

She hadn't touched him since the subway station, which was a good thing. He didn't think he could handle the feel of her hands on him at this point. It was normally difficult being around her without fantasizing about tearing her clothes off and taking her on the Red Fox boardroom table, but this went beyond any fantasy.

She's safe with me, he reminded himself again and again.

He knocked on the hotel-room door. It took a minute before it swung open and Jorgensen peered out at them.

"Finally," he said grumpily. "I thought I'd have to wait all damn night."

Stephen forced a smile to his face and stretched out his hand. "Good to see you, Robert."

He did get a handshake in return, which was encouraging. "Hphmmph."

Jorgensen swept a glance over Ginger, and Stephen watched for any sign that he was affected by the—for lack of a better term—cookie magic. While the man's eyes did glance over Ginger's short, tight black dress and long, sexy bare legs—why was she bare legged in February?—under her cream-colored winter coat, he didn't immediately lunge for her.

Encouraging.

Maybe the magic was wearing off. Then again, he felt it as strong as ever, so it probably wasn't.

Maybe Jorgensen was gay.

Please, God, Stephen thought, *let him be gay.*

It wasn't a prayer he'd ever made before, but there was a first time for everything.

"Can we come in?" Ginger asked.

"No," Jorgensen said bluntly. "I want to go downstairs for a drink. The room service here is atrocious. I ordered dinner fifteen minutes ago and it hasn't arrived yet."

Since room service rarely arrived in fifteen minutes anywhere, this wasn't unexpected.

Stephen fought to keep the smile on his face. "Fair enough."

Moving Ginger to his left in a manner that had her brush torturously up against him—bad idea—Stephen followed Jorgensen back to the elevator and down to the main level lobby bar where they got a booth and ordered drinks from the cocktail waitress.

Stephen was finding it difficult to keep his attention on his troublesome author and not on the beautiful redhead who now sat between him and Jorgensen. Her dress was very low cut and showed off her smooth, creamy skin and a generous amount of cleavage—a sight that made him even harder than he already was. Her tight dress easily revealed the curve of her ass that he always fought to avoid staring at during office hours. Everything about the woman next to him drew his gaze and directed his thoughts in a very unbusinesslike direction. By the high color in her cheeks, he wondered if she might be able to read his mind right now or if it was just that damn obvious what he was thinking.

He wanted her. She knew it.

But at the moment—in the midst of magic and desire—they were stuck in a business meeting. On Valentine's Day.

He forced himself to look at his troublesome author. In his midthirties, just like him, Jorgensen was better looking than his demeanor suggested. He rarely did personal appearances. It gave him a mysterious edge to his author persona. It was obvious to Stephen now that it was purposeful. If kids caught a glimpse of the sour man behind the fun books, it might affect his sales.

"So, you want me," Jorgensen began. He was looking at Ginger and it took a moment for Stephen to realize that he didn't mean it in a crude, sexual way. In fact, at a glance it seemed as if the author was utterly and thankfully unaffected by the cookie magic.

Wish I could say the same, Stephen thought.

His cock twitched.

Behave yourself, he told it.

It didn't listen very well.

"I…" Ginger began, with a careful look at Stephen. "*We* really cherish your books at Red Fox. And we sincerely hope that you will sign the new contract. We know we can do great things for the future of the Blue Monster Mysteries."

"Mmm." Jorgensen slid his index finger absently around the edge of his whiskey sour. "My agent feels the same way. He regrets he was unable to join us here, but he had a prior engagement."

Normally it was the agent who was the cutthroat, the difficult cog in the wheel, but in Jorgensen's case…

Just keep reminding yourself what Jorgensen's books mean to the future of Red Fox Publishing. Without him, you've got nothing.

That didn't exactly put him in a position of power at this very moment and that bothered him deeply.

"Since you came to Red Fox for your last three books, your series has only gained momentum," Stephen said. It seemed like a good place to start.

"Damn right it has. I've done well due to the power of my writing and through the enthusiasm of my fans. Now my question to you is—why should I continue on with Red Fox Publishing? What can you do for me that I couldn't receive elsewhere?"

"One-on-one attention from your editor. Cover consultation—"

"Approval," Jorgensen interrupted. "I want cover *approval,* not just consultation. If you'd seen some of my covers in the past…monkeys wearing mittens at the keyboard could put together something better."

Stephen and Ginger exchanged another glance and he tried not to smile. "I assure you, Red Fox is not currently employing any mitten-wearing monkeys in our art department."

Jorgensen signaled the waitress to bring over another round of drinks before returning his attention to Stephen. "You need me, don't you?"

"Excuse me?"

"I've seen the numbers. Your business is flailing. I'm not surprised. Publishing as a whole is having a difficult time transitioning into this new era. You either evolve or you die. It's like anything, Fox. Plants, animals, people, publishing. How do I know that Red Fox is a publishing house capable of evolving?"

Stephen's jaw clenched. This guy was even more smug than he was on the phone. He knew from the moment they'd met that Jorgensen was the type of person who only wanted people to agree with him and to stroke his bloated ego at every opportunity. He was, quite frankly, the sort of person Stephen despised.

But despising a bestselling author when you owned and operated a "flailing" publishing house wasn't a very good business decision.

Worries about his business were almost enough to take his attention temporarily away from the beautiful and desirable woman seated so close to him that he could feel the warmth of her body.

Almost. His body burned for hers. Every single inch of him was on fire.

"I assure you," Stephen said slowly, "that Red Fox is evolving. And we want you to be a part of it."

Jorgensen snorted. "It must be amazing for you to get the chance to publish my books. The money they make for you means everything, doesn't it?"

I so *hate you.*

Stephen struggled hard to keep the smile on his face. "I won't lie to you, it does. You have a dedicated editor in Ginger who will continue to work with you personally. You are welcome to contact me at any hour of the day with any problem you might have. And, yes, I will give you cover approval. That, plus our generous offer—"

"It wasn't *that* generous," Jorgensen said flippantly as he leaned back in the booth. "I mean, it was decent, but I'm not shouting from the rooftops, here."

Ginger stayed quiet, letting Stephen do the talking. She took a sip from her wineglass in front of her and then stared down into the contents as if it might hold the answers to the universe.

Damn, she's so beautiful. It made his heart hurt.

"Do you think it's a generous offer?" Jorgensen asked her.

Her shoulders tensed. "I do."

"Tell me what you think about your boss here. The honest truth. I'll know if you're lying."

Ginger placed her glass gently down on the tabletop and was quiet for a moment before looking into Stephen's eyes. "He's amazing."

Now his heart began to sing.

"Can you be a bit more specific?"

"Stephen Fox makes coming to work every day a pleasure. He's kind, he's considerate, he's generous, and because of this, I know I work harder every single day I'm there. It's made me love working at Red Fox, and I would do anything to make sure things turn out right for Stephen and his company."

"That's a bit more specific," Jorgensen said after a moment. "If painfully professional."

"How else would I be but professional?"

"How do you feel about Fox here on a personal level?" Jorgensen asked, raising an eyebrow. "You're here on Valentine's Day with him on very short notice. Am I to take it to mean that the two of you have a personal relationship outside of the office?"

"That's none of your—" Stephen blurted, but Ginger placed her hand on his to stop him from saying anything else. The feel of her skin against his cut his words off. A shiver went up his arm and then swirled around his heart before heading straight south to his crotch.

This was absolute torture.

"I consider Stephen a very good friend," Ginger said firmly, without taking her hand away from his. He found it difficult to breathe and his body ached with the need to touch her, to taste her…

"Friend," Jorgensen repeated. "So there's nothing more personal between you? You're not romantically involved?"

"Why do you need to know this?" Stephen demanded, his voice now hoarse.

"Call me curious."

"We're not romantically involved," Ginger confirmed. "Just good friends and business associates."

Jorgensen's gaze rested on her hand on Stephen's before she finally pulled it away. It took everything in him not to reach out and recapture it, to entwine his fingers with hers. At that moment, Stephen blamed this author for every misery he'd ever had in his lifetime.

"I'm glad to hear that," Jorgensen said.

"Why?" Ginger asked.

"Because…" He hesitated only briefly. "Because I want you for myself. Today, tomorrow and always."

"Oh, shit," she said.

4

MAYBE IT HAD BEEN THE eye contact that sealed the deal. Ginger never should have looked into Jorgensen's beady little eyes for as long as she had. She braced herself for him to do something lewd, something threatening—since that suited his loathsome character—but he just continued to stare at her.

"You're beautiful," he announced. "Why have I never realized this before?"

Ginger glanced at Stephen as if searching for help.

He had the audacity to look both disturbed and amused. It was a strange mix.

"I want you." Jorgensen's brow was creased with a frown. "If you want me, I'm yours."

So, Jorgensen wasn't immune to the cookie magic after all.

She'd meant every word about what she'd said about Stephen. He was wonderful, inside and out. She'd do anything for him—and Red Fox Publishing.

Jorgensen had been a pain in the ass from day one, but under contract, he couldn't make quite so many demands. He would be legally obligated to them. Sure, contracts could be dissolved, but it was difficult and took time and money. Once he signed, Red Fox would be okay for a couple more years—time for Stephen to keep building the business.

"This isn't what this meeting is about," she said to him. "We're here to discuss your contract."

"Right. The contract."

"If you sign it, I will still be your editor." She cringed as she said it. She didn't want to make it seem as if she was promising him any more than that. Because she *wasn't*.

"More than my editor," he said very seriously. "You will be my muse."

Stephen groaned. "Oh, give me a break."

She tried to ignore him and instead placed her hand on Jorgensen's shoulder. He seemed to shiver at her touch. "Did you bring a copy of the contract with you?"

"Of course. It's in my room."

"We should go upstairs so you can sign it."

He frowned. "I don't know. Do you really think I should?"

He was currently enamored with her and would be until midnight, if that woman at the café had been right about the cookie spell. Could she get someone to sign a legally binding contract "under the influence"? That didn't seem right, even when it came to this guy.

"That's entirely up to you," she said slowly.

His brow creased for a moment as if he was considering his options. Then he nodded. "We can talk more about it upstairs in my room."

"Okay," she agreed.

Talk was good. Then she could figure out how else to handle this delicate situation.

As she scooted out of the booth after him, she shot a look at Stephen to make sure they were on the same page—no pun intended.

He glared at Jorgensen with a look of unadulterated hatred. His fists were clenched at his sides. Jealousy was now etched into his handsome features.

"Stephen," she whispered. It took a moment before she finally caught his attention. He looked wounded.

You'd think she'd just made out with the other man right in front of him.

"What?" he said sharply.

"Contract discussion upstairs? Are you coming?"

A bit of clarity entered his expression. "Of course I am."

Concern moved through her. Was he going to be okay?

What was she saying? Of course he'd be okay. Stephen Fox was nothing if not professional, even in the most dire situation. He had to see how much was riding on this.

Still, he barely seemed able to hold back his irrational anger on the elevator ride back up to the fifteenth floor as the other man's gaze moved all over Ginger's short dress.

"Wait till you see what I have planned for book nine," he said with a grin as he slid his key card into the lock on his hotel-room door. "The kids are going to eat it up."

"I'll just bet they are."

A busboy rolling a cart along the hall came to a stop in front of the door to the suite and his gaze moved appreciatively over Ginger. "Room service?"

"Finally," Jorgensen said gruffly, then smiled. "Happy Valentine's Day."

"You, too, sir. Shall I bring this in?" The kid sent another friendly look at Ginger, but didn't say anything. She sighed and avoided direct eye contact with him.

"Yes, absolutely! Wonderful." He held the door open to accommodate the cart, then tipped the busboy generously before he departed. "I assumed you'd pick up this meal along with the hotel bill, Fox, so I didn't mind handling the gratuity."

"Of course," Stephen said tightly. "Anything for you."

The sarcasm he normally held back in business settings was out in full view and Ginger shot him another wary look. Stephen stood against the wall by the door, his arms crossed over his chest. He looked uncomfortable and troubled.

Suddenly, their eyes met and held.

No eye contact, he'd warned earlier. It just made it more difficult for him.

She turned, only to be faced with Jorgensen right in front of her. He held the contract in his hand.

"Here it is," he said, his gaze hopeful. "Do you have a pen?"

She swallowed hard. All it would take was a little flirting to get him to sign his John Hancock to the bottom line, but she didn't think she could do it. Apart from it being morally wrong, he would be furious when he woke up tomorrow and realized he'd been taken advantage of. He'd probably think they'd gotten him drunk.

He could sue. And knowing him, he probably would.

"I think we should have that meeting tomorrow morning," she said. "The one you weren't interested in staying for. But I think it's necessary. Stephen has a presentation ready for you that will prove that Red Fox is the right publisher for you and your books."

Jorgensen flicked a look at Stephen. "You do?"

He nodded stiffly. "I do."

"Impressive, Fox. Perhaps I'll consider it, then. In the meantime, why don't you give me and Ginger a little privacy?"

Stephen gave him a thin smile. "Not in a million years. I don't trust you, Jorgensen. I know what you're thinking and she's not part of the deal."

The author looked wounded. "How dare you. I meant that we'll have a nice dinner. I ordered steak and lobster and a dessert of strawberries and whipped cream. I'm happy to share them with a beautiful woman."

"Since I'm paying for that meal as well as this room, don't I have the right to a taste?"

"No," Jorgensen said bluntly. "Three's a crowd. We want privacy."

"Do you?" Stephen's arms were crossed so tightly over his chest it looked painful. "And what about you? Do you want to stay?" he asked Ginger.

She grimaced. "I think I should call it a night."

"Oh, come on," Jorgensen said beseechingly. "Just an hour. I can't believe I've never noticed how utterly delightful you are."

Stephen grabbed her hand and pulled her away from the other man. "I said I'd protect you. I'm protecting you now."

She gave him a look. "You think I'm tempted to stay right now? And even if I was, it's not like I'd sleep with him."

He looked confused. "You're supposed to be with me, not this jerk."

Worry moved through her. He was getting irrational, over-reacting at the thought of her spending time alone with the author.

"Wait, who are you calling a jerk?" Jorgensen snapped.

"Wasn't I clear? *You're* a jerk." Stephen's eyes narrowed. "Actually, you're a sanctimonious prick who thinks he runs the world. Guess what? You don't. Sign that contract or don't sign it, I don't really care. But you're not laying one goddamned finger on Ginger or I'm going to kick your ass from here to Manhattan."

Ginger's mouth hung open at Stephen's tirade. Where had that come from? Out of nowhere, even though it was what she'd wanted him to say for months.

"You *need* me," Jorgensen snapped. "That means I'm the one with the power here. And I want Ginger."

"She doesn't want you."

"That could change."

"Are you in love with her?" Stephen demanded.

"Love?" Jorgensen frowned. "I *want* her, isn't that enough?"

He pulled her toward him and was about to force a kiss on her when Stephen grabbed his shoulder and spun him around.

Jorgensen pushed him. "Don't touch me, Fox."

"Or what?"

When Jorgensen shoved him harder this time, Stephen's tense fist swung forward and connected with Jorgensen's jaw, which shocked Ginger more than anything else that had happened tonight. She'd never see him throw a punch before.

He was surprisingly good at it.

Yup, Ginger thought with a sinking feeling. *That should probably do it.*

Jorgensen didn't waste a great deal of time before he packed his suitcase. Then he made a very dramatic show of ripping up the contract into tiny white pieces, which he then tossed in Stephen's general direction. They fluttered to the floor like confetti.

Then the bestselling author of the Blue Monster Mysteries walked out of the hotel room and slammed the door behind him without another glance in Ginger's direction, snarling something about a personal-injury lawsuit.

She *knew* he'd be the type to sue if given half a chance.

Now it was Ginger who had her arms crossed. Stephen leaned against the wall as if it was the only thing supporting him vertically at the moment. His expression was bleak.

"So," she said, "my suggestion of getting him to come to the meeting tomorrow so we could all approach the contract discussion from a calm and collected direction? Not really in your plans, huh?"

"Looks like."

"You know what you've done, right?"

"Yeah, I think I defended your virtue."

"My virtue?" She sighed. "Stephen, I'm thirty-two years old. My virtue hasn't needed defending for longer than I care to admit."

"He wanted to seduce you."

"He was harmless. I can handle harmless."

"It wasn't cool. Not with me."

She pointed at the door. "You need to go after him and apologize."

He shot her a sharp look. "Never."

"So you're going to just take this lying down? I know you don't generally talk about financials, but I've known for a while that Red Fox is in trouble."

"We'll manage. Jorgensen was a buffer, that's all. A little cash in the bank. I can find new authors, new opportunities. This isn't the end." He broke off, his expression growing more grim.

She pointed at the door. "He needs to sign that contract. Now go after him and try to fix this."

"No."

She let out a muffled scream. "You are so infuriating!" She paced to the other side of the hotel and looked out the window to the city lights below, trying to breathe normally. "Okay, fine. He's gone. Even if you talked to him right now, it probably wouldn't make a huge difference at this point. We need to give him a little time to cool off, then we'll call his agent and explain. Everything will be okay again."

"Everything's not okay."

There was something in the way he said it, as if he wasn't talking about the destroyed book deal anymore. She glanced over her shoulder at him. "What's wrong?"

"That wasn't me. I don't lose control. Not like that. I just saw the way he was looking at you and I...reacted. I didn't want any man to look at you like that. Only me."

His words slid through her like warm water and she met his haunted eyes. "Stephen...what you're feeling isn't real. You know that, right?"

He avoided eye contact with her, frowning down at a spot on the carpet near the room-service cart. "When you got too close to him, I felt really—"

"Angry? Jealous?"

"*Possessive.* Like you're supposed to be mine. I didn't like imagining you with someone else. It makes me lose my mind."

A shiver went through her at the low, sexy tone to his voice. "We should go to the café. We're done with Jorgensen, for now, anyway, and we really have to get to the bottom of this cookie thing."

He let out a shaky breath, but his gaze still fixed on her intensely. "Good idea."

Ginger noticed that he was breathing hard as she walked past him, trying not to get too close. He reached out and brushed his hand against her arm, then wrapped his fingers around her wrist to stop her. His touch was enough to send that shiver straight through the rest of her body, making her nipples tighten.

Her resolve was fading fast. She wished she could blame her own feelings on some stupid cookie, but she couldn't. This was difficult and it would only be more so when the magic wore off for Stephen. Tonight had only made her face her own feelings about him and wish that things could be different between them.

She looked down at his loose grip on her. "We need to go."

"I know."

"You're holding on to me."

"I can't help it."

She looked up at him, into the familiar, handsome face she'd seen nearly every day for a year. Her friend, her protector, her confidant…her *boss*.

Ginger's phone buzzed and it was enough to snap her out of this daze. She pulled away from Stephen and he let her slip easily out of his grip. She fished into her purse and pulled out her phone. The screen read Unknown Caller.

"Maybe it's Jorgensen," she said out loud, jabbing at the answer button and holding it to her ear. "Hello?"

"Ginger, I'm so glad you picked up."

For a moment, she didn't recognize the voice. And then, "Oh, it's you."

Brad, aka Mr. Perfect.

"Look, I feel really bad about what happened earlier. That was lousy of me not to show up for our date."

"No kidding."

"I'm sorry. So, so, so sorry."

"You're forgiven. Goodbye."

"No, wait! Please, let me explain. I was ambushed on my way to you. I was there, right outside the café, but this guy approached me. He told me lies—that you were old and ugly. But you're not. You're gorgeous. Please give me another chance."

She glanced at Stephen who'd walked over to the window to look at the view that was costing him four hundred dollars a night.

"That's ridiculous. Who would do something like that?"

"Some guy. He took me to a bar and bought me a few drinks. It was obvious he was pining for some girl. He took a call from her and he made it seem like he had a woman on his lap with her tongue in his ear. Or something like that. I don't know, I wasn't really paying much attention to him."

Ginger froze. "What did he look like?"

"Do we have to talk about this? Isn't my heartfelt apology enough? Let's meet again. Tonight. Tomorrow. Whenever you like."

"No, tell me what the guy looked like who stopped you from coming to our blind date."

Stephen spun around on his heels to stare at her with complete shock.

It was all the confirmation she needed.

5

WITHOUT ANOTHER WORD, Ginger hung up on Mr. Perfect and dropped her phone into her bag before crossing her arms. She'd stopped breathing as she waited for him to speak.

Stephen gave her a tight smile and spread his hands. "I can explain."

"I certainly hope so."

"I was worried about you. I mean, it's Valentine's Day. Who goes on a blind date on Valentine's Day?"

"Desperate women and serial killers," she said.

"Exactly. You're neither of those things."

"In a moment, I might be both." She let out a shaky breath. "Why would you do this? It was you, wasn't it? The one Brad just told me about? The one who stopped him from meeting me tonight?"

His expression tensed, but he didn't reply.

She let out an exasperated sigh. "Why? Why would you do something like that? You told him I was old and ugly?"

"I was lying."

"That's not much comfort, Stephen." Pain twisted in her gut. This was the last thing she'd expected tonight. Out of all the people in the entire world, she had trusted Stephen. And she didn't trust easily. She'd had more than her share of people—usually men—lie to her face. White lies, mostly. Not supposed to hurt, but they still did. Despite her upbringing with two parents who loved each other deeply, her trust in men didn't really extend very far when it came to herself.

"You knew how much this date meant to me," she said, feeling that lump return to her throat right on schedule. Her eyes burned.

He scoffed. "Right. It was so meaningful, a random blind date with some loser you met online."

"How I meet people is none of your business. It's not like you are interested in anyone seriously."

"This isn't about me, it's about you. And don't try to convince me that it was so damn meaningful to you. It was just a date. It's not like you were going to sleep with the guy."

Ginger held his gaze defiantly. "Then explain the condoms I have in my purse."

He visibly flinched as if she'd hit him. It surprised her until she realized why.

She waved a hand. "You know what you're feeling toward me isn't real. This jealousy or possessiveness or whatever you want to call it. You turned on Jorgensen at the very thought I might stay and have dinner with him alone. You chased away Brad before I could see him. It's all because of that stupid gingerbread cookie."

"You think so, huh?"

"I know so." But then she went silent, thinking through the schedule of the night. She hadn't eaten the cookie until well after Brad was supposed to show. And Stephen hadn't seen her face to face until later.

She shook her head as if to clear it. Things weren't totally adding up for her, but it didn't matter. What mattered was that Stephen had sabotaged her chance with another man.

She let out a breath and tried to calm herself. "Look, I get it. I understand why you did this."

"You do?"

"You're trying to protect me from getting my heart broken. Maybe you thought it would distract me at work too much."

He looked at her as if she'd just pushed a knife into his chest. "Yeah, that's all it is. Just an employer looking out for his employee."

"Thanks, boss."

"Don't call me that. Not now."

She watched him warily. "I think I should leave."

"Yeah, maybe you're right. Go take those condoms and put them to good use."

"You don't have to be a jerk about this."

"Whatever, Ginger." His jaw tensed. "Just being around you right now is difficult for me."

"Touché." She didn't want to let on how much his words hurt her. This was getting out of control. Time to leave and let the magic wear off. Even now, feeling this angry with him, she still wanted his hands on her. His mouth on her. It was like some kind of fever she couldn't shake.

"I'm going back to the café so I can talk to that woman." She turned toward the door. "You stay here. I mean, you already paid for the room so you may as well enjoy it. I'll deal with any whistling men I come across."

"I think you'll be safe. The spell's wearing off. I can feel it lifting and it's not even midnight yet," he said flatly. "What a relief."

Yeah. She was sure it was. But the thought of Stephen no longer desiring her brought with it a deep and painful disappointment. He'd lied to her and tried to ruin her romantic life in one fell swoop tonight.

And still her heart ached.

She grabbed the door knob and was about to turn it when she glanced over her shoulder. "Why did you do it, Stephen?"

"What part? I'm starting to get a little unclear about everything I've done wrong tonight."

"Why did you stop him? It was just a blind date."

"A blind date for which you had a ready supply of condoms."

"Hardly a ready supply. Two."

He glared at her. "Two too many."

"Hey, you had a date tonight, too. Or did you? Brad said that—"

"Let's forget what Mr. Perfect said. The magic is lifting, Ginger. You can roam freely about the city now."

"I can't say I'm disappointed about that." She nodded firmly and turned the knob to open the door. "Good night, Stephen."

"Good night, Ginger."

She walked down the hallway to the elevator with a heavy heart. It felt as if she'd just lost something really important. Something that had been in her hands—like sand—but had sifted through her fingers so quickly there was no way to stop it before it was all gone.

The elevator doors opened and she got on. Jabbing the button for the lobby, she pressed back against the mirrored wall behind her and sighed.

Stephen had chased away her date. He had waited outside that café without giving her any idea of what he was up to. She'd had no clue that he had a problem with her dating. He could have said something at the office this morning when he'd presented the staff with a big heart-shaped cake to celebrate Valentine's Day. She'd told him all about Brad then, even shown Stephen his picture. She'd played Brad up as being amazing, good-looking, successful, sexy…really slathering it on thick.

Why had she bothered to do that?

Come on, a little voice inside her said. *You know why. Stop lying to yourself.*

She'd been looking for some sort of reaction from Stephen. Maybe to spark some jealousy in him.

She'd done it because she was in love with Stephen. And she had been for a very long time.

"Damn it," she whispered to herself as the elevator reached the lobby.

Stephen had wanted to protect her from some guy he didn't think was right for her. He'd gone about it all the wrong way— and she certainly wasn't ready to forgive and forget his underhanded methods.

But why had he really done it? She could understand if it had been after the cookie's magic kicked in, but it was *before*.

She remembered what he'd asked Jorgensen earlier.

"Are you in love with her?"

If the author had answered yes, would it have been different? But Jorgensen simply said he wanted her. The other men had shown interest, but no one else had said they loved her.

Only one.

She stood in the lobby for about ten minutes, the color draining from her face, before this information completely sank in.

"Excuse me, miss?" A man touched her arm.

Ginger turned to look at him. "What?"

He frowned. "Just making sure you're okay. You looked upset there for a moment."

She waited for him to say something like the other men tonight to show that he was interested in her. But instead he just looked steadily at her.

No desire. Just concern.

No more spell. Stephen was right when he said it was lifting. This was the proof.

"I need to…go," she said.

But instead of storming out through the front doors of the hotel and heading back to the café as was her original plan, she turned back toward the elevators, practically running to them. She stabbed at the up button, her heart pounding wildly in her chest.

I love you, Ginger. So much. You have no idea. You never have.

He'd said it. It would have made sense if the cookie magic was some sort of a love spell, but she'd never asked to be loved. She'd asked for men to want her so she could pick who she wanted in return. And they had wanted her—for a short time.

But Stephen had said that he *loved* her.

It felt as if it took forever before the elevator finally arrived. She got on it and then it felt as though it took forever until it reached the fifteenth floor. She had no idea what she was going to say or what she was going to do when she got back to the room and confronted Stephen about this.

The elevator doors slid open to show that he was waiting just outside, his expression anxious.

His eyes widened when he saw her. "You're back."

For someone who worked with words all day long, she was currently at a complete loss for them.

"Where are you going?" she forced herself to say.

He opened his mouth but then shut it as if he'd had second thoughts about what to say. "Out."

"Were you going to follow me back to the café?"

"I wanted to make sure you were safe."

"But the spell's over."

"Yes, it certainly is. For me, I mean. For other men, who knows? You might have been engaged five times over by the time you got three blocks from here." He wasn't meeting her gaze. "Why did you come back?"

"Because I needed confirmation about something."

"Confirmation about what?"

"I—I need to know why you chased Brad off."

He didn't speak for a moment. "Because he wasn't good enough for you."

She had the elevator open with her elbow. She hadn't stepped off it yet. "You could have told me that."

"Would you have believed me? Look, Ginger, he wasn't good enough for you. No guy is, okay? That's just how I feel. Take it as a compliment. I don't normally give anyone else's love life this much thought."

"But you do mine?"

He didn't reply to that.

She swallowed and summoned up enough courage to say what she needed to say next. "On the subway, you said that you loved me. But the cookie magic wasn't a love spell. And you once told me you don't believe in love."

He raised his eyes to meet hers. There was an edge of pain there. "What's your point?"

Suddenly, she wasn't sure. She was horribly afraid she was

making a mistake here that would do great damage to their normally wonderful friendship, something she valued deeply and didn't want to lose. She wasn't usually so completely unsure when it came to men—reading them, wondering what they thought. It had been a rough night for her ego.

"No point, I guess." She let go of the elevator door and it started to close.

Stephen stopped it. His gaze had grown more intense. "What do you want me to say, Ginger? That I'm in love with you? That you proved to me that I can feel that way about someone? That I've been in love with you since first meeting you and making a drunken fool out of myself, in public? That I've pined for you every day we've worked together, imagining what it would be like to tear your clothes off and make love to you on the boardroom table? That every woman I've gone out with since I met you has paled in comparison. That I can't stop thinking about only you? That I wish desperately that you didn't think of me only as a friend and that you wanted me just as much as I want you?"

She gaped at him, overwhelmed by his tirade.

He immediately looked as if he regretted saying all of that and he let go of the elevator door. Before it closed, she slipped off and stood only a couple feet away from him.

"Well, there you have it," he said quietly. "You want to know the reason I scared off your date tonight? Why I'd do it again in a heartbeat even if it means you're going to hate me? It's because I don't think that any man in the world is good enough for you. That the thought of anyone else touching you or kissing you drives me insane with jealousy. No man should be with you, Ginger. No man except me." He laughed humorlessly. "My business is going to hell in a handbasket. Why shouldn't I destroy my personal life, too?"

"So, it's true?" she whispered. "You're in love with me."

"Why else would I act like such a fool on Valentine's Day— with or without some stupid cookie to blame for it?" His pained gaze flicked to hers for a brief moment. "You should probably go now."

"I can't go."

"Why not?"

"Because I'm in love with you, too."

He looked at her so sharply, she almost laughed.

"Don't play with my emotions tonight, Ginger," he warned. "I'm close to the edge."

"I'm not playing. I've never been more serious in my entire life."

A deep frown creased his brow as he continued to stare at her with shock as he took in what she'd just said to him, laying her true feelings out so they were raw and completely defenseless. "Well, in that case..."

He closed the distance between them in two steps, then pulled her against him and crushed his mouth against hers.

6

HER HEART JUMPED in her chest. She'd been so afraid of how this might go. It was a very good sign that coming back up here didn't seem to be a mistake.

His kiss deepened and she kissed Stephen back just as hard, just as passionately. It was even better than when he'd kissed her on the subway—their first kiss, then. Their second kiss, now. Sheer perfection. Did he really think Brad was supposed to be her Mr. Perfect?

He was wrong. So very wrong.

He pulled back a little, holding her face between his hands and gazed at her intensely. "Ginger..."

"Yes?"

"What do you want to do right now?"

"I want you to take me back into that expensive room you reserved for Robert Jorgensen and make love to me on the king-size bed."

He nodded slowly. "Seems like we're in complete agreement."

"First time tonight."

He grinned before it faded just a little at the edges. "This isn't real."

"Oh, yes," she assured him. "It is. Now what are you waiting for, Mr. Fox?"

"Nothing," he said. "Nothing at all."

Stephen lifted her up into his arms and went back to the hotel-room door. It was a blur as his lips met hers again and emotion swelled in her chest at the taste of him, the smell of his familiar spicy cologne and the bare skin beneath it just waiting to be touched. By her.

He scrambled to shut the door and she pulled him back around, hurriedly unbuttoning his shirt to bare his chest. She slid her fingers down the front of him, thrilled at the opportunity to touch him like this.

"How long?" she whispered.

"How long do I have before I explode right now?" He raised an eyebrow. "Not very."

She grinned shakily as he pulled his shirt off completely. "No, how long have you...felt this way about me?"

"How long have I been madly, passionately in love with you despite claiming not to believe in love of any sort?" he asked. Heat came to her face at the intense way he said it. "Since forever."

After she shrugged off her coat, he slipped the straps of her dress over her shoulders. He raked his gaze greedily down the front of her. "That bra is way too sexy to wear on a blind date, Ms. Redman."

She trailed her fingertips over her diamond-hard nipples, clearly visible through the thin-red-lace bra. "This bra?"

He hissed. "Yes, that bra." He slipped a strap over her shoulder, pulling it down slowly to bare her left breast. He cupped it in his hand.

Her breath came quicker, especially when he lowered his head so he could kiss her nipple, drawing it into his mouth and circling his hot tongue around the very tip.

"Oh, hell," she gasped.

He looked up at her. "No, it's definitely heaven."

"I want you."

"Answer me a question first."

"Anything."

He grinned and his expression grew even more heated. "That's a dangerous thing to say."

"Anything," she said again, firmly.

"You know when I fell for you—the beginning. When I saw you that night in the bar, before making a fool out of myself. I didn't know you, only how you looked, how you moved. Physical attraction. The love…it did take at least a couple more hours. I first felt it in the office, when you didn't hold my behavior against me. God, I felt like a fool for hitting on you like that the night before. But what I want to know is when you felt something for me…when *you* knew."

"When I knew I loved you?" His hands on her bare skin made it hard to think, but she tried her best. "I fell for you the moment you apologized for acting like an ass at the bar. Not every guy would take it seriously. You did. And you honestly felt bad about it. I fell for you then and I've wanted you every single day since. But I didn't know for absolutely sure it was love until tonight."

"Tonight?"

"You wanted me, you desired me, I thought it was only because of the magic. It made me realize how much I wanted and desired you, too, how much it would break my heart to know it was only temporary for you."

Stephen shook his head slowly. "Not temporary."

"No. Not temporary." She moistened her lips with the tip of her tongue. "I love you, Stephen. Now stop asking me questions, because I need you so badly I don't think I can keep standing."

It was all she needed to say. Whatever control he'd been keeping a handle on tonight—or for the past year—went out the window. His hands moved to her back to unhook her bra and let it join her coat in a silky pile. He deftly unzipped the back of her dress and let it fall, as well. Her hands moved to his waistband, slipping downward over his erection that strained against the material.

"I need this," she said very seriously, cupping him, "inside me."

He swore under his breath, then lifted her up, his hands under her ass, moving her backward to the bed where he quickly pulled her silky panties off over her legs, baring her completely to him, only leaving her high heels on. Then he swore again as his gaze swept the length of her.

"Where's your purse?" he asked.

She frowned. "My purse?"

"I think you said something about having a couple condoms in it?"

"You don't have any?"

"I wasn't planning on...well, let's just say I'm currently un-prepared for romance of any kind."

"So your date earlier...?"

"Lies," he admitted readily. "All lies."

"No more lies," she said firmly as he began moving down the length of her body.

"No more lies," he confirmed as he pushed her legs apart, kissing her bare stomach, her inner thighs, closer and closer... until he finally stroked his tongue against her heated core.

This time she swore, arching her back and clawing at the bed sheets. "Stephen...oh!"

"Jorgensen said something about strawberries and whipped cream with his dinner." Stephen smiled darkly up at her. "We'll get to that later."

Ginger stopped thinking. Her world grew smaller and smaller. Nothing else existed outside Stephen's tongue against her, driving her insane with every stroke. She was begging him, pleading—not to stop, but for more. Deeper. Harder. She wanted him so desperately she became mindless to anything else. And then her narrow vision exploded as an orgasm rocked through her, leaving her gasping and crying out.

"My purse…" she gasped. "By the door."

Stephen pushed away from the bed, but was back quickly as she recovered from the most intense climax of her life. Colors sparkled around her vision. She got up enough to begin undoing his pants with shaking hands, pulling them down over his hips.

She got up on her knees on the bed next to him and pressed her mouth against his, tasting herself on his tongue in a deep, hot kiss that left nothing unsaid. Her fingers wrapped around his hard cock and she stroked him as the kiss intensified, until he broke it off, gasping.

"Ginger, I want you."

"I think I know that by now." She grinned against his lips. "If I didn't, this would be a clear giveaway." She squeezed him just a little and he groaned deep in his throat.

"My cock," he said mock-apologetically, "doesn't have nearly as much self-control as I try to have."

"Clearly." She kissed him again and pulled him down on the bed so she could feel his weight press against her. He worked his pants off the rest of the way so there was absolutely nothing between them anymore—no clothing, no control…no lies. Just bare skin and heat.

She grabbed his hand and guided it between her legs. "Feel how much I want you. How wet I am."

That earned another dark groan. "I want you, too, Ginger. Every night."

"Just nights?"

He gave her a pained grin. "Days. Nights. Weekends. Leap years."

She nodded, taking his other hand and removing the packaged condom from it. She tore it open and helped roll in onto his hard length. "Prove it."

His gaze bore deeply into hers. "You know how the fairy tale ended, right?"

"The fairy tale?"

"'The Gingerbread Man.' Everyone wanted the delicious gingerbread man, chased him all over town, because they wanted to eat him. He ran from them all—none of them could catch him. It wasn't until he found the fox, who promised that he'd keep the cookie safe, that he stopped running. But the fox was a liar. The fox is the one who ended up devouring the gingerbread man."

Why this tale only made her hotter, she wasn't totally sure. Devouring had taken on a whole new meaning to her tonight. It wasn't something bad, dangerous. It was obsession, it was desire, it was…love.

"I want you to catch me," she whispered as he slowly pushed himself into her an inch at a time. Slowly, slowly, until he filled her completely. And then, without any more to say, he began to move inside of her, making her world narrow once more to only include him. Only Stephen inside of her, making love to her, only the bed against her back. Only the spicy and familiar smell of him, only the addictive taste of his lips, his tongue, as he devoured her mouth with a kiss that confirmed that this was right, so right. She never wanted anyone to catch her again. Only Stephen. Again and again.

It wasn't long at all before his thrusts became harder, deeper. She clung to him, her arms around his shoulders, her fingers pushing up into his silky hair. His hands came to her back and he lifted her up off the mattress, so she clung to him, her legs wrapped around his waist as she felt the slide of him in and out of her. Then, in one final, deep thrust that made another orgasm shatter her entire world, Stephen called out her name before they both crashed back down to the mattress.

His breath came fast and she felt his heart thunder against her as she held on to him tightly.

"So…" Stephen said after a minute.

"So."

He propped himself up on his elbow and gazed down at her. He brushed a lock of red hair off her forehead. "That was…nice."

She glared up at him and tried not to smile. "That was better than nice and you know it, Mr. Fox."

"I didn't want to let it go to your head, Ms. Redman."

"Too late." She drew his face closer to hers and kissed him, long and deep and perfect.

"Happy Valentine's Day," he whispered.

"Best one ever." After another kiss, she brushed past him and got up from the bed. He eyed her warily and there was the slightest edge of doubt in his gaze.

"You're not leaving me already, are you?"

"No, not quite yet." She cast a sly grin over her shoulder. "I'm kind of hungry."

"Oh, yeah?"

"I think Jorgensen said something about ordering room service." She strolled, naked, to the cart the busboy rolled in earlier, feeling his appreciative gaze heavy on her. She lifted the silver, domed lids from on top of the food.

"Steak, lobster and a baked potato," she announced.

"Better eat it before it gets too cold. That is costing me a fortune."

"Not really in the mood for that." She lifted the other lid and picked up the bowl underneath, swirling her finger into the fluffy whipped cream and bringing it to her mouth so she could lick it off. Her gaze flicked to him, where he lay propped up on the bed. The look of arousal on his face was absolutely priceless. She forced herself not to laugh. "I feel more like dessert."

He raised an eyebrow. "I couldn't agree more."

Ginger ignored the strawberries, the steak and the lobster. She returned to his side and dabbed a little of the whipped cream on his chest and leaned forward to lick it off. He groaned.

"Just as delicious as I thought you'd be," she told him with a wicked grin.

She wanted whipped cream, lots of it, all over the man she craved more than any other.

She was ready to take back what she'd decided earlier. Valentine's Day didn't suck at all. It was now her very favorite holiday.

EARLY THE NEXT MORNING, just after six o'clock, Ginger woke in Stephen's arms. Very carefully, after gazing with deep appreciation at his handsome profile for a few minutes, she slipped out of bed and quickly got dressed. She was surprised how soundly he slept. He didn't hear a thing as she left the room. She silently promised to return before he woke up.

She had to see someone and it couldn't wait. She wanted answers.

The Valentine Café was open for business, but the place was empty. The door jingled as she entered and walked quickly and confidently to the counter. A few seconds later, a man came out from the back kitchen area and grinned at her.

"Good morning," he said. "What can I get for you?"

"Information, actually." She glanced around. "I'm looking for a woman who works here. She's sixtyish with white hair. Maybe five-four. She gave me a free cookie."

He stared at her for a moment. "It sounds like you're talking about my aunt, Frances Valentine."

"Valentine?" Ginger repeated. "So the café is named after the family, not after the holiday."

"That's right. But Aunt Frances always loved Valentine's Day. She was a true romantic."

"Can you tell me when she'll be in today? I really need to talk to her."

He frowned. "About what?"

"About that…that gingerbread-man cookie she gave me last night. It—" she wondered how to put it "—it did something strange."

"Aunt Frances gave you a strange cookie. Last night."

"Yes. Look, I know it sounds weird, but I need to see her."

"Sorry, but that's impossible."

"Why?"

It was a moment before he spoke again. "My aunt died a week ago." He studied her. "You're serious, aren't you? You really think you saw her last night?"

"Yes, I saw her," she whispered. "Spoke to her, too."

"And that cookie…did something strange. Good strange or bad?"

Ginger's mouth was dry. How was this possible? She wondered if he was lying to her, but the man's expression was dead serious. He had no reason to lie to her. Frances Valentine was dead.

"I thought it was bad for a while, but it turned out wonderfully."

"Did it help you find your true love?" he asked.

Her eyes snapped to him. "How did you know that?"

He smiled and then glanced around the café in a knowing way. "She's still around. I knew it. Her spirit…her magic. Nobody ever believed her, but she had a way about her. She knew how to help people when it came to love."

Ginger just stared at him, stunned. "I don't understand. How can this be possible?"

He looked pleased, but then he shrugged. "I don't know. Some things just can't be explained. I say, when miraculous things happen, take them for what they are and don't try to figure them out. If my aunt—even now—chose to help you, then be happy."

She opened her mouth to say something else, to ask a million more questions, but then she stopped herself. He was absolutely right.

The spirit of Frances Valentine gave her a magic gingerbreadman cookie that led her straight to the man she loved—a man who loved her in return. All Ginger could do was gaze around the small café and offer a silent and heartfelt thank-you.

7

BEFORE STEPHEN OPENED his eyes, he'd have bet that this was going to be the best Wednesday of his life. Ginger and him— well, last night had been incredible. Better than his best fantasies, and over the last year, he had plenty of them starring the beautiful Ginger Redman.

After he opened his eyes, however, things were different.

Ginger was gone.

"Ginger?" he called out.

There was no reply. Her clothes were gone. Her purse was gone. She hadn't left a note.

He lay back down in the huge bed and stared up at the ceiling.

She'd had second thoughts. About him. About everything. What had seemed perfect last night in the heat of passion, had cooled off in the harsh light of day.

For *her*.

Love had an expiration date. Just like with his parents. Just like with his previous relationships. It didn't last forever. This one, though…he'd thought…

He'd *believed*.

He didn't want to lose hope so quickly, but his knee-jerk reaction was to protect himself. To put his shields up and to be cynical about everything. Ginger was supposed to be different. Every cell in his body had wanted to believe that she was.

Now what was he supposed to do? Pretend it didn't happen? Go back to being publisher and editor at the office. Good friends who had a professional relationship that spilled over a bit to their social lives. Platonically only.

Did she honestly think that was possible now?

Instead of agreeing that she might be right that a night of mind-blowing sex didn't necessarily have to lead to a meaningful relationship, Stephen found that he was furious. And not with himself.

With her.

This wasn't just sex. For either of them. And, damn it, he would fight till the end to prove that to her if there was any doubt in her mind.

He pushed himself out of bed and got dressed, feeling angrier with every piece of clothing he put on. Oh, they'd be having a talk, all right. And Ginger would finally see another side of Stephen Fox—one who'd remind her with a passionate, toe-curling kiss that he was the man for her. Mr. Perfect had been in front of her all this time and she'd finally noticed him. She couldn't deny that. And if she was afraid of what this meant—how big this could be between them—then he'd assure her that she was damn right about that. This was big. And it wasn't something that could just be ignored. Not now. Not ever again.

When his phone rang, he snatched it up.

"What?" he snapped.

"Fox? It's Robert Jorgensen."

Oh, he was so not in the mood for this right now. "What do you want, Jorgensen?"

"We need to talk about what happened last night."

"There's not much to say. The remainder of your contract is scattered on the floor right now. If it wasn't, I'd tear it up myself. You know what you are, Jorgensen? An asshole. Everybody knows it but you, but it's the reason nobody likes you. And you know what else? I'm sick of it. I'm sick of people like you walking all over me. So here's what I want to say about last night— you can go directly to hell."

There was a long silence. And then, "Finished?"

"Not really. I could go on. And, by the way? I've wanted to say that for a very long time."

Another silence. "You're right about me."

Stephen blinked. "I am?"

"I am an asshole. But you're wrong about one thing—I do know it. Sometimes when times are tough, we build up walls that are hard to break through. And when assholes like me are successful, nobody wants to tell them the truth. They just want to sponge off you. But not you, Fox. You tell it straight. I like that."

He blinked again. "You do?"

"Yes. Now, if you're still interested in my books, contact my agent with a new contract. I'll sign it. Goodbye, Fox."

The line went dead.

Stephen stared at his phone. "You will?"

He'd been ready to kiss off that contract and start again from scratch. But this? This was much better.

Maybe a little straight talk would also get through to Ginger. If it worked on Robert Jorgensen, maybe it could work on her, too.

With this in mind, he went to the door and opened it up, shocked as hell to see Ginger on the other side.

She looked up at him. "Oh, you're awake already."

God, she looked beautiful this morning. No makeup, tangled hair and a wrinkled black dress—she was the single most beautiful thing he'd ever seen in his life.

"What the hell, Ginger?" he stormed. "You just leave? Just like that?"

"I can explain."

"Save it. You need to listen to me. I know you think the old Stephen Fox is a bit of a pushover. A nice guy who buys cakes for his employees and pukes on ladies' shoes when he's had too much to drink. Well, that Stephen Fox is long gone. The new one says what he wants to say, he does what he wants to do, and he demands to be treated with respect."

Her eyes widened. "Is that so? And does he also talk about himself in third person?"

"Yes, he does." He glared at her. "You can't just leave. Not after what happened between us. You love me. You said so yourself. If you're scared now about what that means, don't be. I'm not afraid of it anymore, so you shouldn't be, either. You love me and I love you. Nothing else matters, you hear me? And if you run away, feeling overwhelmed by everything, you can damn well believe that I will follow you. We're together now, Ginger. You and me. And I want to make love to you every day for the rest of my life. Do you have a problem with that?"

He tensely waited for her reply.

Ginger just stared up at him with amusement, even though her green eyes shone with tears. "Nope. No problem with that at all."

Her answer shocked the hell out of him. "Really?"

"Yes, really."

"Then where did you go?"

She held up a brown paper bag with the Valentine Café logo on it. "I went out to get some breakfast for us."

"Oh." He stared at the bag. "And my little rant just now?"

"You want me to forget it?"

"Might be nice."

She shook her head. "Not a chance. I loved every word of it. You need to give Jorgensen some of that fire. Maybe he'll sign that contract after all."

He nodded slowly. "Maybe I will. Damn it, Ginger, I thought you left me."

"I did. But I'm back." She shook the bag. "Bearing goodies for the man I love."

He raised an eyebrow. "More magic cookies?"

She peeked inside the bag. "Eclairs. But they're filled with whipped cream."

A grin spread across his face as he pulled her closer to him. "You're as smart as you are beautiful, Ginger Redman."

"Somehow, Mr. Fox—" Ginger kissed him and let the bag of pastries drop to the floor so she could give him her full and complete attention "—I just knew you'd approve."

* * * * *

PASSION

For a spicier, decidedly hotter read—
this is your destination for romance!

COMING NEXT MONTH
AVAILABLE FEBRUARY 28, 2012

#669 TIME OUT
Jill Shalvis

#670 ONCE A HERO...
Uniformly Hot!
Jillian Burns

#671 HAVE ME
It's Trading Men!
Jo Leigh

#672 TAKE IT DOWN
Island Nights
Kira Sinclair

#673 BLAME IT ON THE BACHELOR
All the Groom's Men
Karen Kendall

#674 THE PLAYER'S CLUB: FINN
The Player's Club
Cathy Yardley

You can find more information on upcoming Harlequin® titles,
free excerpts and more at www.HarlequinInsideRomance.com.

HBCNM0212

REQUEST YOUR FREE BOOKS!
2 FREE NOVELS PLUS 2 FREE GIFTS!

red-hot reads!